Praise for *Green Fires: Assault on Eden, a Novel of the Ecuadorian Rainforest*

Barnes and Noble "Discover Great New Writers"
American Book Award (Before Columbus Foundation)

"A riveting novel of adventure and suspense..."—*Kirkus Reviews*

"Marnie Mueller's ambitious first novel succeeds on two important levels: It is a chilling mystery...as well as an ecological education for the reader new to the trials of Latin America...*Green Fires* educates, entertains, and challenges."
　　　　　　　—*The Bloomsbury Review*

"This is a harrowing document and a powerful comment on the problems of our times...a significant novel."—*Choice*

"A rare and rewarding combination of substance and clarity."
　　　　　　　—*National Catholic Reporter*

"An eco-thriller."—*The Hartford Courant*

Praise for *The Climate of the Country*

"The grit, the cold, and the desolation of the Tule Lake Camp provide the setting for Mueller's powerful new novel..."
　　　　　　　—John Marshall, *Seattle Post Intelligencer*

"A vivid and complex tale of divided loyalties and of the consequences of racism and violence..."
　　　　　　　—*South China Morning Star*

"A powerful and relevant story of love and faith put to the test."—Tara Ison, *The San Francisco Chronicle/Examiner*

"...rings with authenticity, both in the historical truth, and more remarkably, in the portrayal of fictional lives in the context of historical events."—David Takami, *The International Examiner*

"What makes this a riveting novel is not only the strong sense of history and the particulars of the racist internment but also the way the politics is played out in family, work, and erotic love."
　　　　　　　—*Booklist*

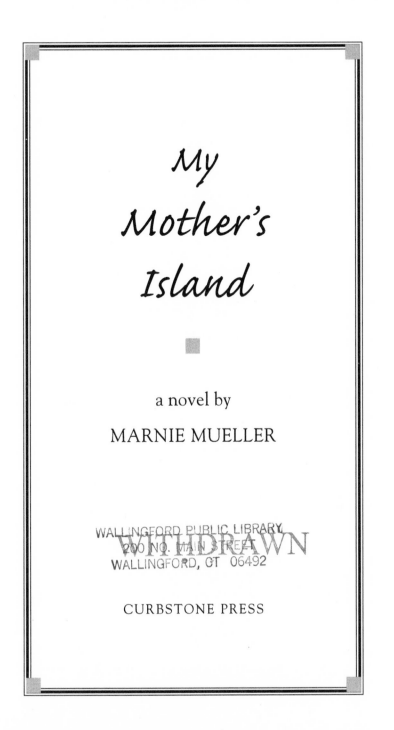

My Mother's Island

a novel by

MARNIE MUELLER

CURBSTONE PRESS

Printed in the U.S. on acid free paper by Berryville Graphics
Cover design by Les Kanturek

This book was published with the support of Worth Loomis, as well as
the support of the Connecticut Commission on the Arts, and
contributions from many individuals. We are very grateful for this
support.

The publishers thank Jane Blanshard for her help in preparing the text
for publication.

Library of Congress Cataloging-in-Publication Data

Mueller, Marnie.
    My mother's island : a novel / by Marnie Mueller.
      p. cm.
    ISBN 1-880684-82-9
    1. Mothers and daughters—Fiction. 2. Conflict of generations—
Fiction. 3. Terminally ill—Fiction. 4. Terminal care—Fiction.
5. Only child—Fiction.   I. Title.
    PS3563.U354 M9 2002
    813'.54—dc21   2001028530

published by
  CURBSTONE PRESS   321 Jackson Street   Willimantic, CT 06266
        e-mail: info@curbstone.org   www.curbstone.org

ACKNOWLEDGEMENTS

Abrazos to my publishers, Alexander Taylor and Judith Doyle, for their care and commitment to each book they publish. It is an honor to be included in their list of fine writers. Every novelist needs a watchdog and mine is Jane Blanshard, who meticulously scours my manuscripts for embarrassing slips. Every author needs an agent and mine is the *simpatica* Liza Dawson, who gently prods me to ask for more. As does Rita Marcus, whose job it is to get the word out, a task she achieves with remarkable success and astonishing optimism. Roberta Allen encouraged me to start writing this book and held my hand along the way; I can never thank her enough for sending me on this emotional journey. I am indebted to Alison Ender Eskow for her insightful reads and invaluable editorial suggestions; it was as though she could read my early, unarticulated thoughts. But where would I be without Fritz Mueller, who keeps me whole, or my friend and colleague, elegant writer and masterful editor, Lorrie Bodger, who helps me see the sweep of my own narrative and the corresponding essentials of form and style, and then pushes, pulls, demands, suggests, cajoles and nitpicks until the manuscript is up to a standard where the public can be invited in.

to Harriet and Ed Nathan
my beloved aunt and uncle

MY MOTHER'S ISLAND

Day One

MY MOTHER SITS on the couch, waiting for me, done up like a little doll in one of her brightly colored cotton dresses; this one is pink and tangerine. Her skin is jaundiced and her face is strained and beaky with the effort of remaining upright.

"Dear one," she says, beaming warmly, creasing her worn skin. "How did you know I'd need you?"

How did I know? Because I've always known what my mother's needs are, and because Lydia Rentas had called me in New York City the day before and insinuated that my mother was beginning to die. *"Tu mami no está comiendo, casi nadita,"* Lydia said in her low, muffled nasal tone that I've learned to understand over the past month of our telephone calls. My difficulty in comprehending her is not because we converse in Spanish to keep our discussions from my mother—I'm fluent in Puerto Rican Spanish—but because Lydia has a badly mended harelip that distorts her words.

This afternoon Lydia sits in the chair by the telephone. The wall behind her is an orangey-gold, a few shades more muted than Lydia's own carrot-bleached hair, and the wall behind my mother is green. Those two bright fields of color come together at the corner by the window where my mother always sits to talk with me, those phone calls when I can hear the bell-like serenade of *coquís* in the background. "Ko-key!" the ebullient frogs sing as we labor through our conversations.

My mother has painted these walls. My mother has painted the walls of every apartment or house we've ever rented, in whatever city, town or village we happened to have

1

settled in. Each summer when she got off from teaching high school, she would say, "I think it's time to start," and we'd go out to the hardware store and buy the necessary gallons; in the early days we used oil-based paint and the house stank for a week even though we'd leave the windows open. Before beginning, she'd slip her slender body into dungarees and an old shirt of my father's, the collar of which she'd turned one too many times. She'd tie a bandanna around her curly black hair, secure paper bags over her shoes, and smear a skim of Vaseline on her glasses. "Paint makes all the difference," she opined in the stillness of those humid afternoons as we swished the wide brushes, and later the modern rollers, down one wall after another. "It conceals a multitude of sins."

My mother is dying in Levittown Lakes, Puerto Rico, an *urbanización* near Cataño, the town where one gets the ferry to go across the bay to Old San Juan. Her little house, a flat-roofed boxy structure, white with a hot pink front door, is on a cul-de-sac of other modest, pastel, cement block bungalows. My mother's street is *Calle Maruja*, the number AE 5. Everyone but my mother and the Haitian family across the street is Puerto Rican. The pink door is open now as I stand in her living room, and the tropical sun bakes my back. Life goes on behind me. Joey Rios, who picked me up from the airport in my mother's car—he is Lydia's druggy boyfriend—straddles our front fence, sitting there waiting to see if he will be needed. Salsa music pulses loudly from next door. Children ride their bicycles up and down the sidewalk before our house, seeking to find out why the *señora's* daughter has come again. Lydia watches me with a host of emotions in her pinched expression: proprietary protectiveness of my mother, concern for me and for *mi mami*, all-knowingness.

"Hi, Mom," I say in my most upbeat voice. "You look good."

"Do I, dear?" My mother smiles, but the way her black eyes dart warily tells me she knows better than to believe what

2

I say. My mother is too smart. Her emotions shift like quicksilver through her intelligence—weighed, measured and packaged—to emerge in what she thinks is an appropriate response.

"Thank you, dear. That's very sweet of you."

"It feels so good to be here again," I say too loudly, flopping onto the Danish Modern couch, its brown-striped fabric scratchy against my sweaty skin. The wooden legs scrape on the terrazzo floor. "It's not as hot as it was in September."

"You know, dear," my mother sighs, "your energy tires me out. I think I'd like to go to bed again."

Lydia and I help her walk into the bedroom, Lydia giving me knowing glances over my mother's bowed head, glances that say, You see how bad she is. I feel the bones of my mother's back as I cradle her. Her arms are deceptively fleshy so I hadn't noticed how much weight she's lost. I help her out of her dress and take off her underwear while Lydia tidies the room, and am shocked anew by the wide purple zipper of stitches down my mother's belly, from beneath her small breasts to the thinning hair of her pubis. The tumor has grown back. Her stomach is distended to the size of a five-month pregnancy. She raises her arms like a dutiful child and I slip her pink gingham nightie over her illness.

"I am so tired," she says, lying back in her narrow bed against the pillows Lydia has plumped. "I've been waiting out there in the living room for two hours for you."

"I'm sorry," I say, old anger and guilt building. "I couldn't get the plane to fly any faster."

"I'm aware of that, dear." She sighs and closes her eyes.

HERE I AM.

Lydia has gone back across the street with Joey. Joey, the junky, is in his late thirties but still lives with his mother Estela in a house directly opposite my mother's. I noticed as soon as

3

I got into the car at the airport that Joey has put on twenty pounds since September, a good sign; he's staying off the stuff. That's what Lydia told me during one call, but I didn't believe her even though I said, "That's great, Lydia, *ojalá* he stays off." "*Ojalá*," she answered solemnly, and then giggled as if to nullify her hope. Lydia, who is fifty but can look and act like a teenager, comes to stay at Estela's on the days she is looking after my mother. I think Lydia saw the job as an opportunity to keep tabs on Joey, to stop him from scoring and make sure he doesn't land back in jail for dealing.

So, here I am again. I spent the month of September caring for my mother in the hospital in San Juan. I returned to New York once I'd settled her back in the house on *Calle Maruja* with a full-time nurse and with Lydia to do the housework and to check on the nurse. Estela had said, tapping the sagging skin below her left eye, "You can never trust an outsider to do the job, you must get someone you know to oversee." I don't think Estela meant Lydia. The last person Estela wants in her house is this woman she claims, "wants my *bebé* Joey, wants him to marry her. She's too old for him." Estela doesn't seem to realize that Lydia is the best thing that ever happened to her handsome, weak, skaghead son.

It was Joey who recommended Lydia to me, which made me have grave doubts about her, but then I met her. I immediately liked this tiny, fit woman with her carrot hair tied in a high ponytail. Her face was ruddy and freckled, suggesting that her hair might actually have been red once. Her teeth were false, so they were as white as a youngster's, and except for her harelip, her face was fine-featured and cute. She was born in Brooklyn and came to P.R. as a teenager when her mother was dying. "My heart was broken," she confided to me at our first meeting. "You know what I mean. I stayed here because in P.R. I felt like I was with *mi mami*. It's the worst thing to have your *mami* die." She had looked at me with such compassion that I couldn't tell Lydia that I didn't think it would be the same for me, that I was certain it wouldn't be. How could I tell her I was afraid I'd be dry-eyed at my mother's funeral?

Today, just before Lydia left with Joey, she gave me a big hug. "I'm your mommy now, Sarah. I'll take care of you like a mommy through this. I'll come every day to take care of you," she whispered in Spanish into my ear, even though my mother's air conditioning was on the highest setting and her door was closed.

I turn on the television and its blare melds into the rising clamor of early evening in the neighborhood—radios blasting, pots and pans clanging, cocks crowing off-schedule, and children calling. There are no real windows in this neighborhood, only louvers that can be cranked open and shut to the outside air. In my mother's bedroom, sheets of thin plastic cover the windows at night to keep the air conditioning in. We live in each others' homes in Levittown Lakes. On this evening in November, the proximity of our lives makes me less lonely as I flip the channels and settle on the Classic Movie station.

The sun streams deep gold through the open front door and across the chalky, cracked terrazzo floor, reaching the dark teal blue chair that we've had since we lived on Long Island. My parents moved down here twenty years ago to retire; after six months my father couldn't stand the idleness, or maybe it was the constant company of my mother that weighed on him, so he went back to work and, a little later, so did she. My father died twelve years ago. My mother is going to die here too, very soon, though right now she's sleeping. How many times in how many different homes I've waited while my mother slept, taking her long stuporous naps through the afternoons. Today it's different. I am here waiting for her to die.

We have lived in so many places, my mother and I. My father, too, but he was rarely around, was either on the road or out late working, "coming home soon." My mother and I, following my father from job to job, settled for a year here or two years there, five years was our longest, in California, Washington State, Chicago, Ohio, Arkansas, Vermont and Long Island, and in those locales we changed apartments on an average of three times per town. Whenever the rent was raised above thirty-five dollars a month, we had to pack up our belongings and move to a cheaper neighborhood. Here we are again, she and I, alone together in Levittown Lakes. This place costs her one hundred dollars a month in mortgage payments—comparable, I'd say, to what we paid in the 1950s.

I have always been my mother's best companion, while she has too often been my enemy. I wonder if she knows how much and how vividly I hate her. I wonder if she knows that I haven't had a child because I don't want another human to hate me as much as I hated her. I dare myself to have these thoughts even though she is in the next room, dying. And then I begin to cry. It is a deep, gut-wrenching weeping that I don't understand, but I do know that it has to do with her dying in the next room and my sitting out here alone in November in my shorts and tank top, watching an old black-and-white movie on television while other people's vibrant lives go on just outside our louvered windows.

Day Two

I WAS UP AND down all night helping my mother to the bathroom. The minute I'd hear her rustling around I would be out of bed and in her room standing ready.

"You don't have to help me, Sarah," she'd say, using my arm for support.

"It's fine. I want to." I don't tell her that I woke up terrified that she would fall on her way, and I would have to lift her off the floor or find someone who could help me.

She was having trouble lowering herself to the toilet and getting up afterward. I noted, too, that she was barely peeing, but I didn't say anything. I knew she couldn't defecate properly. She'd called me a few days earlier. "Nothing will come out," she cried, "no matter how hard I push." Her voice trembled with fear. "Don't push," I said. "Drink lots of water and don't force it. You're getting panicked for no reason." But I knew it was a setback, I knew it was the beginning of the end. I believe it was at that moment when I knew, even before Lydia told me that she wasn't eating. I think I remember saying to myself that the tumor was growing and getting in the way of her bodily functions. But I did nothing.

My mother sits on the toilet in a daze. "Mom," I say, "are you done?"

"Yes, dear." She turns her face upward to me and smiles wanly. I take her in. My mother's cropped hair, which she has always cut herself, is sticking up in a peak on top and flattened on one side. It is still salt-and-pepper even though she is seventy-seven years old. Her tan has faded and yellowed, her nose looks large and very Jewish and her eyes are flat, as expressionless as they used to be when she would go into those fugue states that frightened me so as a child. I would say, "Mommy, are you okay?" and she would answer me, seemingly from another world, "Yes, dear." But her expression wouldn't change.

"Mommy, are you done?" I ask again, braced against the doorjamb in my middle-of-the-night fatigue.

"Yes, dear," she says, not moving a muscle in body or face.

I catch a glimpse of my own face in the mirror as I go toward her. I am a resigned and sad woman in that reflection, but my long brown hair, though tousled, is shining, I note with relief.

"Come on, Mommy," I say as I wipe her dry and tug down her nightie. I position her arms around my neck and tell her to hold tight as I pull her upright. She nestles into my body as though she belonged there. I smell her dense, familiar odor. This is the woman I never wanted to touch and from whose touch I would shrink. I stand still for a moment. I force myself to let her stay close. Finally I say, "Come on, Mommy, let's get you back to bed."

THIS MORNING I help my mother with her shower. Lydia usually does, but I say I will while she changes the bed. In the shower my mother steadies herself with her hand against the tile wall as I soap her bony back with a washcloth, rubbing down over her buttocks, moving into the crack, and underneath. I kneel to wash her legs and feet, then I rise to soap her belly and breasts. She decides that she wants a shampoo. "I feel so dirty," she says. I pour shampoo onto her short coarse hair as she once poured castile onto my thin child hair. I gently work up a lather, massaging her head as she moans in pleasure, and I have a memory of bending over the kitchen sink while she kneaded my head and I kept myself taut, not to give in to the comfort of it. I rinse the suds out and we are finished.

When my mother was in the hospital in September, I became accustomed to attending to her body. In Puerto Rico the family does the nursing in hospitals and since I am the only family, I did it. I gave my mother her bedpan, lifted her on, covering her with a sheet so the nurses would not look askance at such an immodest display if they happened into the room. I wiped my mother for both urine and defecation, took the bedpan away, dumped it and washed it and dusted it with powder for the next use. I dressed my mother in diapers I had purchased at the pharmacy where I had also purchased her bedpan.

At first the nursing staff was suspicious of me, didn't answer my questions, ignored my smallest requests, such as sheets for my mother's bed, never mind making it. We were the only anglos in the hospital; the nurses assumed we were going to demand too much of them. I went about my business, gathering linens, buying the essential items, trying to regulate the intravenous machine that fed much-needed sustenance into her depleted body before the operation. By evening the news had spread that I had come from New York City to *"cuidar a la mamá."*

"We thought you were from here," one young nurse said while another looked on. "Why do you speak Spanish and your *mami* doesn't?"

"I lived in South America, in Peru. And my husband is from Argentina," I said.

"I see," she nodded approvingly, meeting the eye of the other nurse.

"My mother is old," I said, putting on my most forlorn expression, "and my father is dead. It was too hard for her to learn."

The nurses nodded in sympathy.

They would never have to know that in the past she had easily learned German, French and even Swedish when she needed them for traveling in Europe. Somehow Spanish had eluded her. Roberto, my husband of fifteen years, jokingly says it's because of her underlying unresolved hostility toward him. I think it's because she harbors secret anger at my father for getting her to retire early along with him and dragging her down here to live. At that moment it didn't matter which it was; the goal was to garner the nurses' sympathy for my mother. After that they extended themselves, at least as far as time and energy would permit.

It's difficult to be the only family member *cuidando a la mamá,* no matter how well you can charm the staff. There are still twenty-four hours to cover. Leaving the hospital the first evening, two days before my mother's operation, I passed other families moving in for the night. It was seven o'clock, the sun had just gone down behind the hotels on the Condado, and the wind had begun to pick up, blowing across the scorching metal of the cars and the hot macadam of the parking lot. In the family members trooped, solemnly, carrying pillows and blankets for curling up on a chair in the patient's room or on a cot rented from the volunteer service. My mother was in a private room because, as she had said, "I don't think I can bear to have someone else's big, loving, Puerto Rican family in my room."

As I threaded through the parked cars, dread overwhelmed me at the thought of staying all night with my mother after her operation, sleeping on the low cot beside her bed, breathing her air, being responsible for whether or not she survived the first forty-eight hours.

BACK IN THE cheap pension that I'd found a mile and a half down Ashford Avenue, I called Roberto in New York. I imagined him in our apartment, in his office at the far end, transcribing notes on patients he'd seen that day. He'd be in his underwear, his soft paunch, distended after dinner, pushing against the rim of his jockey shorts. If Roberto has a vice, it is loving good food too much.

I met Roberto fifteen years ago, a mere two years before my father died. A friend introduced us at a book party. Roberto wasn't my type, too fleshy, too pale-skinned, and his dark hair was thinning, but in an attempt to make conversation as long as I was stuck with him, I prodded him to tell me something about himself. "You say you've read my novel. So fair is fair," I said, when he kept plying me with additional questions about myself. He finally told me he was a psychoanalyst and a Jew who had had to leave Buenos Aires. "It was either be disappeared by the good citizens, or run away and live, so I opted for existence," he said, with an ironic grimace. I recognized that look; it said, Don't even think about feeling pity for me. "You needn't make light of your situation with me," I said. "I lived in South America. I know how terrible it is right now in Argentina." He stared into his plastic wine glass, his face reddening, his hand clenching the brittle plastic so tightly I thought it would break. "Sorry," he said. "I'm uncomfortable talking about myself. I'm usually the one who listens."

"I can't do it," I cried into the phone. I was supine on the thin, lumpy mattress, staring up at the ominous, water-stained crack running the full length of the aqua ceiling. "I can't stay in her room. I hate her. I'm afraid of her."

"You don't have to be afraid of her. She can't hurt you anymore," Roberto said.

"But I hate her," I repeated.

"Why don't you try not to hate her tonight? Hating only gets you more upset. Sleep. That's what you should do. You're exhausted." I savored the traces of his Buenos Aires accent, with its soft consonants, which I only noticed anymore when we were apart and speaking long distance.

"I wish you could be here."

"I know that, but I can't just pick up without notifying all my beloved crazies. Somehow you have to get through this one alone or forget it and come back home. Let her do this on her own."

"Oh, Roberto, you know I can't do that. She's so sick and helpless and frightened."

"That's the other side of it, isn't it?"

"What do you mean?" I asked, knowing full well what he was about to say.

"At the risk of sounding like a shrink, you have always been attuned to Reba's neediness."

"You mean I've always felt I had to take care of her emotional needs."

"That's right," he sighed. "That's exactly what I mean."

Day Three

WHEN MY FATHER died twelve years ago, my mother asked me to sleep that first night with her, on my father's side of the bed. Whatever my mother asked, I always did without question. Contemplate this: Even though the double bed was really two twins pushed together, I never considered pulling them apart. I lay down on the spongy, sagging mattress, sinking into the indentation made by his body over the years, smelled his odor on the sheets that had not been changed, and was certain I could feel his warmth in them. Terrified, I clutched the edge of the bed all night, keeping myself out of my mother's reach.

She lies in that same room today, on a narrow single bed; my father's half has long since been discarded. We have helped her undress, Lydia and I, eased her down until her head touched the pillow, and together witnessed how she immediately fell asleep. I sit watch over my mother on a floral-patterned club chair pulled close to her bed, with my bare legs folded up into what children call Indian style.

The walls of this small, square, cinder block room have been painted a pale peach by my mother, creating a rosy aura as the afternoon wanes. In addition to the bed and club chair, there is a small table with a lamp, to my left. Behind it, a window looks out onto the house next door where Inez and Jorge García live with their daughters. Inez and Jorge are born-again Christians. She is a teacher at the church school and he is a social worker in the welfare department. Their fervent religiosity doesn't seem to get in the way of my mother's love for their firstborn daughter Lourdes, who is four years old, and who, until my mother became too weak, came regularly for afternoon visits. It's clear that precocious, dimpled and slightly spoiled Lourdes is the substitute for the grandchild my mother will never have. On my mother's bedside table is a small photograph of Lourdes, framed in silver.

A teak bureau stands to the right of the other floor-to-ceiling jalousie window on the far wall. I've removed the plastic covers from both windows. In the back yard, the tree planted in memory of my father, by Roberto and the old man from across the street, Eugenio Castro, has grown taller than the house by many feet. It shades my mother's window and rustles in the merciful breeze that always picks up off the ocean in late afternoon here in Levittown Lakes. I think, Daddy is watching over us. He'll take care of us. He'll help us find our way through this last part. I think this, knowing full well that taking care of us was not his strong point.

The beach is a mile and a half from the house, and I long to be on its crescent spit of land where the wind blows so hard that your hair is whipped around your head, and the sand sprays up and coats your wet body after you emerge from your swim to stand with your back to the sea, looking out across the choppy waters of the bay to the golden skyline of old San Juan. It is my mother's favorite beach, and before she got sick she used go each day to swim sidestroke up and down the shoreline for half an hour. I can see her head in her white bathing cap, her eyes half closed and essentially blind without her thick glasses, cutting through the undulating turquoise water. After her swim, she told me, she liked to sit on the beach for a while and watch the children playing or just look up at the sky, "the most beautiful sky in the world," she said. "In all the places we've ever lived, I've never seen such marvelous cloud formations." I can imagine how she walked up from the water, her body angled forward against the wind and the slope of the beach. When she reached her towel she would have bent to get her glasses from inside her shoe. That's where she always left them, as far back as I can remember, and that's where I leave mine as well. I can see the water beading on her oily skin, how the tips of her hair would be wet when she pulled off her cap, how she wiped her arms first and then her legs before wrapping the towel around her shoulders to protect them from the sun. She would have looked longingly at the small children, and she will tell me in great, loving detail, when we next talk on the telephone, how sweet and beautiful they were, always adding, "But of course none of them is as lovely as Lourdes."

When I was seven we vacationed for a week on the coast of Maine, my mother, my father and I. We rented a little cabin under white pine trees within walking distance of the long flat beach. For days I played happily at the edge of the water, running in and out, racing the waves. My mother kept saying, "You should go out beyond the waves, where it's calm. You don't have to be afraid." But I said no, I'd rather stay there playing in the surf. My mother grew impatient on the third day. Emerging from the water, she stood over me, tall and slender in her red-and-white seersucker bathing suit, her dark, springy, backlit curls glistening with droplets. "You know how to swim. You're strong enough. You simply have to be brave for a moment as you pass through." The next day she was angry—I saw it in her face, in the menacing look in her eyes. I was questioning her authority. She grabbed me around the waist and dragged me into the icy water. The grip of her arm against my skin was unrelenting and her fingers bit into my bare midriff as my bony hip thudded against her own. The water rushed up around us, engulfing our bodies and I heard the screams of children just before a wave crashed down on us in a whirlwind of heavy pounding water filled with thick swirling sand. It pushed us down and around until we emerged into the calm on the other side, the calm she had promised. The sun was too bright. My eyes stung as she turned me onto my back and told me to breathe deeply. Her hand remained under me on the narrow of my back as we lay in the swelling waters. My terror then was greater than when we had been under water. I couldn't look at her, didn't want her touching me, didn't trust that hand underneath my spine. She could drown me out there and who would know? I had to get away from her. I flipped over onto my stomach and began to swim toward shore, flailing my arms and legs, gasping for air. She kept up with me. "Good girl," she was saying. I swam faster, my fear of her giving me strength. She came up on my left side and I thought, If she grabs me, I'll bite her, when a wave took me and I rose on the top of it and for a moment I was as free as a fish slipping across the water, hanging suspended, looking down onto the beach filled with laughing, playing people, and my mother was nowhere near. The wave was kind to me and deposited my skinny body on a bed of rolling foam sweeping me safely back to shore.

My mother sleeps. She is curled on her side with her hands pressed in prayer under her cheek; dark twists of hair cling to her sweaty temple. She could be twenty-one years old, the way the wrinkles have fallen from her peaceful face. My mother has always slept as an escape—long hibernation from which she wasn't easily roused. The five-hour "naps" frightened and disgusted me as a child. I would want her to wake and make me dinner, and at the same time I wished she would sleep forever so I could go alone into the evening and next day and on and on in my solitariness, entertaining myself with the stories I made up.

Soon I will have my old wish; soon she will never wake.

LYDIA BECKONS ME from the bedroom door. I meet her in the kitchenette, the area that leads out to the *marquesina*, the roofed and iron-gated terrace that is attached to every house in the development. Most people use them as porches, sitting around on beach chairs eating and listening to music, playing dominoes or just *charlando* the evenings away. My mother keeps her car in hers. The floor is stained with grease and the whole place smells of the male cats who spray their territorial scent. For a while my mother liked having the cats around, she liked their company, until a pack of them got into an open window of her car and she could never get the stench out and had to sell the car. After the incident, whenever we'd drive into the *marquesina*, my mother would snap at me to roll up the windows. "I don't want those damn cats getting in again and ruining everything," she'd say. "How many times do I have to remind you, Sarah?"

Lydia is stirring a pot on the stovetop. She wears cut-off jeans and a white halter. I can smell red beans.

"I made this for you, *nena*," she says, grinning at me with her too-perfect white teeth. "Estela told me you love Puerto Rican food."

"I love it a lot," I say, leaning forward against the counter, my elbows holding my weight.

"What do you love? *Arroz con pollo, plátanos? Qué cosa?*"

"I love the *ensalada de pulpo* at Luquillo Beach the best."

We laugh together.

Lydia lifts a lid off another pot. The funky odor of greasy, garlicky rice comes to me.

"I was wondering," she says, this time not looking my way, "can you let Joey and me borrow Mommy's car for a little while? I need to go back to my place to pick up some things."

All I can think is that Joey is going to use the car to score some dope.

"Joey doesn't have any ideas about going over to the Condado, does he?" When Joey picked me up at the airport he drove off the highway and into the Condado, around the all-night Walgreen's near my old pension and up the narrow street under the highway. He told me that this was the place the "big bad dealers hang out," as though I didn't know he was a user.

She continues not to look at me. "I wouldn't never let him do that. I'll be with him the whole time, *nena.* You can trust me. I couldn't do nothing to hurt you or your mommy." With that Lydia comes over and puts her arms around my shoulders, pulls me down to her and holds me really close. I smell fresh garlic on her skin as if she's wiped her cooking hand along her bare neck. "I'm your mommy now, remember?"

IT'S FOUR HOURS later and Lydia and Joey haven't returned with the car. Lydia told me the whole trip would take an hour and a half. I am furious at her. If she came up the driveway now I would yell at her to get the hell out of here with her junky boyfriend. I'm angry with myself for not having a driver's license and being dependent on Joey to get around. I don't drive because I'm afraid I might lose control and kill someone on the road, and now I want to kill him.

I go out to the *marquesina* without turning on the overhead light. I need to calm down. The night air is soft and moist, a sweetness glides by from the gardenias growing next door. I step onto the driveway and look up at the stars, listening to the whooshing of palm fronds in the distance. The air and the sounds soothe, but they also bring a melancholy. It is November. It smells and feels like November in Puerto Rico. November was the first time I came to this island. It was on November 23, 1963, the day after Kennedy had been assassinated, my second day in the Peace Corps. Still stunned by the events, we, the new recruits in Puerto Rico for a month of training, walked down the wheeled steps off the plane onto the hot tarmac, under the relentless sun. On the roofs of hangars were sharpshooters, and coming toward us across the black pavement was Muñoz Marín, the governor.

He wept as he embraced us one by one. This island is where my adulthood began.

Puerto Rico is also where I met the best friend I ever had. Her name was Lucy Brady and we sat together on the rattling bus that drove along the road toward Arecibo, the same road that borders Levittown. The bus turned up into the mountains just before Arecibo and bumped along narrow roads, passing tiny shacks. By then it was dark and the only lights were the kerosene lanterns inside the *casitas*, illuminating photographs of Kennedy. I heard my first *coquís* that night, their calls mingling with the mournful sound of dirges playing on transistor radios in house after house all the way up to our training camp in Utuado.

Lucy and I stayed best friends after we returned to the States. We lived in the same tenement in the East Village. I was downstairs in a tiny apartment with a bathroom in the hall, hers was larger and had plumbing inside. I adored Lucy, loved listening to her stories of the rich alcoholic father who'd left her when she was ten and the bohemian mother who had one affair after another, brazenly hiding nothing from Lucy, not even the acts. Lucy had a way of telling her family stories that made them sound romantic. She'd purse her lips in a manner I thought of as French, one hand driving nervously through her dirty blonde bangs as she rested her head on her other hand, her skinny arm and pointy elbow poised on the kitchen table. After she'd finished with a particularly horrendous tale, opening her teary blue eyes wide, she'd suddenly laugh, the same self-denigrating laugh I'd heard that night I met Roberto. "Hey, guy," she'd say. "It could've been worse."

The drug dealers visited Lucy's apartment all the time. "You're too much of a prude," she'd say when I implored her to stop taking so much. "I'm losing you," I'd say. "When you smoke all that dope you go too far away from me. It's not good for you either." She'd swear she was going to cut back.

But it wasn't only marijuana she was using. Her main drug was heroin. How could I have been so blind, I've asked myself a million times since then. I saw her nodding off. Saw that life was getting harder and harder for her. She couldn't pay her bills, and her apartment was filthy. One night she came back from visiting her mother in Seattle for three weeks and called me on the phone.

"Sarah, please, I need your help, guy." Her voice, so weak and plaintive, made me think someone had died. "Please come upstairs and help me."

I entered the apartment. The walls moved. They were black with cockroaches. It was the middle of July and she'd forgotten to take three open bags of raw garbage out when she left for the vacation. This time we both toked up and began to spray and swat and spray, running to the bathroom to vomit and back to spray and whack with brooms and rolled-up newspapers. We flicked at them with towels until they showered onto the floor and then we stomped and smashed them like grapes, cracking them beneath our feet. They fell from the ceiling onto our heads and shoulders and arms. We shrieked at the top of our lungs as we worked, to release our horror. We blasted the Stones song, joining them, screaming, "I can't get no satisfaction," to keep from losing our minds. We swept and shoveled the dead off the floor into paper bags. All the time our faces were screwed up in grimaces of agony. When we thought we were done, that the kitchen was scoured from top to bottom, Lucy turned on the oven. She could at least cook the piece of salmon she had brought with her from Seattle, so it wouldn't go bad. The cockroaches began to crawl out of the oven, darting from around the closed oven door, coming up in armies from the burner plates while those trapped inside cracked and cooked into a dusty, acrid stench.

After the incident, Lucy was more distraught than ever, calling me in the middle of the night to say she could feel the roaches crawling over her. When I'd go up to check, there were no roaches to be found, only the reek of dead carcasses lingering in the air. I began not to pick up the phone when it woke me after one in the morning. Then the calls stopped and for four days I didn't hear from Lucy. I was relieved. Her endless neediness had, for the first time, become a burden. But when five days passed and she hadn't called and every time I phoned her no one picked up, I got worried and went upstairs to her apartment. I yelled her name through the door. There was no answer, but there was a horrible stench coming from inside. When I opened the door with my key I was overwhelmed by a shocking rankness, like the rotting smell of a huge dead rat. I followed the revolting odor, down the narrow dark hall and into the kitchen, and there I found Lucy at the long table where we always ate together, slumped over her paraphernalia with a needle still stuck in the decomposing flesh of her neck.

I HEAR MY MOTHER'S moaning cry and rush back inside the house. I find her trying to sit up in bed. The front of her nightgown is covered with black and brown vomit. She'd proudly eaten dinner tonight and drunk half a glass of Coke to keep her nausea down. She is crying.

"Mom, I'm here. I'm sorry, I went outside to the *marquesina*."

"Maybe next time you can stay closer," she whispers. "I threw everything up. You didn't hear me."

"But I'm with you now, Mommy. Let me clean you up."

I decide to cut her nightgown off, rather than lifting it over her head. I calculate that she has twenty of these little cotton nighties and that, judging from what the doctors have said, she may not last twenty more days. Which will make for perfect symmetry, at least for me; in nineteen days it will be November 23rd.

"What are you doing?" she asks, her voice filled with alarm. "Are you ruining my nightgown?"

"I'll stitch it back together once it's off. I'll use your sewing machine. I don't want to get your hair dirty again." I can smell the Coca Cola mixed with vomit and bile from the bottom of her stomach.

"Are you certain you know how to use the machine?"

"Yes, it'll be fun." I wad the nightgown into a ball and carry it out to the garbage in the kitchen. I hear the car pull into the drive. There's no time to confront Lydia and Joey right now.

My mother lies back against the pillow, her small breasts flat against her bony chest, the purple scar peeking out from the soiled sheet. I have begun to soap her with warm sudsy water when Lydia looks in.

"I'll see you tomorrow, Lydia."

"How's Mommy?" she asks.

"I'm fine, Lydia. Sarah is taking care of me very well." My mother smiles.

When Lydia has left and my mother is in a fresh pink nightgown and the top sheet has been changed, she takes my hand. I steel myself against her touch; the old phobia returns and makes me want to shout, Let go of me.

"You are my light," she says. "I don't know what I would do without you. How did you know I'd need you through this?"

August 1950

THE SUMMER SARAH turned eight her mother went to Europe. It was an opportunity she couldn't miss, Reba said, this group tour sponsored by the teachers' union. She went by boat and was to return in two months by airplane. There were photos taken of her on the ship, looking happier than she'd ever been, her slender body in a long, loose gabardine coat over a rayon dress. The wind is blowing, catching the wide skirt of her coat, lifting it behind her, and with her hand she holds a half-moon-shaped felt hat in place on her head. She wears rimless glasses one can barely make out and her smile is open and welcoming. No flattened affect, no dead eyes of the months leading up to the voyage. This is a woman on her own, a woman finding pleasure in the wind and sunlight and perhaps in the person snapping the photograph.

Sarah was left at home in her father's care, though as usual he was busy traveling around Vermont, day and night, organizing farmers into rural fuel co-ops. After a week of shuttling Sarah from person to person along his route, he made arrangements for her to stay the rest of the time with the Allbrights, Quakers who worked a farm outside of Colchester. They had a large, white Victorian house surrounded by fields of hay and corn, and enough acreage for ten head of cattle. Each night Sarah helped them herd and bring in the cows for milking. She worked alongside Cordy, short for Cordelia, little Ephie, short for Ephiginia, their older brother David, and their dog, an old fleecy sheepherder who was so gentle the cows ignored him.

It was late August on the night Sarah's father was coming

to pick her up and take her back home. The light was half summer and half autumn, the evening coming on earlier each day with a melancholy that even at that young age Sarah could feel. The fields were infused with red as she climbed over small hillocks in her worn-soft dungarees and striped tee shirt, skirting the cow pads, running herd and slapping the Holsteins' black-and-white muddied haunches with her tan hands.

David, his auburn hair a deep magenta in the glow, raced ahead to make certain the barn doors were open for their arrival. Cordy and Sarah moved along together. The light caught Cordy's wild head of golden curls, bringing out the fire in each coil. Sarah admired how her freckled face glowed as though made of some shiny material that reflected the sun. Wordlessly, Cordy and she split apart and spread out to intercept and shoo in the strays while little Ephie remained in the rear with Tandy, the dog—short for "in tandem," Mrs. Allbright said—both of them yelping rhythmically at the cows if they loitered over a clump of grass or if they acted just plain stubborn about going for the barn, though usually to no avail. But on this night the cows were eager to get their teats hooked up to the machine and find relief for their tender, ballooning udders, so they heeded the urging.

They entered the sweet and sour, funky smelling, intoxicating indoor world of cows. Sarah, in work galoshes, squished through the manure, urine and straw-laced mud on the floor. It was degrees warmer in the barn from the electric lights and the animals, especially compared to the temperature outside, dropping quickly with the setting sun. The children's father, Grant, yelled, "Get those milking machines going, kids." The squeezing, churning, sucking sound began and the milk rose in the tubing as Cordy and David positioned each cow in her metal stall, and Sarah helped attach the tubes to the teats. She was careful to stand free of any hoof. She knew not to trust even her most beloved cows, those that would affectionately turn their big noses to nuzzle her hair and push against her shoulder as she worked on them.

When all the cows were rigged up and the machines doing their work, she received her reward. She was allowed to put her hand inside the cows' mouths, the way Cordy had taught her, and let them suck while she gloried in the soft feel of their rough tongues and the pressure of their own pleasure on her flesh. She could have let her entire bare arm slip up into the mouth and throat of her favorite cow Tilly, and if possible let her whole body be pulled in like Jonah into the whale to live in one of those little compartments where Tilly put her cuds to save for later chewing. She could ride around in there as the old cow slowly lumbered back to the field the next morning at dawn, to be spit out gently with the slippery cud, sliding down off her wide rough tongue to drop onto the dew-soaked grass with its hair-thin strands of spider webs covered with pebbles of amber water. Sarah imagined sitting among the warm cows, watching the sun rise over the mountains through eyes as deep brown as their own, as though Tilly had birthed her and she was one of them.

But her father was coming to take her back down to their shadowy, empty apartment in Burlington. It was another new home, this time in the poorest section of town. Tomorrow they were driving to New York City to pick up her mother at a place called Idlewild Airport and Sarah wasn't sure if she wanted to see her mother again.

Cordy and Sarah walked from the barn toward the house on their final trip home, not speaking, either one of them. Sarah smelled milk on her friend and felt Cordy's plump arm hooked into her own skinny, bony one. The moon was rising in the east up behind the hill of corn. The high tasseled stalks were silhouetted against the huge orb, which was painted orange by the sun setting on the opposite horizon. Around her the air was turning an intense purple. A love for Cordy and this last night together and the house with the lighted windows, the scent of cows, the corn they were to eat for dinner, all this overwhelmed Sarah so that she wanted to call out, wanted to hug Cordy close and feel the golden springy curls against her face. Instead, Sarah kept walking, not speaking, fighting the tears that rose to replace her ecstasy.

They were gnawing the bare cobs and sucking up the butter from the holes left by the corn kernels when Sarah heard her father's car pull into the drive. She recognized the motor cranking in the old Plymouth, the creaking of metal as the door on his side opened and the exact way it sounded when he slammed it shut. She didn't want him here so soon.

The screen door slapped closed and he was in the bright kitchen looking just like her daddy always did. He stood there smiling. "Daddy," she cried and ran to him, desiring nothing more now than to have him put his arms around her, and to hear his laughter. She leaned into his belly, smelling the summer sweat on his wrinkled white cotton shirt, mixed with the dust of the roads he drove down.

"How's my chicken?" He held her away to get a look.

"Okay," she whispered.

"Okay? You look beautiful." His hand was on her cheek as he kneeled. His face was tan and his eyes, dark and adoring. He had a stubbly, two-day-old beard and the top of his high forehead, where his hair was thin, had blistered and peeled, revealing pink, sore-looking patches encircled by brown skin.

"Have some food, Scott?" Mrs. Allbright asked.

"Haven't had a decent meal all summer," he laughed and stood. He kept his hand on Sarah's shoulder. She snuggled in closer yet, wanting to melt into him, become a part of his old dusty clothes, walk on his shoes the way she used to do.

"What the heck have I got here?" he laughed, but he didn't move away.

"Looks like somebody missed you," Mrs. Allbright said. "And I'll bet she'll be glad to have Reba back as well."

LATE THAT NIGHT her father tucked her into bed in the new room, pulling the silky quilt that used to be his and her mother's up under her chin. In this apartment she was to sleep in the attic in the big brass double bed that once was theirs, while they slept downstairs on Hollywood beds in two different rooms. She'd spied the setup when they'd walked through the long dark hall lined with stacked cartons that her mother hadn't had time to unpack before leaving for Europe. She'd glanced into the rooms and seen the bed in the room where the telephone was and in the living room its twin was made into a couch with throw pillows and a wedge-shaped bolster.

Her father smoothed the peach-colored quilt, folding it in tightly around her body. He didn't say anything for a while as he played his hand over her forehead. She stared warily at the shadows in the dormer windows and wished she dared ask him to stay with her tonight. There was a little cot by the bay window where he could sleep.

"It hasn't been an easy summer for you, has it," he said.

Tears had started to dribble out of the sides of her eyes. He wiped them away.

"I missed your mother a lot too. A hell of a lot. I sure hope she'll be glad to get home."

Please sleep on the cot, she wanted to say

"Tomorrow will be better, chicken, for both of us." He bent down and kissed her damp cheek.

Please stay. I want you to stay.

"See you tomorrow bright and early. Now get your sleep." Don't go.

"Night, button nose," he said, standing in the lighted door.

"Night, Daddy," she said.

"I love you."

"I love you too."

The hall light went out. It was completely dark in the

room, and the night pushed against her eyes. The stairs creaked as he went down. The door, at the bottom of the staircase, which separated the second floor from her attic area, clicked shut. She wanted to call, Daddy, leave it open, but no words came out.

NEW YORK CITY had a sweet, dirty odor, like none she'd ever smelled before, and her eyes burned from the hot air as they raced between cars and trucks on a highway that had solid rock walls rising on both sides. Her blouse stuck to her back and her panties felt as if she'd wet herself. If it hadn't been so noisy with horns blasting and metal clanging every time they hit the bumps and her father swearing, she would have sunk into a deep sleep to escape the intensity. She had no reserves left after her wakeful night of terror in the upstairs room and the long trip down from Burlington.

Her father pointed out the tall buildings of the city against a white sky as they raced over the longest bridge she'd ever been on, and out along another highway where the air became fresher and cooler. There were sailboats bending with the wind on a wide bay of choppy navy blue water. She heard the roar of an airplane and thought they were there, but her father said, "Not yet." They continued driving until they pulled up next to an open area with high grass and what seemed to be a wide highway that her father said was the runway.

They sat on the hood of the car in the scorching midday sun and waited. Only a low, wood-slat fence separated them from the field.

"That's it! I think that's it. It's the Scandinavian Airline," her father shouted and then his voice went quiet and almost sad. "She'll be here with us in no time now."

Sarah's heart was pounding and she bet his was too. He didn't get down off the car, but sat with his arms wrapped around his chest and his hands tucked into his armpits.

The huge silvery plane came blasting onto the black highway far off to their right. The ground trembled beneath their car, and the grass on the field was smashed flat to the earth by the intense wind. The plane slowly taxied toward them and came to a stop dead ahead, a good two hundred yards in the distance.

They watched, without moving as five men ran pushing a big set of stairs toward the plane. The door swung open and out came people exactly as they did in newsreels on Saturday afternoons. One by one, and two by two, they descended the stairs, the wind blowing their skirts and ties. Sarah's heart hammered.

"There she is," her father yelled, standing up on the fender. "Reba, Reba, over here." He waved both arms over his head.

She wore a dark hat and a pale blue two-piece dress, her favorite seersucker summer suit. She didn't hear their calls and didn't look their way. She was busy talking to a woman on one side of her and then to a tall blond man behind. She didn't look for her husband and her daughter sitting there. She didn't seem to be expecting them.

"She must think we're inside," Sarah's father said, his voice falling in disappointment.

Sarah took his hand so he wouldn't feel bad. His palm felt as soft and rough as a cow's tongue.

He half smiled. "That's a girl. Don't worry, honey, we'll have her with us in no time."

WHEN REBA STRODE through the glass door she saw them immediately. Sarah ran and flung her arms around her mother. Reba pulled Sarah close and put her face down on the top of her daughter's head. Sarah was shocked to find how easily her arms encircled her mother's tiny waist and how high she now came on her mother's narrow chest.

Reba's fingers combed through Sarah's snarled hair, as Sarah pressed her head against her mother's breast, feeling this foreign heart beat as though it were her own.

"For God's sake, Scott." Sarah heard her mother's voice echoing cruelly through the walls of her chest. "Haven't you found time to comb your daughter's hair even once since I've been gone?"

Day Four

IT IS JUST AFTER seven at night and all color has suddenly disappeared from the sky. I turn on the lamp beside my mother's bed. She is propped up against a pile of pillows, her face a stark chiaroscuro, darkness on one side, illumination on the other. She holds a small, old-fashioned teddy bear between her breasts. She strokes it tenderly, kissing it from time to time. I brought the bear with me from New York and gave it to her on her first day in the hospital, saying he could keep her company when I had to go back to the pension. She grabbed the soft brown bear and kissed it more passionately than she'd ever kissed me. "Oh, isn't he darling," she said. "Isn't he just the dearest thing."

It has been a better day than yesterday. My mother has eaten three tiny meals, including a small omelet with sliced avocado on the side. That was an hour ago, and there are no indications that it won't stay down. Today she decided that she wants to go to San Juan to see Dr. Gold, her oncologist, to find out what her options are. "I need to know if there is any hope. But if it means a long, painful chemotherapy or radiation, I don't think I'm interested. I don't want to lead that kind of life."

I know that there is very little hope. When I went back home to New York after her operation I took her files and CAT scans to the foremost doctor in uterine and abdominal cancer at Mount Sinai to see if I should make arrangements to bring her north. My mother had said she didn't want to move from Puerto Rico, that the trip would be "devastatingly strenuous" for her, but I felt I had to try. I never actually saw the doctor, only spoke with him on the phone after he'd studied the results. His voice was sober as he said to me, "The type of sarcoma your mother has is a rapacious cancer and the rate of growth that I see in your mother's case is unusual. Given the information I'm looking at and her age and the sudden onset, I would say it would be futile to intervene. And rather cruel." When I hung up the phone, I sat for a long time looking out the window at the branches of the trees behind our building, watching as their thinning October leaves came loose in the wind and blew away. The mother he spoke of was the mother I'd wished dead so many times in my adult life. His news hurt more than I'd expected, but I tried to imagine what such a verdict would do to a daughter who loved her mother. What could he possibly have been thinking as he told me point-blank that my mother was surely going to die?

My mother's olive-complexioned face is small and heart-shaped, narrowing to a delicate point at her chin. If you look at pictures of her from university days, you see that there was a lively Semitic beauty about her, an intelligence radiating from her dark eyes. Over the years her expression became dulled by depression and twisted with anger. Even the pictures of her standing before the classroom where she taught high school show a sadness or a lack of affect, a faraway longing in her gaze, a flatness. I mull this as I sit beside her bed, because I know she thrived on teaching, relished the work she did. As a five-year-old, sitting in the back of a neighbor's car, I heard my mother say, "I can't stand staying home with a child. It's such a deadening experience. I have to get back to teaching."

We have called and made an appointment with Dr. Gold for four days from today. I've arranged for a friend from her bridge club, Esmeralda Jijón, to pick us up and drive us in. Still irritated with Joey, I don't want to rely on him.

"I'm so glad you'll be coming with me," my mother says, her chin resting on the top of the bear's head. "It was too difficult last time by myself. I had to wait in his office for five hours before he could see me. I was freezing in the air-conditioning and it was so hard to sit up."

I am gripped with fury. He's a kind man, and has been a decent doctor, but it's unconscionable to have made her, a post-operative elderly woman, sit there waiting for five hours. Even though I've already heard this story, I am overwhelmed by sorrow mixed with shame at not being here for her. I see her small, sick and pale, with no one to accompany her. I hear everyone speaking Spanish in the waiting room. I imagine her ingratiating smile, her formal politeness. She hadn't wanted to impose on anyone so she had driven into town herself. It is an hour-long journey. She hadn't had the strength to drive back so she called another bridge friend, Pearl Simon, who heard the exhaustion in her voice and took my mother into her Condado condo for the night.

Increasingly, feelings of pity for her are taking me over. It is her sadness and fragility that bind me to her these days, whereas throughout my life it was her remoteness and cruelty. Or perhaps, as Roberto says, it always was her neediness that held me captive.

I've pulled the club chair to the end of her bed and sit slumped down with my feet up on the mattress, my knees partially blocking my view of her.

"You know, it was twelve years ago that Scott died," she says in a distant voice.

I'm surprised to hear her say this. Back in September, she seemed oblivious to the coincidence that the day scheduled for her operation, September 21, was the anniversary of my father's final heart attack.

"Yes, I know," I say.

"He died on the day of my operation. Did you realize?"

"Yes, I did, Mom."

"I wondered if you didn't."

The wind rushes through his memorial tree in the back yard as if my father has heard us.

"Do you remember the dove in the hospital?" I ask.

"Of course I do, it was so strange."

We'd been waiting, my mother lying on her gurney, in the partially open-air ramp area above the operating room and overlooking the interior garden, when a dove flew up and landed on the railing beside us, peering at us with peculiarly crossed eyes. The orderly, a plump middle-aged man in pink scrubs, became frantic.

"Ay, I've never seen such a thing. I must get the *paloma* out of here. *Váyase, paloma,*" he shrieked, waving his arms. At first the bird remained arrogantly unbudging. "*Váyase!*" The orderly charged the dove, this time succeeding in sending it fluttering down the ramp, only to land on the banister twenty feet below and remain glaring up at us. "*Nunca lo he visto tal cosa,*" the man continued to mutter to himself, making feints at the bird, until we were called into the operating room.

"You know what I thought when I saw the dove?" I say to my mother, hesitant to admit my romantic thoughts to her. She hated it when any of my childhood remarks "smacked of sentimentality."

"What is that?"

"I thought, It's Daddy, come to watch over us." Like the tree outside, I say silently.

My mother beams, even laughs. "It's just like him, isn't it? Insinuating himself into a place without being invited. Demanding that business be taken care of. Oh, Scotty. I still miss him. The pain isn't what it was at first. Every day I used to feel I'd been socked in the stomach so hard that I could barely breathe. I didn't tell you, but I collapsed in the corridor of the hospital when they said he was dead. They wanted me to identify him, but I couldn't. I told them that he'd been Scott when he was alive. He wasn't Scott anymore now that he was dead."

We sit in silence except for the soft murmur of the tree and the far-off beat of a bass. I hadn't known this. I hadn't known that she'd grieved so.

My mother falls asleep sitting up, still holding her teddy bear. I turn out the light and remain in the darkened room, remembering my sullen anger during that week of mourning she and I spent together on *Calle Maruja*.

September and December 1981

ON THE EVENING of my father's death I flew to Puerto Rico. I cried all the way down. The plane was dark and a middle-aged woman in the seat next to me asked if she could help.

"My father just died." I said. "I can't stop crying."

"Oh, *señorita,* I understand."

I was inordinately grateful for her simple reply and for letting me weep without interference, because once I arrived at my mother's house, I knew I wouldn't be able to show my grief freely.

To my surprise, when the car service drove up to the house on *Calle Maruja,* I found my mother standing in the *marquesina* with all the houselights on, waiting for me, her fingers clutching the iron bars, seemingly, to hold herself upright. How long had she been there like that, I wondered as I paid the driver.

"Darling," she collapsed into my arms when I opened the gate. "How good of you to come, and so quickly."

But the next morning my mother rose early and sat at the dinette table with a cup of black coffee, robotically writing letter after letter to people in the States informing them that my father had died.

By midmorning, colleagues of my father's and neighbors and teachers from my mother's school were stopping by to pay their condolences. Only much later, when Roberto made mention of it, did I see that we'd unconsciously replicated the tradition of sitting shiva. For exactly one week, we entertained guests who'd come to pay sympathy calls, bringing food and succor. None of them knew my mother was Jewish. She hadn't yet met the Jewish women in the bridge club. She had no identity as a Jew here in Puerto Rico, but then she'd had very little life as a Jew all the time she'd been married to my father.

As soon as each visitor left, my mother returned to the table and immediately wrote a note thanking him or her for coming by.

Late in the afternoon, she looked up from her letters and stared at me. Her pallid face was set in the odd familiar sternness I recognized from my childhood, when an order was about to be given.

"I want you to gather all of Scott's clothes. Get everything from the closets and drawers and put them into large garbage bags. The bags are in the lowest drawer to the left of the sink. I think three should do. Esmeralda Jijón said she can give them to Cuban refugees. She'll pick them up tomorrow."

"Already? Isn't it a little soon, Mom?"

"I want them out of here, the sooner the better." She went back to her writing.

I stared at the top of her head. "Don't you even want to sort through them? Maybe you want to keep some things."

"No, Sarah. I want them gone. I don't want to have to tell you again. Do what I say, please."

"Where do you want the bags, then?" I asked. My voice had gone hollow. Stop your damn writing, I cried silently. Come look at his clothes, feel them, say good-bye to the fabric that touched his body. Have some emotion, for Christ's sake.

She looked up. "Out in the *marquesina*. Haven't I made myself clear? I don't want to see them."

I carefully folded his formal shirts, his *guayaberas*, the pale blue and tan pants he bought at the Roosevelt Fields shopping mall in San Juan. I kept a gray wool sweater for myself. His underwear was in a ratty state with yellow stains and frayed elastic. All his several pairs of shoes were scuffed and worn down at the heels, with holes in the soles. This was a man who took as little care of himself as he did of his family. I put the underwear and shoes in a separate bag to be thrown out. No Cuban refugee would deign to wear them.

I found his hearing aid in the bag of his personal items my mother had reclaimed from the hospital. I opened the blue plastic box and doubled over with the sadness of seeing it; this fleshy blob of putty had been wedged into my father's ear not two days earlier.

It was I who finally convinced him to get the hearing aid. I'd picked a spot on his favorite beach for the task. My mother was with us, but she sat off to one side, abdicating the role of telling him he was going deaf, just as she hadn't confronted him years before when he was drinking too much. She'd left it to the doctor to offer him the choice, stop drinking or die. My father stopped cold turkey. But that day on the beach in his bathing suit, his fleshy shoulders rounded forward, his belly in horizontal rolls, his skinny, knotty legs folded to one side, he'd kept his head down and had played his brown, age-speckled hand round and round in the sand.

I'd said the words, "Daddy, your hearing is going. You're always asking people to repeat things, and I can tell you don't understand a lot of what is being said. And you talk too loud to compensate. It's not good to continue this way, especially if you want to be effective in your work."

He didn't answer for a long spell, then he shook his head, his dark eyes finally meeting mine. Big cow eyes, I thought, mournful, filled with love and shame.

"I hate the idea of those things," he said, so quietly that it surprised me; I'd grown accustomed to his shouting. "They're so damned unsightly. Wouldn't it look ugly?"

"No, Daddy, they say they're tiny now. You can hardly tell. No cord, nothing. I really think it would be better to get fitted for one."

"It's stupid, but I have a little trouble with looking ugly."

"I thought appearances were secondary with you leftists," I said, laughing.

He chuckled. "Don't let us fool you, we're as vain as the rest of them." He sobered and gazed long at me before speaking again. "Me particularly. I was sort of shy as a young man, had trouble thinking I was even halfway decent-looking. Your mother changed that though," he said, reaching over to take my mother's hand.

I DRAGGED THE plastic bags through the living room and kitchen. My mother never looked up. Out in the *marquesina* I settled down on a paint-spattered wooden chair from the kitchen set we'd moved from apartment to apartment for thirty years. The set had finally been relegated to this outdoor area, like my father's clothes. The table, warped from the dampness of tropical rains, held a laundry basket, old buckets of house paint, a huge box of washing machine detergent, and paint trays with stiff unrinsed rollers and brushes. I had known this kitchen set as red, pale blue, yellow, green. Every time my mother painted the walls she gave it another coat. If I chipped the paint with my thumb, I thought, I could reveal our sorry history.

Sitting there, I breathed in balmy, pungent air, and looked out at the lemon tree, heavy with fruit, hanging over the neighbors' chain-link fence to the right. *Jíbaro* songs came from the house of the neighbor directly in back, where laundry hung out to dry on the fence and three scrawny kittens lay in the dirt sunning themselves, and chickens pecked beneath a mango tree.

Mr. Castro's identifiable whistle brought me back.

"*Hola, don* Eugenio," I said, without getting up.

He unlocked the padlock on the front gate of the *marquesina* with the key he used when he put out my mother's garbage. He entered and limped around the car, back toward me.

"*Hola, niña.* I am sorry for your loss." He pushed his straw hat off his forehead, revealing a lighter shade of brown skin. "We all miss *don* Scott. He was a great man." He spoke in Spanish to me. With my mother he used an elementary pidgin English.

"Thank you, *don* Eugenio. Your words are a comfort."

As we exchanged more sad remarks, he poked his knobby finger into the plastic bags. "What's in here?"

"My father's clothes."

"Hmmm," he said.

"My mother has someone coming to take them tomorrow."

"Are there no little presents for the people of the neighborhood to remember your good father by?" His skinny arthritic body was bent low over the largest bag.

"*Señor* Castro, my mother would be very upset to see you dressed in my father's clothes."

"Child, I wouldn't wear them in the neighborhood. She would never have to see."

Señor Castro had no place other than the neighborhood to wear these clothes. He had no money to go anywhere. His children were all in New York, so even if he had money, he had no one to come and pick him up and take him out.

He plucked one fine *guayabera* after another from the pile and held each up under his stubbly chin measuring the length of the sleeves against his arms. He smiled flirtatiously at me when he tried the fancy embroidered ones that my father saved for weddings and other occasions. They were exactly the shirts my mother would recognize.

"Okay, *don* Eugenio, take these three, but promise you won't let my mother see you in them."

"I will never let her see, my child." With that, he pulled a plastic shopping bag from his back pocket and stuffed the shirts in, then he lifted out a couple of trousers that he held up to his skinny waist, gazing plaintively in my direction.

"Okay, you can have those too. She'll never recognize them."

I BECAME AS emotionally cut off as my mother as the days went on, not crying for my father, having no sympathy for her. When Roberto arrived on the fifth day and saw my state of mind, he insisted that I go to the beach with him.

"I'm taking you out of this house by force if I have to," he said when I balked, saying I was in mourning and that it wasn't appropriate to go swimming.

But the minute we got in the car I felt I'd been rescued from an isolation ward. We drove west along the road following the ocean; the air blowing into the car was as soft as vapor on my skin. The vegetation looked greener and lusher than usual to my eyes, the palms taller and more majestic against the sky. Music blasted us as we passed cars parked on the embankment facing the sea. Legs clad in work pants were stuck out the windows to cool. I'd forgotten that people always pulled off to the side of the road in the evening to eat their dinners or just drink beer and soda and watch the sun reflected on the water. I put my arm on the window ledge and my head on my arm, glorying in the warm wind on my face.

When we arrived at the beach, broad beams of sunlight were slanting from the west through openings in the great heaps of white and gray cumulus clouds. It was an unearthly light, as if my father were sending it down to bless and envelop me, his golden girl. We parked on the road and scrambled over the rocky edge onto the narrow stretch of beach. Far out over the ocean was a huge cloud, as black as night, the sea beneath it green-gray with choppy whitecaps. Closer the water was calmer and turquoise, with rippling lines of apricot. The waves made a hissing sound as they hit against the shore. A hundred yards to our left a Puerto Rican family of mother, father and five small children ran in and out of the surf. They were all short and round-bodied and fully clothed, the mother in a dress, the children and father in shorts and tee shirts. The children's shouts came to us on the strong westerly wind. Calls of *"Papi, Papi, llévame, llévame, Papi."* Daddy, Daddy, lift me, carry me. Roberto wrapped his arms around me from behind and I felt his smooth, warm skin against my own, his slightly spongy flesh, almost as soft as my father's had become in the last years, and I cried aloud, *"Llévame, papi, llévame contigo,"* tears streaming down my cheeks. Roberto squeezed me more tightly. I felt his own tears on my back as he pressed his face to my shoulder and rocked me while the foam lapped our legs and our feet dug deeper and deeper into the shifting wet sand.

THREE MONTHS LATER Roberto and I returned to Puerto Rico to be with my mother over Christmas, to see her through this first holiday without my father. She didn't want to be in the house on *Calle Maruja*, nor did she want to stay in the cabañas in Boquerón on the southwest corner of the island where for years we'd spent Christmas when I'd come from New York to visit, living out on the beach in a rented cement block house, dressing in nothing more than bathing suits and shorts. "I don't want to see anyone right now," she'd said, meaning the large group of anglos: retired union organizers, social workers, university professors and even college presidents who came down from the mainland every year to live like vagabonds in the tiny cabañas for a month or two, moving from *casita* to *casita* under newly acquired names for each move, because the rule was one week to each customer. This was a state-run park intended for poor people. Each cabaña cost one hundred dollars for the week and you could put up as many people as you could fit into your house for that time period. Puerto Rican families slung hammocks in every conceivable space and squeezed up to fifteen people into a cabaña at one time. I used to envy those jam-packed scenes, with the lyrics of *jíbaro* songs accompanied by mountain instruments spilling out, and the smell of roasting pork, lard and beans wafting over you as you walked by. I would try to replicate that family feeling: I'd trek to town along the beach through the palm tree allée and buy my supplies, including sofrito and achiote to spice my pots of beans and rice and chicken. Then I would invite the entire expatriate clan to our bungalow, and at least for the duration of the dinner party I felt the neighbors didn't have pity for our tiny family group.

My mother didn't want to go down to Boquerón, I suspected, because she didn't want to be reminded of those times, the happiest in my recall, nor did she want to be at a disadvantage among these couples of thirty years or more. She was the first to become widowed, and they were my father's friends. He had gathered them in with his casual hearty being, his infectious laughter, and his love of political wrangling. She would remain in our shadows at these events. I was the star in the kitchen and he the center of attention at the long table we would set up on the outdoor patio.

Instead she had found us rooms in a *parador* near Quebradillas to the west of Arecibo. My mother picked us up at the San Juan airport and from there Roberto took over the driving. Just beyond the turn for Levittown Lakes we passed our favorite chicken stand.

"Let's stop," my mother said, eagerly. "I'm starving. There may be nothing along the way because it's Christmas."

Roberto swerved the car in beside the chicken truck with the large tin sign announcing *pollos ornados* in irregular red-and-black hand printing. The aroma of *picante*, spit-barbecued chicken filled the car.

"Scott loved this chicken," my mother said.

We ate our greasy chicken and drank the milk of coconuts at the lone picnic table with paper and other slightly disgusting refuse swirling around in the breeze, but I didn't care. This was what my Puerto Rico was about, and this was what my parents had been best at, relishing these ordinary pleasures, eating roadside chicken, looking out at the wide open Atlantic Ocean with its blue-green undulations and pounding waves, and being serenaded by the blasting, heart-rending island *canciones* from the owner's tape deck. *"Mi Puerto Rico,"* I thought, *"Mi borinquén."* I'd been coming here to visit my parents for nine years, longer than we'd ever lived in one place as a family.

"This is it," Roberto said, raising a chicken leg in my mother's direction. "This is why I married your daughter. She introduced me to another Latino culture. I thank you and Scott for that, Reba." He flashed a melancholy smile my mother's way, his eyes as dark and liquid as my father's had been.

My mother managed a begrudging smile. "Yes, Scott had a great appreciation for Puerto Rico, as do I." Her voice had turned cold and formal. Though her eyes met mine I knew she wasn't seeing me. In that instant she had begun to disappear from the world outside her being.

"I think Roberto meant that in a good way, Mom. He didn't mean disrespect. He wasn't making light of Daddy's death. He was just recalling how wonderful Daddy was. He's as sad as I am." We're losing her, I thought. I've got to get her back.

"I'm sorry, Reba. I loved Scott. I miss him terribly." Roberto reached across the table and patted my mother's hand.

She didn't respond to his touch. Her gaze turned away toward the ocean, profile to us, her face tiny against the vastness of the open sky, her nose rounded and prominent, her full lips pursed as if about to speak to some interior voice. I watched as she slipped further from us into a world of which I knew nothing. When I was a child, if I caught these states coming on, I would work double-time to keep her from disappearing there, chattering, telling funny stories, trying to get her to look at a drawing or at the food on my plate or at the kitten, when we had one. But I always failed. Her face would tilt toward mine, her expression blank and her eyes flat, and she would slur, "wha's that?" before going far away, abandoning me to the frightening aura of her nothingness.

"Where did she go?" Roberto mouthed, looking concerned.

I shrugged and went on eating, forcing myself to concentrate on the comforting warmth of the sun on my head and shoulders.

"Can she hear us?" he asked quietly.

I looked over at him, but just turned my lips down and raised my eyebrows.

"She seems to be in a trance," he whispered.

I nodded, fighting back tears. Big-deal shrink, I thought. I could have told him that much. Oh, why did I have to be alone again with her weirdness? God damn you, Daddy, for going away and leaving me with her again.

"It seems like a variation of a dissociative fugue state in which a person carries on an activity that he doesn't remember when he comes out of it." Roberto had moved closer to me. His face in profile to my mother, he shielded his mouth with his hand as he spoke.

My mother continued to sit erect and immobile across from us. Only her eyelids fluttered as though blinking reality away.

"There's a category for it?" I asked.

"I'd have to look up the exact symptomatology, but by all indications, I'd classify it as pathological."

I wrapped my arms around my waist and put my forehead on the table. There was a name for this eerie exercise of hers that I'd had to contend with all my life. It was pathological. It wasn't anything I had done wrong.

"Are you okay?" he asked, rubbing the back of my neck.

"Yes," I said, breathlessly. "I'm very okay. Thank you for that diagnosis."

After about fifteen minutes she shook her head and stared at us, slightly addled. She seemed to barely recognize us or this chicken rotisserie spot on the side of the road. Smiling shyly, she began to eat again.

"Have you finished already? My, you two eat so quickly," she said, wiping perspiration from her upper lip with her forefinger.

THE *PARADOR* WAS a dark wood roadhouse slung low along a cliff above the ocean. My mother brightened when we entered the open-air reception area, with its view of the beach where the high waves broke against boulders and sent dramatic sprays of froth into the air. "Scott would think this was much too grand," she laughed, her face alive with possibility. From that moment she was in a fanciful mood, so charming that it was as though a childlike joy had been released from captivity. I felt proud and pleased that Roberto was seeing a more pleasant side of her, and I dared to hope for the future.

She sustained her good cheer for the entire week and it continued on the drive home. She chattered from the back seat, where she had graciously situated herself, saying, "you two should sit together. I'm perfectly happy back here."

We drove in the late afternoon, passing miles of pink-plumed cane fields on our right, and beyond the fields the emerald green mountains of the Utuado and Dos Bocas region, where I'd climbed the dark roads in a bus with Lucy on that night in 1963; the ocean was a brilliant aquamarine and the sky above was a deepening blue, with billowing pink, lavender and orange-tinged clouds way out at sea.

My mother hung forward over the back seat. "It's so beautiful here. Look at those clouds. The sky in Puerto Rico is the most beautiful anywhere, and Scott and I have been all over the world. I don't think I could ever get enough of this view, of the ocean and the palms and sky. And look," She pointed out the front window toward Punta Salinas, her beach. "Look at those tamarisks, the way their boughs float in the wind. I am so happy that I stayed here after Scott's death.

Everyone said how lonely I would be, but it hasn't been that way at all. Everyone in the neighborhood has been as dear as they can be, so I'm. . ." and on and on she went.

We had decided that we would go home with my mother, spend the night with her, and take a taxi to the airport so she wouldn't have to return alone to an empty house after her first vacation without my father.

As I was unlocking the padlock on the *marquesina* gate, Estela came running across the street in her housedress and slippers. She dipped down to the car window to say hello to my mother, but then immediately came over to me.

"Something is wrong, *niña* Sarah. You might not want Mommy to go into the house."

"What is it, Estela?"

"I think Mommy's house was robbed. That's what *señor* Castro said. He took out your garbage and was checking the house today and he saw a big mess inside. You go in, *niña*, and look for yourself." She had hold of my arm as she spoke, her head close to mine. "Don't let her see it first."

I expected my mother to refuse Estela's protective solution, but instead her face crumpled with fear and she became childlike.

"Oh, no," she gasped. "Please, Sarah, you and Roberto go in and look."

The house had been completely trashed. Every drawer pulled out and overturned, and closets and cupboards ripped apart. The floor of the entire house was knee-deep in her belongings—dishes broken, photographs strewn, clothing thrown all over, with pockets turned inside-out, prints and paintings torn off the walls, mirrors shattered—as if a cruel, vengeful tropical storm had whipped through.

Still shaken by what we'd seen, I went back out to the *marquesina*. Estela and my mother were where I'd left them beside the open gate, my mother wrapped in Estela's arms.

"Is it that bad?" My mother asked faintly.

"It's pretty messy," I said, trying to keep my voice light. "Why don't you let Roberto and me straighten up a little before you come in."

"Reba, you come with me," Estela said. "You can sit in my house while Sarah and Roberto put things in order."

My mother nodded. Her face was ashen with fatigue and fear. She let Estela lead her across *Calle Maruja* and through the gate to the *marquesina*. My mother's hunched back disappeared into cascades of orchids of every imaginable variety, which hung, fragrant and showy, from the ceiling and all along the ironwork sides of Estela's carport.

"*Niña, niña*. Dr. Roberto. *Los malos han robado mami!*" *Señor* Castro shouted, hobbling stiff-legged down the curb and across the street. He wore my father's most colorful *guayabera* with cross-stitched embroidery down the front, one my mother was sure to recognize.

"Did you see anything, *don* Eugenio?"

"No, *niña, nadita*. They must have come in the middle of the night like *ratones*." He fanned his hand to indicate robbers. "I bet they were those addicts," he said, ever so slightly shifting his eyes toward Estela's place.

He followed us into the house.

"You don't have to bother, *don* Eugenio, we can do this ourselves."

"No, *niña*, let me help you and Dr. Roberto." And he continued shuffling in. "*Dios.*" He shook the fingers of his right hand, letting them crack through the air. "What a bad world."

While Mr. Castro poked around aimlessly, Roberto and I tried to get the house into some semblance of order, putting clothing back into drawers and drawers back into dressers, folding everything as best we could in our haste. We hung dresses in the closet, using the bent and broken hangers we found flung around the rooms. I picked up my mother's meager collection of costume jewelry, odd beads and brooches, dusty bracelets, nothing of value. I scooped up brittle slides that my father had taken on every trip they'd gone on and never bothered to look at afterward. The family photographs were scattered about. All of them fit into one small plastic briefcase, the kind given out at the yearly conferences of the Co-operative League of America that my father attended. The story of our constant uprooting seemed to be told in these meager black and white photos that no one had taken the trouble to put into an album: one or two pictures of the places we'd lived, tiny snapshots of my grandmothers whom I'd met only once or twice in my life, a photo of me in a playpen in front of our barracks in the Manzanar Japanese American Prison Camp and one of my father standing at the door of a mess hall in another camp in Arkansas. These last depicted an important piece of the history of America, but this rampage through the little bungalow diminished our existence. My parents had made history with their lives, working with the Okies during the 1930s. My father had set up co-operatives in the Japanese American prison camps and organized rural energy co-operatives all across the country and limited equity co-op housing in New York City. Even here in Puerto Rico my father had worked on consumer and environmental concerns affecting the island. He was a hero to many people, but it all felt churned to nothing in the mess of this room.

"Look at this house," I said angrily to Roberto, who was squatting by the desk, tossing scraps of uncatagorizable papers into a shoe box. "It's like all the small, shitty, poor places we ever lived in. What good does it do to save the world if you have to end your life in such a crummy, cramped, dusty excuse for a house?"

Roberto swiveled around to frown up at me. "Sarah, whatever your father's failings, and he had his share, he was a moral man. He gave back to the world much more than he took out. By my way of seeing things, that's more worthwhile than owning a fancy house."

When we felt it was safe for my mother to return, Roberto called Estela on the phone. "You can bring her over now," he said.

My mother held Estela's arm as she walked tentatively across the street. I met them at the door and led my mother into the living room. She stood surveying what remained of the wreckage, her face frozen in a mask of grief. "Oh, my. Who could have done this to me?"

We set her up at the dinette table to go through the receipts and bills we'd rescued from all corners of the house. Estela took on the bathroom as her job, and Roberto and I continued working on my mother's bedroom. Mr. Castro dragged garbage bags out to the curbside for pickup the next day. In the midst of our silent efforts my mother's piercing shrieks reached Roberto and me in the back room. We raced out to the dinette, but she wasn't there. The cries were coming from the *marquesina*. We found her standing at the iron gate, angrily railing at a short, delicate boy who was cringing on the other side, his shoulders drawn up toward his ears, bewildered, trying to explain, "But, *señora*, I not know you go away."

"Mom, what is it?" I cried, standing back, afraid to approach her.

Estela and Mr. Castro had rushed from the house after us and Estela went immediately to my mother's side while Castro, his head thrust forward, inched timidly toward her. Roberto slipped over to the far side of my mother.

My mother whipped around, her eyes darting, and then, finding me cowering behind the others, she seared me with her fury. "He wasn't supposed to deliver the paper this week. I expressly told him not to deliver it. He will never learn," she screamed at me.

"Reba, please come inside," Estela pleaded.

Mr. Castro shrank back, grimacing.

I couldn't move. I couldn't answer my mother. Estela and Roberto stepped in closer and took her arms, maneuvering her gently away from the gate and the frightened boy.

"But he must learn," my mother screeched, gesturing with pointed finger at the recoiling child. "If I have to beat it into him, he will learn."

"*Señora, señora,* we will take care of this," Estela crooned as she urged my mother into the house. Roberto was bent forward, speaking quietly to my mother. I could only watch.

"YOUR MOTHER IS very agitated. Dr. Roberto is with her," Estela said when she emerged again. "But she will sleep." She shook her head, as if comprehending yet not quite approving.

Meanwhile I, in numbed embarrassment, had calmed the boy, paid him the money he had innocently come to collect, and sent him on his way.

Very late that night Roberto and I crawled exhausted into bed. The air conditioner whirred in my mother's room, giving us some privacy in ours.

"It's because of my father's death that she acted that way. And the robbery. She must have thought the piled-up newspapers showed the robbers that she was away. It was all too much for her. I can understand that," I said. I curled into his body, shifting around to get comfortable, but I felt all elbows and knees, and my shoulders ached with tension.

"Let's assume that stress caused her to act inappropriately," Roberto said, sounding like the ponderous shrink he usually refused to be to me. His formality set me on edge.

"What are you getting at?" I snapped.

"I'm wondering why it bothered you so much. You were immobilized with fear. You looked terrified. What did it remind you of?"

I didn't answer him. Why did he have to intrude this way?

"Is that how she used to turn on you as a child? The boy was a child, after all."

I could barely breathe.

"That boy was just a child," he repeated. "I don't want to push you, Sarah, but did she yell at you that you had done such and such wrong and that she was going to beat the right way into you?"

I couldn't answer him because I'd become four years old, in my mud-caked overalls out in the vegetable garden in New Philadelphia, Ohio, where we had moved from Chicago in the winter. I am gleefully weeding in the early morning while my mother sleeps, singing to myself that I am helping Mommy, when from behind—I didn't hear her approach across the muddy lawn—she grabs me by the collar, choking me as she twists it tighter, shaking me, screaming words I don't understand until their meaning penetrates the howling, whirling anarchy in my head. "You've pulled up all the pea seedlings, you stupid, ignorant child," and then she begins to strike me across my behind and my knees and in the center of my back. "How am I ever going to make you learn not to destroy things without beating it into you?"

"Yes," I said to Roberto. "Yes, she sometimes spoke to me that way."

"That's an unconscionable way to discipline a child, so destructive," he said. "You've told me that you hate her. But you've never let me in on these details."

"Because I'm ashamed for myself and for her. I don't want other people to know."

"But Sarah, I'm not just other people."

"Oh, yes, you are. In these matters, everyone is other people."

Day Five

WHEN LYDIA ARRIVES in the morning I am formal with her, verging on cold, still angry with her for keeping the car out so long. She confronts me in the kitchen.

"What's the matter, *nena*? Why aren't you talking to me today?"

I'm washing up the dishes from my mother's breakfast. She has had some dry toast with a skim of jam. So far she's kept it down. I move the blue sponge over and over the Franciscan Ware plate, over the pink roses with green stems and yellow stamens that I know so well. When my mother dies I will take this set of dishes and the Fiesta Ware chartreuse salad bowl and nothing more, I decide.

"*Nena*, talk to me," Lydia begs in her nasal voice. "I'm sorry if you're mad at me."

"You said you'd get the car back in one hour," I say, my voice as icy as my mother's can be. I feel like my mother as I speak. I am my mother as I stand with my back to Lydia. "You promised and I trusted you. Do you know how upset I was? What would I have told my mother if you'd wrecked the car? She didn't even know I'd lent it to you."

"I'm sorry," Lydia cries, her voice like a long croak. "But I stopped to see my son. My Ladito. He lives with me, *nena*. He was all alone because I stayed later with you. I brought him back last night to meet you today."

I don't believe her. "You don't have to tell me all that," I say. "Just admit it, damn it, you kept the car out longer than you said you would. Who knows what you were doing." I feel pleasure in these harsh words. I want to hurt her. Subdue her. I turn to see the damage I've done and find her slumped against the refrigerator, hugging the towels she has just taken from the clothes dryer in the *marquesina*. Her eyes have filled with tears and her small face has shrunk into itself, pinched and bruised with sadness.

"You think I'm lying, but I'm not. It's true. He's my baby, my Ladito. I took him in because his *mami* has *SIDA*. I'm all he has. He's seven years old. I couldn't leave him there all alone. His *mami* lives out on the street. She sometimes comes looking for him. She steals things from me, even from him, for drugs. I can't leave him there overnight." The tears spill down her cheeks.

My paranoia is lifting. I don't feel compassion yet, I don't completely trust her story, but I am beginning to come back to my old affection for her.

"Here," I say, handing her two sections of paper towel.

She takes them and wipes her face.

"I'm sorry I got mad," I say. "But I don't need that kind of worry right now."

"I know that, *nena. Yo sé, nena.* I didn't mean no trouble. And Joey and I didn't do nothing bad like you were thinking. We respect you too much. We wouldn't do that." She blows her nose. Her hair is stiff and strawlike today.

I watch her, thinking, Here is this woman with nothing, taking in the child of a drug user who has AIDS. At the same time, I'm still wary that she's conning me.

I put my arms around her and she sinks against my chest. As I hold her, feel her warm body against mine, the last vestige of suspicion seeps from me, and I realize that my anger isn't related to her and the dumb car. It's an old fury that I've had from childhood, one that could erupt and swamp me without notice. It's about my terror of people not coming back when they say they're going to, about not being able to count on anybody, about being left all alone. I almost laugh as I recall what my mother said was my first sentence; "Daddy go away car car." People just drive off and never return to me, like my father, and Lucy, and now my mother who is dying in the other room.

"You're a good person, Lydia. I'm sorry I spoke to you that way."

"I love you, *nena*. I'm your *mami*, too. I can have two babies. Don't you worry, I'll take care of you."

I DECIDE TO GO for a run, feeling that it's safe to do so with Lydia in the house. In my room I dig through my small suitcase that sits precariously on a desk chair, and which I've not yet unpacked. Even if I did unpack, there'd be no place to put my things. The closet, a narrow indentation in the wall, with a rusty, ill-hung louvered door, is filled to capacity with old winter clothes my mother hasn't worn in years and dusty luggage we shoved back in after the robbery. There is no bureau, only a desk piled high with papers and odds and ends: my father's old slide racks, my mother's discarded handbags, stacks of dog-eared paperbacks, and a folder stuffed with photographs of my father standing alongside various community people in the States and in Puerto Rico. There is a cobalt blue bookshelf crammed with more books. On top, laid on their sides, are dozens of yearbooks from my mother's years of teaching. My bed is a narrow cot with a trundle bed beneath it. When Roberto is here and we open it out, there is no space to move at all. As I do each time I change my clothes, I pile my khaki shorts and tee shirt on top of my suitcase.

Once I'm dressed in running shorts and a singlet, I tell my mother that I'm going.

"I'll be back in half an hour, Mom," I say, standing at her door. We've taken the plastic off the window to let in fresh air. The morning light pours in. My father's tree is fresh and glistening from the heavy rain in the early hours of the *madrugada*. Yesterday, I heard Estela say that the rainy season is ahead of schedule this year.

"That's fine, dear," my mother says. Her head lies back

on the pile of newly changed pillows, her eyes closed. I note that her face is gaunt and yellow. "But don't take too long, please."

This won't be as good a day as yesterday. I wonder if she'll be strong enough for her appointment with Dr. Gold on Tuesday.

I run around the cul-de-sac of *Calle Maruja* and out onto the road that borders the canal. A slight breeze blows off the murky water. Otherwise the air is hot and humid with the sun almost at midpoint in the pearly sky. I keep pushing, feeling free and happy to be out of death's house. I am soaked with sweat by the time I reach the end of the road, and turning left I keep going until I'm at a small park with a track and baseball field. I do a couple of turns on the oval, running intervals, speeding up, slowing down until I can go no further and begin to walk. Around and around I continue, thinking of nothing much except to wonder at the skinny teenage boy jogging counterclockwise who wears heavy navy blue sweats, more appropriate for winter in Central Park.

I feel as if I've run a hundred miles, the house seems that far away, until I remember my mother in her bed with her head on the pillows and a cry escapes from me like a bird that has fluttered up from hiding. I walk off the track and over to the cement risers, shaded by a roof, where I sit.

Where and when did it go wrong for us? I wonder. Did I ever love her? I longed for her, that much I know. I used to stand in the doorway of her bedroom on weekday afternoons during my early teens. This was after we moved to Long Island and were living in the first house my parents had ever owned. Immediately upon arriving home from a day of teaching, my mother would go to her bed with a plate of toast and jam and a glass of milk. She'd curl in under the covers and read magazines until she fell asleep. Hers was a single bed, separated from my father's by a bureau. They'd not slept in the same bed for years, something about my father being a light sleeper and my mother kicking in the night from violent dreams in her deep, druglike slumber. Sometimes on a Saturday or Sunday morning if I happened in, I found them in one bed together. Usually my mother had crawled in with him and was wrapped around my father from behind. But on the weekday afternoons, I'd stand in the doorway trying to make conversation. She would answer my questions distractedly, not looking up from her reading, until finally she'd sigh and say, "Sarah, I'd really like to have some time to myself. It's been a long hard day."

The boy in the heavy clothes continues to circle the oval. As I watch him, I have another memory of that house of those same days. My father calls me from the bathroom at the top of the stairs. My mother is downstairs in the living room watching television. I am in my bedroom doing homework. I go to the closed bathroom door and call in.

"What is it?"

"Could you come in here a minute, honey?"

Reluctantly I open the door. My father is sitting in the half-filled tub, naked. He smiles sheepishly at me.

"Do you think you could wash my back? I don't want to bother your mother."

The bathroom is tiled in yellow. Very plain. I kneel on the pale pink bathmat and take the washcloth he hands me.

"Just soap the rag, honey."

I dip it into the gray water with its skim of dead skin floating on the edges. I dip it behind him. I soap the yellow washcloth and move it as quickly as I can over his mole-covered shoulders, his back and torso.

"Not so hard, honey. Take your time."

I want to hit him on his spine, smash my fist into his flesh, scratch my nails down his back. But I slow a bit and then I abruptly stand and say, "I think you're clean, Daddy. I'm going back to do my homework now."

The boy is finished with his run and has gone over to an area of dry, dead grass where he sits with his legs extended wide and begins to touch his toes.

I shiver in the shade. It has become too cool where I sit.

MY MOTHER IS asleep when I return. Lydia is waiting for me in the living room. She has taken everything out of the teak credenza. She is sitting on the rug my parents bought when they visited me in Peru when I was in the Peace Corps. In a ragged circle around Lydia are stacks of dishes, souvenirs from other trips, and a package of canceled checks, bills, receipts and old checkbooks. I join her on the floor and flip through a pile of old bills.

"I decided to clean this out. Every day I do another cupboard."

I wonder what she means by cleaning them out. She can't throw anything away. Only my mother can authorize what must go and what must stay. Again paranoia intrudes. I have the uneasy feeling that Lydia is casing the place, finding if there is anything valuable or useful here.

"I love these dolls," she says, meaning the large shadow puppets my mother bought on her first solo trip to Bali after my father died.

Lydia rises to her knees and takes one of the puppets down from its stand on the credenza. She manipulates the sticks that make the figure bow. I crawl over, angle the lampshade beside the couch, and turn on the light. Even in the sunny room a shadow image appears on the green wall. Lydia laughs with delight. She makes the puppet stand up and then jerks it into another bow. I lift the companion puppet from its pedestal and begin to move the sticks. For minutes our alter egos spar above us, jabbing heads, lifting arms threateningly, backing off in fright, eventually joining together in an awkwardly intimate dance while Lydia hums a flat, nasal tune.

"Tell me about your son," I say after I've put my puppet

back and turned off the light. I'm sitting beside Lydia on the floor as she carefully dusts her puppet, which is in her lap.

She smiles, not looking up.

"Ladito is very sweet. He doesn't have AIDS. He was born before his *mami* got it. But she's no good for him and she knows it. She asked me to take care of him. He's the same age as my daughter's boy. I'm too old for this but I love him. I think you have to do for people when they ask. Don't you think?"

"I guess so. I've never been in that situation." I think of how I didn't help Lucy, didn't take notice of how troubled she was.

"You're helping your *mami*. You gave up everything to come down here. She says so. She says you're very busy."

"She told you that?"

"Yes." Lydia rises to her knees to set the puppet in its holder. "She was so happy when you said you were coming down. I was here when you told her. She said, 'When I had the operation, Sarah just turned on a dime and came down here and now she's coming again. I'm so lucky to have her.' She said, 'Not everybody's daughter would do the same.' That's what she said, honest."

I finger the stylized jaguar image in the Incaic pattern of the rug, thinking how I had put aside the novel I was working on and had turned down a well-paying magazine article. Even so, it was easier for me than for other people to adjust my schedule; I didn't have a nine-to-five job.

"But I had to come. There was no one else to take care of her. I'm her only child."

"It's the same with Ladito. His daddy is dead. His grandma doesn't even know he exists. His mommy's brothers and sisters live in New York City. I couldn't say no. That's the way life is sometimes. You do what you have to do. But love takes over after a while and it's like you're glued to the person and it's not possible to unstick. That's how it is with me and

Ladito. We're just stuck together. And he's so cute. You'll see. I'll bring him around for you to meet."

I SIT IN MY mother's room while she sleeps. She has not wakened for lunch. This means she's been out for over five hours. It is three o'clock and the sun is on the living room side of the house. Her room is in shadow. By six it will be dark. I wonder if she will wake before night falls.

I watch her sleep. Her skin is yellow and dry, but the wrinkles have once again fallen away as though she has already been released from gravity. She doesn't look pretty. Her mouth is slackly open and her nose appears large and puttylike. Her hair is matted to her skull. She has drawn the cover up under her chin and her clutching fingers look like little paws. She breathes on and on. I am wondering at what Lydia said about how pleased and excited my mother was by my coming here, when Lydia enters the room and stands by me, putting her hand on my shoulder.

"She looks peaceful," she says quietly in Spanish.

"You think so?"

"Yeah, to me she looks real peaceful. But by the end it could get real bad."

My stomach lurches at her mention of the end.

"What do you mean?"

"I've been with lots of people at the end. The whole thing inside them just explodes and it can be real ugly. You should think about that, *nena*. Be prepared for it." She sits on the arm of the chair and pulls me close to her. "I'll be with you. You can trust that. But maybe you should think about getting the nurse back so you won't be alone in the middle of the night."

Lydia leaves and I remain sitting with my mother. This is not the first occasion I've been told to be prepared for my mother's end. Between the time when my mother had her operation and when I returned for this stay, I had a conversation with my friend Phyllis. I told her that if it came to it, I would help my mother to die, that I would get an overdose of pills and feed them to her. We were sitting in a quiet restaurant off Ninth Avenue in the forties. "Sarah, I wouldn't jump into this so fast, like you're prone to. Like diving into the pool and then finding out you can't swim. It's not that easy to help a person commit suicide," Phyllis said, putting her fork down on the plate and looking at me with her sympathetic, deep gray-blue eyes. "I think I could do it," I said, though already feeling queasy now that she'd put the word suicide to the act. "Look," she said, "you saw what I just went through with my mom's death. You saw how hard it was for me and my brother. And that wasn't even suicide, that was just pulling out the support that was torturing Betty." Phyllis rubbed her cheek under her left eye. It was her nervous habit anytime she was going to cry. "Not everyone dies the same way," I said, "and I can imagine my mother wanting to end it and asking me to help." Phyllis shrugged, her eyes filling with tears. "I'm not religious or sentimental. But I saw Betty's soul leave. I saw eighty years of life, almost fifty years of her being my mom, go out of her. I don't know what I would have done if Tommy hadn't been with me. Believe me, it's a frightening experience, no matter how cool we want to think we'll be. So my hope, as your friend, is that you'll have someone with you when your mom dies, even if you're lucky and she just peacefully slips away. I know you, Sarah, you're very emotional, very feeling. I don't think it's going to be easy for you, however it happens."

ROBERTO CALLS later in the evening.

"I can't get down there. The airline strike is still on. They say Clinton is going to step in, but he hasn't yet."

"If he does settle it, just buy a ticket, any ticket even if it costs five hundred dollars. I need you down here." I start to cry.

"Well, this is progress. You admitting to needing my help."

"That's not fair. I always need you. You know that. It's other people I don't need."

"Correction. It's other people you can't admit you need, *cariña*."

"Roberto, stop pushing me. I don't need you pushing me."

"I'm not pushing you into anything. But you could call some of your hundreds of friends who keep phoning here and asking what is going on. They want to help."

"No! I don't want all their damn advice. Anyway, I can't have them calling here every five minutes. Do you know how many calls I'd get if I let them? Twenty a day. What would my mother feel if the phone kept ringing for me all day long? I'm not going to do it, so quit getting on me about this."

THIS NIGHT I'M unable to sleep. I lie in bed with the air conditioning off and the door to my room open. I listen for my mother. I get up every hour and wander into her room, checking to see if she's still breathing. I sit for a while in the club chair with my feet tucked under me and the polyester quilt up to my chin against an onslaught of freezing air from the whining machine in the window. It's as cold as a morgue in here, I think.

October 1948

THE YEAR SHE was six, Sarah used to play at being an orphan. After school, while her mother was still up at the high school, teaching, Sarah would change from one of her three dresses into blue jeans and a plaid shirt. She would go outside to sit on the cement stairs before the two-family house where they had an apartment in the French Canadian section of North Burlington, Vermont. Hunching over her knees, she would watch for the few people who walked along their street. When she saw someone, Sarah would imagine them asking her, "What are you doing there all alone, little girl?" She would pretend she'd answer, "I'm an orphan. I have no mother and father." Then the person would sit down beside her on the step and talk with her and say how good she was and invite her home to eat. This was a calming fantasy because in real life Sarah was loath to let anyone know how lonely she was and how much she wished she had a mother to care for her tenderly.

It was an especially angry year. Sarah had no baby-sitter because she had been sent home by the woman up the street who watched children in the neighborhood; Sarah had said piss and shit too many times in the woman's house, even after the second and third warnings. Sarah's parents didn't have enough money to hire a private sitter. The one housekeeper they did have for a short time had left in a huff after she'd found Amos La Fontaine and Sarah naked on her parents' bed in the room Sarah shared with them. Sarah slept on a low cot shoved up under the front windows, which placed her a mere foot from the double bed she and Amos played marriage on. There was a problem also with the doctor's daughter, a child with a home Sarah could have gone to after school, except that she'd bitten the girl so hard in the arm she'd drawn blood. Sarah's mother, who seemed amused by this aggressive behavior, had cheerfully explained that she mustn't bite people, only animals did that. In all of the incidents it seemed as if she liked Sarah's feistiness and subtly rewarded her us-against-them actions. But when her mother responded that way, how could Sarah tell her about the uncontrollable, whirling rage that had risen in her at the girl's fussy, frilly dresses and the self-satisfied expression on Mary Ann's face and the fact that Mary Ann's bedroom was filled with toys while Sarah had none, neither bedroom nor toys of her own in the tiny apartment that had barely space enough in the living room for them to walk between the couch and two easy chairs.

This is not to say that Sarah's mother didn't try to do her best with her daughter during that year. One day, when Reba got home from school, she found Sarah crying in the bedroom. Sarah told her that a bully, Jean Devereaux, kept saying he was going to beat her up. "Then it's time I taught you how to defend yourself," Reba said, leading Sarah into the tiny kitchen that looked out over an empty lot to the back of the Catholic funeral parlor.

"Your father doesn't believe in physical fighting, but I do." Reba lifted her fists into boxing position. "Certain situations call for extreme measures."

Her mother's usually sallow cheeks were flushed with the excitement of the battle, her slender body taut and coiled to spring as she sparred with Sarah. "You've got to show him you're not afraid of him, otherwise he's going to continue threatening you. Keep moving all the time, one foot forward, and keep your head low," she said as she danced toward Sarah and back, butting Sarah with the top of her dark curly head, jabbing her with her fist. "Keep your fists raised and feint and dip and dodge his blows like I'm doing, until you see an opening. Then hit him with your left fist, it's your strongest punch, then follow through with your right and clobber him with your left." Sarah laughed loudly, holding her fists high and her chin to her chest as she danced in step with her mother, loving that Reba was paying her this much attention, but intimidated and challenged by her mother's prowess and intensity. Her mother could teach whole classrooms of high school kids. Sarah's father said she was the smartest teacher in all of Vermont. She sewed every one of Sarah's dresses. She could drive a car across the whole country and back again. And now she could throw a punch like Sarah had seen men do in movies.

The next day Sarah went to school and Jean Devereaux came after her in the playground and she ran away, over to the side door of the school where other children were congregated. After classes she ran all the way home instead of lingering to watch the kids playing marbles in the dirt field behind the three-story, soot-blackened building.

Sarah sat in a puddle of shame at the kitchen table, too frightened and dejected to go out to the front steps, dreading her mother's homecoming, looking out onto the grim view of the vacant lot behind their place, with its weeds and saplings growing up around tires and an old wrecked, rusting carcass of a truck. Glass shards glittered in the late afternoon sun and a line of ragged and patched clothes hung from a rope along the house to their left. Her mother hated this view, hated this apartment, and told Sarah's father so. On weekends Reba would sit as Sarah was sitting, looking out the window, her expression flat and her skin slack, her fingers circling round and round the pattern on the oilcloth. Sarah's father was rarely with them on weekends, or any time for that matter. There were always people he was trying to get to some meeting or other. "The best time to catch farmers is on a Saturday or after church on Sunday," he would say. Or in the evening on any day. Sometimes Sarah and her mother went with him on the weekends, driving around the countryside, down to Barre or Randolph, or thereabouts, stopping at one farmhouse after another to "see this or that fellow." Sarah's father would stand by the fence if he found the farmer in the field, his foot up on the rung of the split wood, talking to the man who'd come down off his tractor. All the while she and her mother remained in the car, her mother's patience finally running out after three such stops of an hour's duration each.

That afternoon of Sarah's failed fight, her mother found her in the kitchen with her thoughts.

"I expected to see you outside."

"I stayed in. I was tired."

"Tired? From what?" Reba laid her books on the table and put her hand to Sarah's forehead, then bent down to place her cheek to Sarah's. Sarah could smell cigarette smoke on her breath and imbedded in her clothing.

"From beating up Jean Devereaux," Sarah said in her brightest voice.

Her mother laughed. "Good girl. You see. He won't be bothering you anymore."

"I punched him in the face and then hit him in the stomach and he went running away from me. He's really a baby, Mommy."

"That's what I told you," her mother said, taking off her coat and dropping it on the chair. From her purse Reba got her pack of cigarettes and settling across from Sarah she shook one out and lit it, sucking in the smoke, then blowing it out and at the same time picking a piece of tobacco off her tongue. "You only have to stand up to bullies to find out what cowards they are. Unfortunately, that's the way this world works." Reba sighed and turned to stare out at the back yard.

For the rest of the school term, Sarah used her wiles to stay clear of Jean Devereaux, and then that summer her parents moved out of the neighborhood to a better apartment up by the university in Burlington proper. It was an area of single-family houses, large, hundred-year-old clapboard

structures with gracious porches and wood-paneled rooms.
Here the children played in the quiet streets and all had their
own bedrooms, the boys with cowboy motifs, the girls with
organdy-skirted dressing tables and miniature doll col-
lections. Their mothers stayed home and cooked and dusted
and vacuumed. They had lawns and large maples, elms and
firs in front of their houses. Sarah and her mother and father
still lived in a multiple-family house, the only one on upper
Brookes Avenue. Sarah continued to share a bedroom with
her parents, but now her alcove was curtained off from their
space by a heavy upholstery fabric patterned with richly
colored roses. When her parents weren't home Sarah would
pretend it was a stage curtain and open and close it on her
solitary performances.

Day Six

PEARL SIMON, my mother's bridge partner who's lived in Puerto Rico for forty years, drives out from San Juan to take me to the local shopping center. I am in the kitchen washing the dishes from the breakfast my mother didn't eat when Pearl pulls up in her yacht-sized 1975 Lincoln Continental. "A woman needs a big car," she told me one day during the week my mother was in the hospital. "Men don't respect you on the road, especially Puerto Rican men don't, if they see you in a little compact. In this car, I'm somebody to reckon with."

I watch her walk up the short path from the sidewalk, her legs spread to keep her balance. It's only when she walks that she seems old to me. She's quite a woman, or a dame, as my father used to say way back when; she has bright red hair, exaggerated eye makeup, a lighted cigarette hanging from her mouth. At seventy-five, one can still recognize the sports-writer and the gunrunner for Israel that she once was. On top of that, she's a voracious reader, devouring six serious books a week. "On the Sabbath I rest," she says, letting loose with her raucous laughter.

"Hi, darling." Pearl kisses me, pressing her cheek against mine. "How is she?" she asks conspiratorially.

"Not too good. She's having a hard time eating."

"I brought my lunch. We'll eat together when you and I get back. Maybe that will encourage her."

"Pearl, I don't know how to thank you for this."

"Don't you worry. Just be glad baseball season is over or you'd be up a creek without a paddle." Her full-out laughter ends in a crescendo of coughs. "Damn, do you have an ashtray? I know Reba gave up smoking, but she must still have one here." The long ash falls to the floor.

She deposits her pink plastic lunch bag and bright red thermos in the refrigerator. My mother has already explained to me that "Pearl will probably bring her own food. She's always trying to lose weight."

"I also brought some food from Ana Mendez for you and Reba. She's a good cook, Ana is. What do you bet she sent *arroz con pollo*? What else?" Again a belting laugh as she adds a Tupperware container that she's pulled out of her large plastic carryall. "Let me go in and say hello to Reba and then we'll be on our way in the chariot."

I watch her familiarity with the kitchen and the house. The surprise to me is that she has spent time here. My mother has never had friends before. No one ever came to our apartments or house just to hang out and have coffee. The few people who visited for dinner were my father's friends from work. She had no women pals to go out with casually on weekends or after school; I had to fill that need. But when I was with her in the hospital and since I've been out here, the phone has rung with women and the occasional man from her bridge club calling to see how we're doing. There may actually be people at her funeral.

PEARL AND I DRIVE the back way through miles of urbanization built by Levitt, block upon block, cul-de-sac upon cul-de-sac of the same cinder block, stucco-slathered structures, some of which have been added to over time, a second story here and there, a *marquesina* closed in to make a room, a few with elaborate gardens in front and back, the majority with bare patches of failed lawn. The sky is a brilliant, cloudless blue and the air drier than usual, but inside Pearl's car, which has no cooling system, the atmosphere is suffocating. She lights one cigarette after another off of the last. The engine pours out more heat and toxic fumes. Pearl races her vehicle like a stock car driver, careening around corners, slamming on the brakes when the car she's been tailgating stops for the light. She has no seat belts in this car. I clutch the burning metal of the window frame to keep from being thrust into the dashboard or through the already cracked windshield.

"You're quite a driver, Pearl." I laugh nervously.

"That's what I told you. You have to be aggressive or they'll massacre you, these Puerto Ricans. Your mother's getting better at it. I taught her some tricks." She winks at me.

"Pearl, you're going to get her killed." Then I realize what I've said. "That was terrible. I'm sorry."

Pearl reaches out and pats my leg. "Take it easy on yourself. You're under a lot of pressure, honey."

In the parking lot we circle for a good fifteen minutes before we find a space close to the door, so we don't have to walk. I would have liked nothing better than to stretch my legs.

When I told Lydia we were planning to shop today, she looked at me as if I were nuts. "You know what it's like on Sunday? Everybody's getting their shopping done on Sunday. I never go to the supermarket on Sunday unless I have to."

This is the biggest supermarket I have ever seen, even larger than suburban stores in the midwest of the United States. The aisles are numbered one to forty. The store appears to extend a mile from where I stand and the aisles are at least sixty yards long and ten feet wide. Even so they are clogged with people pushing chest-high shopping carts the size of Eastern Bloc automobiles. The carts are mounded with groceries high over the shoppers' heads. There are families pushing an entire fleet, sometimes five carts in a row. Everything seems to be sold in bulk. The smallest bag of rice is twenty pounds. There are three-gallon jugs of cooking oil and ten-pound cans of beans. The chickens are sold in threes, and ground beef is in ten-pound packages.

"What can I say," Pearl laughs when she sees my reaction. "Puerto Ricans like to shop and eat."

What could my mother have felt coming in for her tiny purchases, pushing her almost empty cart among these large families? Even I am tempted to fill the cart to bursting so that no one will know how meager our family is. But I can't, not with Pearl here. Already she has started to question my purchases. "Four steaks? What do you need that many for? You said Reba isn't eating." I put them back and pick up a two-pound package of lamb chops. "I can freeze what I don't use," I say. "And anyway, sometimes I cook a little for Lydia."

"She's a very nice girl. It's a mitzvah that you feed her," Pearl says.

My mother has especially asked for S & W baked beans. Before we left, she said, "I would love it if you could make them for me. You must buy an onion, half a pound of bacon and a package of brown sugar. I'll tell you exactly how to make it. Oh, my how I look forward to the taste."

We find a reasonably sized jar of the beans but have to settle for a three-pound package of bacon and a five-pound box of brown sugar. And then it is time to check out. The aisles have become more difficult to navigate, but it's only when we try to go to the front that we find ourselves in a massive traffic jam.

"It's a gridlock alert," I say, as we push to the back of a line, squeezing by alarmingly stacked carts, calling *"permiso"* over and over to people standing jabbering in our way.

"This is exactly what they do on the roads—stop their cars in the middle and have a conversation," Pearl says at top volume. We get some nasty looks.

After much maneuvering and aggressive bumper-car action, we finally stand at the end of a twenty-five-cart line.

"This will take nothing less than two hours, sweetheart, and I'm going to have nicotine d.t.'s if I don't have a cigarette," Pearl says.

I'm getting irritated with her. Why does she have to be addicted to those damn cigarettes? My mother used to smoke as much as Pearl does, and I think sometimes that's why she got cancer. She stopped five years ago, but it was probably too late. She was left with a deep hacking cough that could have been a symptom of undetected lung cancer. It could have metastasized to her abdomen, though nobody wants to say that, nobody wants to take responsibility for missing it in the first place. I'm standing here in the middle of this ridiculous supermarket in Puerto Rico having these thoughts that I've not let myself have before, because it would mean I hadn't acted responsibly either. But I had. I'd gotten after her time and again to stop smoking. My father had, too, but she'd just brushed us off. Even after my father died and she woke me up one night with her cough and I went into the bedroom and said that maybe the time had come to stop, that Roberto and I wanted her alive for a few more years. I said that almost meaning it as the words came out. She looked up at me over the Kleenex she was spitting phlegm into and said, wiping her mouth, "Maybe I don't want to live that much longer." But six months later she stopped. She went with a couple of people in the bridge club to get vitamin B shots into her ears and up her nose. She said it had been so horrific that she didn't want ever to start smoking again, for fear she'd have to revisit the pain of the cure. But her cough persisted, even up to the day she went in for her operation. I was terribly concerned about her cough and how much agony it would cause her after the operation if she went into her usual paroxysms. I asked the surgeon—a young Puerto Rican, Harvard-trained man—if he could do anything about it. He looked solemnly at me and said, "This is the least of your mother's problems. I don't think you should worry about that." But she didn't cough after the operation, and she hasn't coughed since. I don't know why, though perhaps it's because she went off her high blood pressure medicine, but whatever, she has not coughed for two months. There is mercy in the world, I think, as I come back to the reality of the freezing supermarket and Pearl, who is covering her own cough with a white handkerchief embroidered in pink around the edges.

"I was thinking, Pearl, that I'd like to buy my mother some roses. She loves roses. It might brighten up her room. I saw a florist when we came in. You hold the fort and when I get back, I'll stand guard and you can go out for a smoke."

"You're a peach," she says, already feeling around in her oversized straw purse for her pack. "On your mark, get set, goooo."

As I walk through the crowded aisles toward the front of the store, I feel like sobbing. I don't even know why, except that memories of what happened during her operation are coming back to me. I sat in a waiting room, devoid of furniture but for five rows of straight-back plastic chairs and a large television hanging from the ceiling on a steel bracket. There were three other people in the room: a teenage girl, an old man and a middle-aged woman. For hours I watched the television without seeing it. About three hours into the waiting a sudden sorrow came over me. She's dead, I remember thinking. She just died. Tears were pouring out uncontrollably and the girl was sneaking peeks at me as if I was weird and scary. But I couldn't stop. I put my head down and simply gave in to the convulsive weeping, the tears filling me to overflowing like rain gutters in a torrential storm. An hour later, when the doctor came in, my crying had subsided. He was still in his scrubs. There was blood down the front, my mother's blood. His face was pallid and sweaty. He looked like a patient in shock. "She almost died," he told me, his hand on my arm. "There were a few minutes about an hour ago when she lost so much blood that we didn't think we could save her." I felt faint as I stood there listening to him go on, realizing that I had sensed the moment when life almost left her. "You have no idea what we found in her. It was an enormous, grotesque tumor, slimy, oh, I have never seen anything like it." He held his hand six inches apart, like a fisherman showing the size of his catch. He sat down suddenly. His head was in his hands. I wanted to comfort him, to say it was not his fault, that I was grateful to him, but I was too filled with shame to speak, ashamed of what he had found inside her; despite my hiding her failings throughout my life, this young Puerto Rican doctor had discovered their source and had named it repulsive. How could he want to receive succor from the likes of me? "May I see her?" I asked. He looked up, shadows of the horror still in his eyes. "She's in the recovery room. It's pretty awful in there." I told him I'd like to go in, but I had one huge favor to ask of him. "What's that?" he asked, his face regaining tone and color. "Could you get her into the Intensive Care Unit? I don't have it in me to care for her alone." He stood, gave me a hug, and said he would do what he could, that it was very difficult, but he would use all his pull to get her a bed.

The woman at the florist stand agrees to break up two bunches so that I can make a bouquet of six yellow and six salmony-pink long stem roses. I have told her that my mother is dying and that she loves pink and yellow roses, which isn't exactly true, but I want to put the roses in the high-necked Franciscan Ware coffeepot she got as a wedding present fifty years ago, and the pink and yellow exactly match its country pattern of wild roses. "It's very kind of you, *señora*," I say as she lays the roses out and carefully wraps them in blue paper. "I can do no less for a daughter whose mother is dying." She smiles sadly. I think, How lucky I am that my mother is dying in Puerto Rico, where sentiment abounds.

An hour and a half later we're back in the car.

"They're beautiful," Pearl says. "Let me get a sniff."

She burrows her face into the flowers as I watch the road for any catastrophe.

"She'll love them," Pearl says. "She'll love her daughter for thinking of them. You're such a good daughter. My son says you're making it impossible for the rest of the sons and daughters of the bridge club members. Howard says he'd never be able to compete." With this she laughs. "You're like one of those damned goody-goodies I used to hate in high school and college."

"Oh, Pearl, I'm not so good." I have an urge to confess that I cater to my mother's needs in order to cover up my anger at her, my hatred of her. But I know I can't say anything. This must continue to be my secret. For my mother's sake. I want her world of women and her neighborhood to think I do it out of love. I want them to believe that she has earned my love by a lifetime of caring for me. But then, I think, why did I cry like that in the waiting room? Why is the bond between us so deep that I knew the exact instant when she almost died?

The recovery room was like purgatory, with gurneys of writhing, moaning people under bloody sheets. I found my mother immediately. "Sarah, Sarah, help me," she groaned. Her face was gray and splattered with tiny dots of blood, her mouth was slack. She grabbed my arm. "I'm thirsty. I need water. Please help me." Terrified of her, of the room, of the possibility that she would die if I didn't get her water, I ran to the nurses' station. "My mother needs water," I said. The nurse came out from behind the counter, and, taking my arm, escorted me through the swinging doors into the silence of the hall. "It's best if you don't go back to your mother. She can't have water. It will only upset her more if she keeps asking you." "But she needs me," I said. She shook her head. "You can't do her any good right now. She doesn't need you. She just needs to need."

I turn my head away from Pearl, pretending to look out at the passing view, but I am hiding new tears. She just needs to need, the nurse had said, meaning, not me in particular, just the universal need of need. I've always wanted her to need me. Maybe she never has.

"HOW LOVELY," my mother says when I bring the roses into her room. "They're so hopeful."

But I see she is not as overwhelmed by their beauty as I

want her to be. They are just roses to her, I tell myself. To you they are a bountiful gift, an attempt at giving her life, saving her, bringing her joy. To her, they are "lovely" roses. Whose need of need is operating now?

I cook the S & W beans while my mother chats with Pearl. I do them exactly as she has asked, sprinkling on the brown sugar, carefully placing the strips of bacon on top.

"Mmmm, I can smell my beans," she calls from the bedroom when they are almost done.

"They'll be ready in five minutes," I call back.

I spoon out a small portion on a salad plate and give Pearl and me the same amount so my mother won't notice how tiny her serving is.

When I carry in the dishes and put them down on a TV table I've brought along, Pearl says, "That's *trayf*, Reba. You may do it, but I can't eat *trayf*."

"Pearl is observant," my mother says. She is sitting up higher in the bed than she has for some time. She looks perky and bright-eyed. "Maybe you should get her something else."

"No, nothing for me," Pearl says. "I've eaten my salad. I'm on a diet anyway. I always forget that your mother's not religious."

"No," I say, "not very. But it's interesting, Roberto said that when my father died, we replicated shiva without even knowing it." I glance at my mother and find her studying me. She looks away. "He said we sat in the house and received visitors for exactly one week."

"I don't know about that," my mother says.

"You didn't cover the mirrors, did you, Reba?" Pearl chides gently.

"Of course I didn't." My mother takes a prim bite of her beans. "I don't know what Roberto's talking about."

"I guess he was just saying that traditions hold even when you don't practice the religion," I say, daring to take the next step into this forbidden territory. We never speak of religion, she and I.

"You see, Reba, you see what I told you. She married a Jew. Right? Do you remember what I told you?"

"Pearl, I'd rather just enjoy my baked beans right now. It was such a lovely thing for you to do, Sarah, to make me my favorite beans."

I watch her eat, thinking, This is the way she does it, this is the way she avoids any issue that comes too close to the center of her being.

AFTER MY MOTHER finishes half her portion of beans she begins to lose energy. Pearl chats on, but my mother slides down lower in the bed and her eyelids begin to flutter. I signal Pearl when they close, indicating that we should leave. In the living room Pearl lights a cigarette. She hasn't smoked in the bedroom. She inhales deeply and lets out a stream of smoke with a long sigh. Her lipstick has worn off and I can see the freckles on her thin lips as she frowns.

"My friend isn't doing well," she says, quietly.

"No, she's not."

"Darling, you see a sorrowful woman before you. I love your mother. We have a lot in common, even though she hasn't been true to her heritage. But we both believe in working for a better world. We've both lived committed lives, fought for progressive movements. There's no one else here whom I can talk to about these things who understands. But this religion business. Did you notice that she has a menorah? Did you have a menorah in the house when you were growing up?"

We are standing beside the credenza where the menorah sits next to one of the puppets from Bali. It is a cheap bronze object, six inches wide, hardly big enough to be noticed. I pick it up. "No, never. We celebrated Christmas."

"Reba bought that menorah when she went to Israel. And what I was referring to back in the bedroom, about your marrying a Jew? Reba told me one day that she didn't think you wanted to identify with being a Jew. And I said, but you married a Jew, that must mean you have a connection to your Jewish heritage and to her."

"What did she say to that?"

Pearl's mouth twisted into a defeated half-smile. "Nothing much. She said she'd think about it."

"She's never seemed to really like Roberto. And he's such a nice man. I think she doesn't trust him."

Pearl stubs her cigarette out, chuckling to herself. "He's a psychoanalyst, am I right?"

"Yes."

"Doctor?"

"Yes, he went to medical school."

"The doctor part's good, but otherwise he's every Jewish mother's nightmare. She gets herself a doctor and he turns out to be a shrink." She laughs. "What could be worse, a son-in-law who can read her thoughts."

I'M PICKING UP the dirty dishes in my mother's darkened room when she says my name.

"Sarah, is that you?"

"Yes, Mom."

"Has Pearl left?"

"A while ago."

"Oh, my, I must have dropped off. I hope she wasn't insulted. She gets insulted very easily."

"No, she wasn't, Mom. She only hoped she didn't tire you."

"Not at all. If she calls be sure to tell her she didn't tire me at all. Isn't it lovely how everyone is being so attentive? I never would have thought it would be this way. They seem to really care."

I put the dishes down again and sit. "They care very much. Pearl said how much she loves you."

"Did she? My, isn't that nice."

"She said you're the only one who understands her when she speaks about political things, progressive things, I think she said."

"Yes, we have a lot in common. I can tell her about the sort of life Scott and I lived, the adventure, the ideas, the commitment, and she knows what I mean. That's been unusual for me, to have a friend like that."

"I know that, Mom."

"Do you, dear?"

It is very dark in the room. I haven't turned on any of the lights in the rest of the house, so there is no ambient glow to help me adjust to the darkness. It's just as well I think, for both of us.

"I've often wondered what it felt like to leave your entire family behind. I've wondered what your life was like before you married Daddy." Please answer me, I think. For once don't avoid my questions.

"Oh." She pauses. "I think I've told you. Mother was very difficult, cruel really, but I got a lot of support from all the aunts and uncles and cousins and especially Grandma. Grandma was my savior."

"Did you have seders and other holidays?"

She is silent. Ten heartbeats go by.

"Yes, we had large family seders filled with wild political wrangling. They were really quite marvelous," she says wistfully. "We went to temple on the high holidays, fasted on Yom Kippur, and broke the fast at Grandma's. Do you know about breaking the fast, dear?"

"Yes, I do, Mom. I've never fasted, but I have been to services a few times."

"I didn't realize that."

"Mom?"

"Yes, dear."

"Did you miss all that when you left with Daddy? Did you miss the big family events?"

"Oh, I suppose so," she sighs. "But you must understand that in those days it wasn't easy for a gentile to marry a Jew. Certain compromises had to be made for love. I'm not sorry for any of it. Your father and I believed we were changing the world, and I suppose we did in our small way. I wouldn't give up any of that for a few seders."

My heart is thumping as I ask the next question.

"Do you think maybe you'd like to call your sister?"

"Hannah?"

"Yes."

"I haven't spoken to Hannah since she called me after Scott died. It was good of her to call after we hadn't talked for years. Why would I call her now, dear?"

What do I say? Because you are dying? I can't believe she doesn't know why she should speak with her only sister, even though they've been estranged. They've never really fought, my mother would never have a direct confrontation with her. But they seem to have no love for each other. That was destroyed long ago in their mother's house.

"It might be nice for you to hear her voice. I've spoken with her a few times recently. I think she'd be receptive."

"You've spoken with Hannah?" Her voice sounds like a little girl's.

"I have. I called her when you were in the hospital. What do you think? Should we call her?"

"Let me sleep on it. May I do that?"

"Of course, Mommy. That's exactly what you should do. Go to sleep now and we'll talk about it tomorrow."

June and August 1951

SARAH'S COUGHING began the summer she turned nine and her parents took in a college student to live in their apartment. She was moved out of her attic room and into the little dining room. The low cot that had been in her bay window was brought down and set up in the corner by the swinging door to the kitchen. To make it look like a couch during the day, the cot was covered with the rose-patterned drapery material from the apartment on Brookes Avenue. Her clothes shared the closet with their meager supply of linen. And that was it.

The student was Ira Rosenblatt from Brooklyn, New York. He went to City College and had come up to the University of Vermont to participate in a special program in group dynamics that her father was teaching. As it was explained to Sarah, Ira Rosenblatt was learning to be a political organizer like her father, and they were helping this student by giving him a place to live.

Even though she had been lonely living on the third floor, she didn't like giving up her bed to this large, dark, hairy person who wore sandals with socks and even walked around outside in shorts. She'd heard the neighbors downstairs derisively say, "What a nature boy, he's probably a Red," and laugh at the idea of a grown man wearing shorts. Sarah didn't understand what a nature boy was or a Red, but she agreed with them about the creepy shorts and sandals.

"This isn't my idea of summer, Scott," Sarah overheard her mother say late one night in the kitchen when she was supposed to be asleep in the next room.

"You don't have to do anything for him. He can take care of himself, honey," her father said, sounding whiny.

"That's ridiculous and you know it. We should at least charge him for the food he wolfs down, if not for my labor."

"I don't want to do that, honey."

"And why, may I ask, don't you?"

"Because I didn't set it up that way."

"Oh, God."

"I can't help it, honey." He was still whining.

Sarah's mother hated whining.

"Damn it, Scott, we have no margin for this, even with my summer school salary. You could be the next to lose your job, the way it's going. I don't like giving away what little extra we have to that. . .bloodsucker. That Jewish prince." She slammed something down on the table.

"Reba, please," her father pleaded.

Sarah began to cough. The tickle had been building in her throat and the pressure had started in her chest. She'd tried to hold it back because she knew it would annoy her mother, who hated Sarah's cough. It reminded Reba of her younger sister's asthma. Long before Sarah's cough developed in the early summer, her mother said, "I'm only grateful you don't have asthma. I always thought Hannah used it to get her way."

But Sarah couldn't stop her cough once it began. It would double her over as she tried to catch her breath. When she drew air into her lungs, the hacking became worse. And so it was that night when her mother pushed open the door to find her in the wedge of kitchen light; Sarah, on her knees, bowed forward, was clutching the sheet, gasping and wheezing.

"Sarah, control yourself, please," Reba said. "Don't let it get the better of you."

Sarah held her breath, lips tight together, her forehead pressing into the mattress, begging herself to stop when a harsh bark burst through setting off a worse attack of coughing.

"Sarah, try to calm down." Her mother knelt beside her, placing her hand on Sarah's back. "Breathe shallowly."

Sarah's chest bone was raw and her weak lungs seared. The coughing continued, one seizure followed by the next, until she silently asked to die. Shortly after the wish for death, the attack stopped and a peace spread through her lungs, calming the spasms, and she curled into herself with her head still down and her hands in loose fists beside her thighs.

"Sarah, you must try to control these episodes. You have to relax." Her mother's hand made circles on Sarah's back.

"Is she going to be all right?" her father asked. "That sounded terrible. How are you, button nose?"

"Okay," she said, into the mattress.

"Of course she's all right. She simply can't give in to the coughing."

Her mother told her to lie on her back while she went into the kitchen to get a damp cloth. Sarah heard her say, "I think she's using the coughing for attention."

She soothed Sarah's face with the cool cloth and played the game of lifting Sarah's arms and telling her to let them become so limp she couldn't hold them up by herself, and then her mother released her skinny limbs to flop softly onto the bed. She followed with Sarah's legs and feet. When she touched Sarah's chest, on the spot that felt as sore as chapped skin, Sarah wanted to say, No, take your hand away, you're making it hurt more. But she couldn't chance provoking her mother's anger or hurting her feelings. Instead, she concentrated on the lacy shadows projected on the ceiling by streetlights shining through shifting leaves. Soon her mother lifted her hand and Sarah could breathe easily again.

Her mother taught summer school classes at the high school from eight to five, so Sarah was on her own every day. Her best friend, Jane Smythe, was vacationing at her family's farm in St. Albans. Her other best friend, Leah Goldberg, went away for weeks at a time to a cabin on Lake Champlain. Even if they'd been in town, they weren't allowed to visit Sarah's apartment. One day in April, Sarah had asked Jane if she'd like to come over after school to play. "My mom says I can't come by anymore," Jane answered, avoiding Sarah's eye; she just kept tugging on her dark red bangs and poking the toe of her saddle shoe into a muddy indentation on the playground.

An electric vibration went through Sarah's body. They've found out I'm Jewish, she thought. She'd figured no one would discover her secret because their last name, Ellis, her father's name, wasn't Jewish. Only her mother had a Jewish name.

"That's okay," Sarah said, looking down.

"But my mom said you're welcome at our house any time."

This last was true. Sarah was still invited for dinner and overnights. At first Sarah told herself this was better, because her mother wasn't enthusiastic about having children over anyway after she'd taught all day at school. Her mother didn't enjoy cooking dinner for Sarah and her father, those nights he came home, so she would be happier not having other mouths to feed. But shame over this unexplained rejection gradually won out and Sarah began to decline most invitations. She didn't want pity from anyone, least of all Jane Smythe. In late spring she spent solitary hours after school on her cot up in her attic room, eating maple sugar candy and black olives from the can, reading forbidden true confession magazines—all of which she shoplifted from the stores along Church Street—and masturbating incessantly. To punish herself for this newfound comfort and pleasure, she would spray Evening in Paris cologne, also stolen from the five-and-dime, onto her genitals, causing smarting pain.

IN JUNE, SHORTLY after Ira Rosenblatt arrived, Sarah, her mother, her father and Ira went out to breakfast with Mr. and Mrs. Allbright, who had come down from their farm in

Colchester, and Dr. and Mrs. Samuelson. Dr. Samuelson taught at the medical school. They were in the Flamingo Restaurant on Church Street, settled into a large, curved, red leather booth by the window when a newsboy walked by shouting the headlines.

"I guess we better take a look," her father said, sliding out of the padded seat.

Ira got out too, and followed her father, tucking his escaped plaid shirt tail into his pants. Sarah was happy Ira had at least worn long pants to the restaurant, although he'd forgone the jacket and tie the other men had on. Her father stayed outside reading the paper with Ira standing right up against him, Ira's hand on her father's shoulder. They were both shaking their heads as they read.

"I wish they'd get back in here," her mother said, foraging in her purse for a pack of cigarettes. She shook one out and offered the pack around the table. Only Mrs. Samuelson took her up on it.

"It's fine, Reba, let them read the horrible news. We all must do the same." Judith Samuelson lit Reba's cigarette with a gold lighter.

"But not on the street for everyone to see. People will take the allegations as truth if they see him so eager to read about it." Her mother puffed nervously, plucking tobacco from her tongue after each draw.

"They already do, Reba." Dr. Samuelson spoke in his usual soft voice. Her mother always said, If Dr. Samuelson were a practicing doctor rather than a brilliant researcher, he'd have a wonderful bedside manner.

"Well, they're all imbeciles," her mother said. "Scott's the most democratic person in the world."

"Of course, Reba. We all know that to be true." Dr. Samuelson said.

"I certainly hope so," Sarah's mother said under her breath.

Her father looked ill when he came in, his face the color of dirty ice, but he was sweating. The door whooshed shut behind him as he walked toward their silent group. Further back in the restaurant, in the main section beyond the long liquor bar that was closed in the morning, the other patrons continued with their normal chatter. The lights seemed brighter back there than in their curved booth, even though the sunlight was shining so intensely into the plate glass window that the letters OGNIMALF EHT were printed sharply in black shadow on the white tablecloth.

Sarah's father slapped the paper down in the middle of the letters.

"What's black and white and Red all over?" he said in a way that seemed both angry and funny and hurt.

"A newspaper," Sarah answered, wanting to make him laugh.

"Oh, dear," Mrs. Allbright said, putting her arm around Sarah and rubbing her cheek. "Maybe this is not the best time to talk," she said.

The waitress arrived with their food and set the heavy white crockery plates down before each of them. Sarah had pancakes with as much maple syrup as she wished; nobody told her to stop as she poured it on. All around the table the adults dug in hungrily. Mr. Allbright reached for the newspaper, folded it in half, and, propping it up on his water glass at the far side of his plate, began to read.

Sarah, who sat between the two Allbrights, began to read also. She got to the place where it said a Mr. Julius Rosenberg was killed in an electric chair, that a current had been put through his body until his life ended. His wife was killed after him.

"What's an electric chair?" Sarah asked Mrs. Allbright.

"Grant, would you put that away?" Mrs. Allbright said.

"Yup. Sorry," he said, tucking the paper in under his thigh where it stayed while he continued to eat.

But Sarah already knew what the paper said. The man had walked into a glaring, white-walled death chamber. A rabbi had been in there with him saying "the Lord is my shepherd, I shall not want," but then the man had to sit in that chair where they gave him the shocks. Her imagination took great leaps as the silence at the table grew. She remembered a book she'd found one day this past winter in her parents' shelves, filled with sickening stories and photos of what Germans had done to Jewish people in Europe, how they had experimented on them and tortured and killed them. While reading the pages, dark clouds formed in her eyes until she couldn't see the print. Her genitals began to burn the way they had when she'd put Evening in Paris cologne there, except this time it was from a sort of icky excitement, and she began to shake so badly and feel so sick to her stomach that she closed the book and never looked at it again. Thinking of the electric chair caused her to burn down there again and feel sick and it was an effort to keep eating so the adults wouldn't know what she was thinking. What she couldn't understand was why a rabbi had been with the man in the death chamber. A rabbi was Jewish. Would a Jewish man torture people too? Was the man in the chair Jewish or German? She wanted to ask these questions of the adults, but they'd begun talking again, and the discussion had shifted: how the cows were giving at the Allbright farm, how her mother's classes were improving, whether the Samuelsons would be staying in Burlington or moving to some more "habitable place," as Dr. Samuelson put it. This was the moment when the talk veered back into the dangerous area. Sweet Dr. Samuelson frowned, his face becoming cruel-looking, "I don't know how long before the bastards come after me as well."

"Let's not talk about that now, Herman," Mrs. Samuelson said, giving a meaningful glance in Sarah's direction.

Sarah's father had remained silent through the conversation. He was usually the center of most discussions, challenging people, prodding them into changing their opinions. Sarah loved those times when she was privy to seeing how people gravitated to him, listened to what he had to say, admired him. "Scott, you really put me on the spot on that one. Made me think about it in a whole new way." Today he ate solemnly, without a word, looking into his plate most of the time, except when his dark eyes would rise and he'd concentrate on one person or the other, as though he were trying to enter their heads to understand better what they had to say. His face sagged, and his mouth turned down. He kept rubbing his hand through his thinning hair and it stood up around his head in a messy way.

ONLY SARAH, her mother and father drove back home in the car. Ira said he wanted to air his brain.

"I'd like to stop off at the office," her father said when they got in the car.

"You want to clear it out now, Scottie?" Reba said. "Don't you think it can wait till next week?"

Sarah liked that her mother said Scottie.

"I'd rather start when nobody's around. This isn't going to be easy."

EVEN THOUGH a couple of weeks later her father was no longer teaching the course in group dynamics at the university, Ira Rosenblatt continued to live with them. Instead of going to classes Ira traveled around the state organizing farmers into fuel co-operatives with "the great Scott Ellis." Ira got a tiny smile from her father with that one. Her father rarely smiled these days. "At least the whispering campaigns haven't touched the Farm Bureau yet," her father said.

When everyone was out of the apartment, which seemed to be more often than ever, sometimes for an entire day on the weekend, Sarah would sneak up to the bedroom that Ira had taken over from her. He kept it tidy, she had to say that for him. The bed was made, his clothing hung neatly in the closet and his underwear, socks and shirts were nicely folded in the bureau, each category of clothing in a different drawer. On top of the dresser he had a comb and a brush. She'd never seen a hairbrush for a man. Beside the brush were stacks of coins. Each time she snuck up to the room she snitched a quarter for herself—rent, she figured, for the use of her room the whole damn summer.

On the mirror were two photos of a lady. In one she was dressed in winter clothes, with a fur collar and cuffs and more fur on her hat. She was dark and pretty. She could almost be Sarah's mother's younger sister but with a bigger nose than Reba's. In the other picture the lady wore a bathing suit that showed her large bosom, which was much different than Sarah's mother who had almost nothing there. "Two fried eggs on a skillet," she'd heard her mother grumble to her father once. "Honey, I love them," he'd said and her mother had laughed and then cried.

Sarah was intrigued by the summer photo and always took it down carefully, easing it from where it was wedged between the mirror and the mahogany frame. By the window she inspected every item: the car the woman was reclining against, the wide open area behind her that looked like a parking lot, the way her long dark hair blew up into the air and how her hand was raised as she tried to pull it down. Around her neck was a star, but not like your usual star, this one had one extra point. She'd seen such stars at Leah Goldberg's house where there were many objects from a place called Israel. Sarah had once asked her mother why the Goldbergs had those things in their house and her mother had answered, "Because they're Jewish, just as I am, and just as you are on my side, only we don't flaunt it." Her mother had been cooking, and she turned off the fire under the frying pan and sat at the yellow kitchen table where Sarah was drawing a picture. Reba said quietly in her teacherly voice, which made Sarah feel squirmy, "I'm Jewish and Daddy isn't. We decided when we got married to give up all religion so we wouldn't fight about it. That's why we don't go to church on Sundays or any time."

All Sarah knew about Jewish was that some children at school had begun to make fun of Jewish children. Jane Smythe had told her that the Germans had killed the Jews and it was a good thing. Sarah's lesson from her mother in being Jewish happened shortly before she found the Nazi book on her parents' shelf and a month prior to an incident in school when Jane Smythe, Stephanie Hinkley and James Wakefield started saying that Leah Goldberg stank. They walked past Leah's desk holding their noses. "Peeuew, it sure stinks here," Jane said. "Must be because there's a Jew here, the kind that Hitler killed." Sarah's jaw began to buzz and she felt dizzy enough to put her head down on her arms on her desktop. What if they found out that she was Jewish too? She sneaked a look at Leah, who sat with her head bowed, her thick black bangs hanging over her eyes, her spindly arms crossed at her waist. A week later Sarah went to Leah's house, never mentioning what had happened nor admitting that her own mother was Jewish. She surreptitiously examined the elaborately designed metal objects that seemed out of place in a New England house, those items that came from Israel and identified the Goldbergs as Jews. Sarah was grateful her mother had no such unsuitable objects filling their apartment.

But as Sarah stared at the photo of the lady who must have been the person Ira Rosenblatt called "my fiancée Sonya," she was transfixed by the star at the base of Sonya's throat. Even Leah didn't wear such a star to school. The few French Canadian kids in the neighborhood wore crosses around their necks, but they went to Catholic school. Protestants wore nothing religious. But here was a beautiful, shapely lady with a Jewish star on her bare skin for everyone to see. What kind of a place was Brooklyn, New York, where you could show your Jewishness so freely?

Slipping the photo back into place, Sarah saw herself in the mirror. She had light-colored hair, a small nose that held her new, clear plastic-rimmed glasses, and a very high forehead like her father's, which everyone said "bespoke intelligence." She didn't have her mother's too-curly black hair and fleshy nose. She didn't have Leah Goldberg's large lips, big nose, low forehead and big sticking-out ears. And she didn't smell Jewish, she didn't think. Leah's house smelled of exotic food and mothballs. Ira Rosenblatt's room had a slight odor of mothballs too. She decided that when she moved back up to her room, she would open all the windows, steal another bottle of Evening in Paris cologne, and spray it in the air and in every corner.

As the summer progressed, Sarah had increasingly intense coughing episodes. In the middle of August she was invited to visit Leah's family's place on the lake. Sarah's mother was teaching in the second summer session and her father had obtained another position teaching a special symposium at Goddard College. Ira was already at the college and her father was to drive down on the very day Sarah was to go to Leah's.

"You can take the few extra minutes and drop her off at the Goldbergs'," her mother said. "I don't have time to take the bus out there after a day at school. It's grueling, Scott. I don't think you realize that."

"Of course I do, honey, it's just that..."

"It's just that I have to do everything." Reba began to cry.

It was early morning on the day Sarah was to leave, and she was in bed in the dining room. They must have thought she was asleep. She tried to concentrate on the comforting late-summer cawing of the blue jays outside her window, mixed with an occasional car driving by. She began to feel the need to cough. She pressed her hand to that raw place on the surface of her chest, keeping it there as she told herself to calm down, the way her mother would. It worked. She could breathe.

Her father drove her. They passed by the old farm in Shelburne where they used to live when she was a little girl and would waken in the night with dreams of fire engulfing her, when her mother would have to sit with her and explain that dreams weren't true. But to Sarah they were very true. Even awake with her mother by her side, she had felt the terror of being burned alive.

"Chicken, I'm going to have to ask a favor." They were almost at the turnoff to Leah's. "I'm going to have to drop you at the top of the road. I'm in a big hurry. If I don't head right out, I won't get to Goddard in time for the class. Mr. Goldberg always wants to have a conversation. I'll never get out of there. What do you say?" He plopped his hand on her knee.

"It's okay, Daddy." It wasn't, though. She didn't want to show up at the Goldberg's door without him, like some orphan.

"That's a big girl. Thanks for this." He pulled over to the shoulder just before the dirt road merged into Route 7.

Sarah got out, opened the back door, and lifted her small suitcase out. It was blazing hot. The August midday sun was a huge white disk in a heat-hazed sky. She scuffed her shoe in road dust as she watched her father drive away. It was dead quiet except for the buzzing of bees and the whine of cicadas down by the creek that ran to the lake, way over by the huge far-off oak tree. Once when she was little, when they'd lived in the farmhouse, she and her mother had had a picnic under that oak tree, and her mother had made a tiny acorn doll for her and told her a story as she moved the doll like a puppet on her thumb. Overhead, the sun had come through the leaves and warmed her skin in spots. She'd fallen asleep on the blanket with her mother asleep beside her. It had been nice.

Sarah started down the dirt road where the alfalfa, rising

high over her head on either side, was mixed with goldenrod and purple asters. Twenty steps along, the pressure began to build in her chest and she coughed involuntarily. She told herself to breathe in slowly, but the necessity to cough didn't cooperate, instead it grew greater. She coughed intentionally thinking it would make the tickle go away, but the hacking went deeper and she lost control. She gasped for air. She gagged as she tried to draw it in, wheezing, almost vomiting. I'm going to die if I can't breathe, she thought, out here under the sun on this dusty road. She dropped her suitcase in the middle of the road, not caring about it, and fell into the alfalfa with the idea that if she lay there quietly it would pass. But it worsened. She rolled over in the prickly stalks, smelling the sweet scent she usually loved, but which now began to frighten her. Trying to pull air deeper into her lungs and belly, she rolled back and forth, but still she couldn't breathe. The air wouldn't enter her burning, aching chest. Black clouds formed in her eyes. She knew she was dying and she just gave in to the idea. And then, as it had happened in the past, at the moment when she decided there was no hope, the spasms and pain subsided and with tiny bursts of breath and hoarse gasping sounds, she brought the air back into her lungs.

She lay there for the longest time. The roadside was safe again in its grassy sweetness, the stalks such a pretty golden color against the gray-blue sky. Her eyes were as dry as straw, but in her heart that beat too fast in the still-delicate chest, she was as lonely and sad as she'd ever been, thinking of her poor father driving off toward his meeting with no idea that his daughter had almost died out here.

After a while, she decided it was safe to begin walking again. She rose onto her knees tentatively, trying out her breathing when she was upright. Though a tickle threatened, it quickly passed and she got herself to standing without a relapse. Her head felt woozy and her legs weak, but she knew if she started moving she would feel stronger. She went back for her suitcase, relieved that a car hadn't come by to smash it to bits, and she continued along the sloping road toward Lake Champlain, glittering in the distance.

When she arrived at the Goldbergs' cottage, she knocked on the kitchen door. Mrs. Goldberg appeared in her white bib apron. Her long black hair, white at the temples, was pulled up and away from her round flushed face and knotted in a high twist in back.

"Sarah, I didn't hear a car."

"My father dropped me at your driveway," Sarah said, telling herself it was only a sort-of lie. "He didn't have time to stop in. He had a meeting."

Mrs. Goldberg frowned and looked past Sarah, checking for the dust clouds that should be left as evidence. She examined Sarah more carefully, plucking bits of hay from her hair. Sarah flushed, afraid she'd been caught in her half-truth.

"Come in, child," Mrs. Goldberg said. "Let's get you into a bathing suit and cool you down."

AT THE END of August, plans were made to go down to New York City for four days. They were driving Ira Rosenblatt home, but there was quiet talk between Sarah's parents of possible jobs in the city. She'd overheard her mother in the kitchen arguing, "I'll only move on the condition I can get a job outside the city. I will not teach in a New York City school." It seemed that Sarah's father had finally lost his position with the Farm Bureau, "due to all the dirty McCarthy business," she'd heard him say. An article had appeared on the front page of *The Burlington Free Press*, calling him a communist and saying he was a "stain on the good name of the Vermont Farm Bureau."

On Saturday, the week before they were to leave, Reba said Sarah had to help clean the house. Her mother was so angry, stomping around the apartment, that Sarah didn't put up any fuss. She began immediately to vacuum the living room. The machine was roaring so loudly that Sarah didn't hear her mother come up behind her, and the next thing she knew, her mother had yanked the vacuum cleaner from her hands, hitting it against her thigh. Reba banged the stand-up machine out into the hallway and slammed it down. She came back to the living room, grabbed Sarah by the shirt and dragged her to the hall, jerking her violently from side to side, her clenched fist thudding into Sarah's chest.

"How many times do I have to tell you that the hallway must be vacuumed before you do the rooms? Are you becoming an imbecile?" Her fist pounded at Sarah's bony breast again. "Now do what you've been told for once, for Christ's sake."

Reba whipped around, and Sarah stared numbly after her as her mother strode down the hall to the kitchen. Sarah put her hand to her bruised breast bone. She pressed into it, making it hurt even more.

Sarah found her mother sitting at the yellow kitchen table, her head in her hands. Sarah hesitated in the middle of the high-ceilinged room, taking in her mother and last night's dishes piled in the sink and the dirty, scuffed and gooey linoleum. Her mother's unruly black hair stuck out every which way, her fingers tightly entwined in the curls.

"It's okay, Mommy," Sarah said. "I'll do it right."

Her mother looked up finally, but her eyes didn't find Sarah's. They stared unseeing past Sarah's right shoulder. This frightened Sarah more than the blows, to have her mother there and not there.

"I'll go finish the vacuuming, Mommy. Okay?"

Reba inhaled deeply and nodded slightly, but her eyes still didn't connect with Sarah's.

THEY DROVE DOWN to New York City in the jam-packed Plymouth. Reba sat in the front passenger seat. "I will not be relegated to the back," she had said to Scott when they were packing the car. Ira and Sarah rode in the back with their feet propped up on his stacks of books and their bodies wedged in between the bundles of Ira's clothes that hadn't fit into his suitcase. By the time they hit Rutland, the smell of sweaty underarms and dirty shirts worn once too often rose up around them in the sultry heat.

They drove to the place called Brooklyn that Sarah had wondered about, and delivered Ira to a steamy, cramped apartment on the ground floor of the brick building where he lived with his parents. All the living room furniture was covered in thick transparent plastic that stuck to Sarah's skin in the heat and made a sucking noise when she stood up. Reba sat stiffly in the room, refusing everything that was offered by the Rosenblatts, which seemed to upset Ira's mother. When Sarah and her mother were together for a moment, Reba muttered, "I don't think I've ever seen such terrible taste." But it was at the Rosenblatts' that Sarah got to meet the lady in the pictures. Sonya came through the door and screamed. Ira picked her up and twirled her around, her foot and hefty calf kicking up in back, just like in the movies, Sarah thought, delighted. She looked much younger in person and not as dark-skinned, and her face was wide and freckly. She had the broad nose and full lips of the photo, only in real life her lips were painted bright red, and when she smiled, which she did a lot now that her fiancé was back, her teeth showed chalky white against the scarlet. Leaning down to Sarah, she held out the six-pointed star she wore around her neck. "Ira gave me this Mogen David two years ago. It's beautiful, isn't it?"

On their second afternoon they went to the Lower East Side in Manhattan to meet a man her father told them was a great old socialist who'd come up against the authoritarian communists. "Leibowitz was with Trotsky in Mexico the day Trotsky got his head split open," he said knowingly to Ira.

The man lived in a five-story building, a tenement, her

father called it. Inside it smelled of garbage, old rotting wood, and cooking. The walls were painted a glossy dark yellow. "Just the cheapest color that exists," Reba muttered as they climbed the sloping stairs. They were dripping with sweat by the time they reached the fifth floor landing. It had been dark on the staircase, but, at the top, light flowed down from a window in the ceiling. It was all very romantic to Sarah, being here with Ira and his fiancée in this unusual place.

The large kitchen looked out on a backyard where tall trees grew and lines of laundry looped from window to window. The stooped, gray-haired man was not much taller than Sarah's great-grandmother in San Francisco and he talked as she did, in sentences that ended with question marks. Mr. Leibowitz wore a spotless blue shirt with long sleeves, even in the intense heat, and brown gabardine pants.

They sat around his Formica table, drinking purple wine from a heavy glass decanter etched with deeply gouged roses. Mr. Leibowitz ceremoniously poured the purple wine into matching glasses and had Ira squirt bubbly water into them from a sapphire blue bottle, the exact color of the New York City evening sky that Sarah had seen the night before from a boardwalk somewhere in Brooklyn.

She had never tasted anything so delicious. Immediately her head became wondrously fuzzy and she didn't care that her mother frowned and looked bored, as though she thought she was too good for the surroundings. Sarah forgot why she hadn't liked Ira Rosenblatt all summer as she leaned against Sonya's soft, fleshy arm without seeming to, so as not to irritate her mother, and listened to her father and Ira and Mr. Leibowitz talk about Joe McCarthy and Roy Cohn, who was a "snake in the grass" and "a discredit to his people," and how it was a sin that the Rosenbergs had been killed by the state. Even her mother relaxed as the afternoon wore on, and the adults drank more of the homemade blackberry wine. Reba later moved over to sit next to Sarah and let Sarah put her head in her lap and kept patting her cheek, and late in the afternoon, as orange sunlight touched the table, Reba said in a wistful voice, "this reminds me of Grandma's house. I haven't felt so at home in years." If Sarah could have spoken when her mother said this, if she hadn't been almost paralyzed in half-sleep, she might have added, "and so safe too."

ON SUNDAY, Sarah, her mother, Sonya, and a Mrs. Bernstein, the wife of a man her father was meeting, drove out to Jones Beach. They went in Mrs. Bernstein's station wagon because her father had taken the Ellis' car. Reba was very happy. She liked talking with Mrs. Bernstein, whom she called by her first name, Doris. Sarah knew her mother thought the discussion was of a high caliber, talk of teaching techniques—Mrs. Bernstein was also a high school teacher—experiments in learning, and laughter about the stodgy ways of those who were not progressive in their thinking. Sarah sat in back with Sonya, who knitted sections of an afghan for her trousseau.

They parked the car in a huge lot that was as big as three blocks in Burlington. They gathered their belongings and wove in and out between the cars until they reached a beach as wide as the deserts in Sarah's geography book, with sun that pressed down on them and sand that burned through the soles of her sneakers. A few yards down the beach a tickle started to take hold at the base of Sarah's throat. They couldn't even see the water yet when the first cough came. With every breath, even shallow ones, her chest filled with smarting particles. A horrible whooping sound erupted as she dragged for air.

"Sarah, no, not now, you haven't coughed in days." Her mother slowed her pace until Sarah reached her side.

Sarah couldn't stop. The coughing was as bad as on the road to Leah's. She doubled over to get the next bit of air.

"The poor thing," Mrs. Bernstein said, walking back to them. "Is she allergic to something? Should we leave?"

"Certainly not," her mother said.

Sarah sank down onto the burning sand, her face low to the ground trying to find a purer, less dangerous layer.

"It's the ragweed and the sea air," her mother said. "She'll be better off up in the car. I'll take her to the parking lot and come back down."

"How can she stay in the car?" Sonya asked.

"I'll open the windows. She can take a nap."

Sarah's mother took her wrist after Sonya and Mrs. Bernstein had been persuaded to go on their way and put up the red-striped umbrella so Reba could find them on her return. Her mother pressed her fingers into the flesh of Sarah's arm, dragging her across the vast expanse of glaring white sand that shimmered in the noonday sun. Sarah wheezed and gasped for breath as they raced over the scorching flats toward the parking lot. Trying to keep pace with her determined mother, fear ricocheted through her body. Perhaps it was that terror and the adrenaline it pumped at the base of her throat that ultimately saved her, because by the time they'd reached the wood-paneled station wagon she was barely coughing.

Without a word, her mother unlocked the car with the key Mrs. Bernstein had handed her. The heat in the car was tremendous. Her mother rolled the back windows halfway down.

"You'll be better in the car," she said. "You don't seem to be coughing up here. I've counted on this time at the beach. I won't have it ruined."

With that she left. Sarah watched her walk back toward the water until she got so far away that it was impossible to distinguish her white blouse from among the other shirts and cover-ups. The car grew hotter. Even the breeze that came through the window was hot. She began to feel the way she did when she had a fever, slightly sick to her stomach, a little dizzy. The families walking by with beach umbrellas and large, colorful plastic balls all seemed to be laughing and enjoying being with each other. Sarah decided they were pretending they were happy together. They were only acting that way so everyone would think they were perfect families. She grew very thirsty and wished her mother had thought to leave some water. At first she perspired, soaking her tee shirt and shorts. She stripped down to her bathing suit, but felt uncomfortable with the scratchy upholstery against her bare skin and put her clothes back on. She stopped sweating. She stopped being thirsty. She touched the skin on her arm, on her neck, on her cheek. It was hot. Was she going to die, burning up like a leaf in fall, shriveling in the sun? It wouldn't matter anyway. She didn't care. The cars in front of her became blurry from the tears welling unbidden. She didn't want to cry. She tried to stop the tears but they slipped over the rims of her eyes, washing down her cheeks, first hot, then cool as they dried, crusting her skin with salt.

After a while the sun moved and blasted like fire through the side window. She couldn't keep her eyes open in its suffocating heat. Her head kept rocking forward and then she'd jerk awake.

AS THOUGH IN A dream the car door opened. Someone called Sarah's name.

"Sarah, sweetheart." It was Sonya. "Come, you must get out of this inferno."

The air outside felt cold. Sarah shivered.

"Let's go to the bathroom, sweetie," Sonya said, bending down so her face was close. Her lips were pink without the lipstick, her face more freckled. She fluttered her fingers over Sarah's forehead. "Let's get you a Coke. You're not sweating. You should be sweating."

WHEN THEY RETURNED to the car after a hot dog with everything on it and two large Coca Colas with ice, her mother and Mrs. Bernstein had arrived.

"Well, she doesn't seem any the worse for wear, Reba," Mrs. Bernstein said, looking relieved. "It seems you made the right decision after all. No need to have been concerned."

Her mother, who had tanned two shades darker, looked relaxed and contented to Sarah, as if she hadn't thought of her daughter at all, and had only pretended to Mrs. Bernstein that she'd been worried.

Protected by Sonya's hand on her shoulder, Sarah thought, My mommy hates me. I almost died and she doesn't care, and she doesn't even feel sorry. Sonya, with her soft body, pretty freckles, and her Mogen David at her throat, had sat across from her at the metal table in the cool shade of the umbrella, filling her with food and drink and love, and had muttered under her breath, How could she do such a thing to you? Sarah thought maybe she could stay forever with Sonya and become her daughter when Sonya married Ira. Next week she'd turn nine. She'd learned a lot about cruelty this year, and too much of it happened too close to home. In Sonya's house, she could be safe and maybe even fussed over a little.

Day Seven

THE SOLE PHONE in the house is in the living room.

"Would you like a phone by your bed, Mom?" I ask her in the morning. "That way when your friends call you could talk with them from right here instead of having to go to the living room."

"I haven't gone to the living room in a week, dear," she says, looking up from the book she's reading. She has the teddy bear hooked under her right arm. Her fingers are circling his ear, the way she used to trace patterns on her own skin, round and round her thigh, or the inside of her arm. It seemed to me that she was caressing herself, giving herself some lewd pleasure. It used to drive me mad, make me have to leave the room. But I am not irritated or repulsed by the way she is touching the stuffed animal. On the contrary, I find it sweet, feel thanked for having given it to her.

"That's why I'm suggesting it," I say. "If you're going to spend most of your time in here, it would be nice to have the lifeline to your friends."

She grins sardonically. "That's one way of putting it."

It feels for the moment that she has her old self back.

"See if Joey can do it," my mother says. "If nothing else, he's handy in that way."

I don't want him to do it, but I also don't want to tell her that I'm irritated and don't trust him.

"Sure," I say. "That's a good idea. I'll ask Lydia when she gets here."

"YEAH, I CAN do that," Joey says, when Lydia and I go over to Estela's house.

We found him sitting on a plastic chaise longue in the

marquesina amid Estela's hundreds of orchids, watching a soap opera on the large television in the corner. Even the television has pots of yellow-flowering exotic species sitting on top. He stood when we came in, hiking up the waistband of his long, psychedelic orange boxer shorts. He wears no shirt.

When I ask him how much he wants for the job, he says, "Nothing. For your *mami* I do it for free. She's a good person. She's treated me well. Been good to Lydia too."

HE LOOKS HEALTHY, I think, as I watch him take the measurements from outside my mother's bedroom window along the wall to outside the living room window in order to jury-rig the connection.

"No reason to pay the company any more than they're already stealing from us," he says.

In the two months since he's been off drugs, Joey's belly has ballooned out and it flops over the elastic waistband of his shorts, his shoulders are padded with thick flesh. His hair is well cut and glistens in the harsh morning sunlight. It is Indian-straight, a testament to some Taíno blood. His skin, usually a pale brown, is now sunburned to a ruddy dark shade. He shuffles through the grass wearing thongs on his thick, blunt feet. Not a handsome man, but I can see why Lydia is attracted to him.

"You're sure the phone company won't catch us?" I say.

"Nah, and what if they do? What'll they do, sue you?" He grunts as he kneels at the front window. His shorts pull down, revealing cleavage.

By then I'll be back in New York City, I think. "Just don't tell my mother. She's a stickler for honesty."

"That kind of honesty is a waste on this island," he says, standing, taking a felt-tip pen from behind his ear and scrawling numbers on his forearm. "But don't get me wrong. I admire that she's a truthful woman."

"Sarah," Lydia calls me from around the front corner of the house. She peers through the bars that connect one house to the next. "I have somebody I want you to meet."

"It's the kid," Joey says. "She wants you to see her precious Ladito." He winks.

I return to the backyard, passing my mother's window, to find Lydia and the little boy at the rear gate of the *marquesina*. He stands in front of Lydia, his body snug against hers. He is small for seven years old, with black hair cropped close to his head, delicate features, his chin with just the hint of cleft at its point. His chest is narrow and bare.

"Oh, what a beauty," I say and mean it.

"Say hello, Ladito, shake *tía* Sarah's hand."

He reluctantly leaves Lydia and, head cocked shyly to one side, he comes to me with hand outstretched.

"*Hola. ¿Qué Tal?*" I say.

He brightens, hearing the Spanish. "*Muy bien, gracias,*" he says in a barely audible voice, with a tiny smile.

"Would it be all right if he plays for a while in the yard?" Lydia asks. "He doesn't have a yard at home."

"Of course, Lydia. You don't have to ask."

"He'll be quiet. He won't bother Mommy."

"If he does, we'll tell him to quiet down. Is that a deal, Ladito?"

"Yes," he whispers, taking a pink rubber Spalding ball from his pocket and throwing it up into the air. The ball falls a few feet from him. He looks to Lydia. When she nods, he runs to fetch it.

Lydia and I go around to see how Joey is doing. She bends over him, touching his back.

"I need some more wire," Joey says, looking up at her, "and then I'm done. I've got it at home."

"It looks good, Joey," she says. "Looks like you did a good job. He's very handy," she says to me. "He's starting a course in refrigerator repair next week, aren't you, Joey?"

"I am," he says, standing with a groan. "Can get good money doing that."

"That's great," I say. "I'm glad to hear it."

"He'll be a good provider then," she whispers to me as we leave him. "Maybe we can get a place together. A house with a back yard, maybe."

When we come around the corner, I spy little Lourdes standing on the far side of the chain link fence, watching Ladito. Her dark eyes follow his every move. She is dressed as usual in a fussy dress, layers of lavender and white organza with a pink-checked pinafore over top. On her feet are white patent leather Mary Janes and ruffled lavender socks.

"Hi, sweetheart," I say. "Do you want to come over and play?"

"*Sí*," she says in her loud deep voice, startling coming from a four-year-old. She nods solemnly.

"Call Mommy for me." By now Ladito has approached the fence.

"Mommy," she booms, throwing her head back.

Inez comes out. "I didn't go to work today," she says. "The baby is sick." Inez is in her late twenties, with short, dark, nicely styled hair. Her face is beautiful—placid and open. It could almost make me reconsider my prejudice against charismatic evangelical sects. She told me once that she and Jorge found peace in the church, that it had changed their lives. "How's Reba?" she asks, lowering her voice, since my mother's window is close.

"She can't hear with the air conditioner on," I say. "We're going to the doctor tomorrow to see if there's anything to do."

"God willing, he has something to offer," Inez says, her eyes squinting with concern.

"I don't hold out too much hope," I say. Lydia has moved in close, and proprietorially links her arm in mine.

"She's not doing so good," Lydia says.

"It's in God's hands," Inez says. "I'll pray for you."

She brings Lourdes around and through our carport. When I worry aloud that Lourdes will get her beautiful dress dirty, Inez says it doesn't matter. "She's got plenty more. Her grandmother can't buy enough for her. She spoils her more than Reba does."

Joey leaves to get the extra wire and we three women remain standing in the yard in the hot morning sun, watching the children begin to play tentatively. Ladito hands the ball to Lourdes. Lydia still holds my arm.

"Do you think Reba would like to see Lourdes?" Inez asks. "Lourdes keeps asking about *tía* Reba."

"My mother's lost a lot of weight in the last couple of weeks. I don't want to frighten Lourdes."

"Oh dear God, I know that," she says, frowning in sadness. "I was thinking maybe she could stand outside the window so Reba could see her and Lourdes could hear Mommy's voice."

"A TELEPHONE, and seeing my dear Lourdes all in one day. What else could a woman want?" my mother says, smiling. She shows more animation and energy than I've seen since I arrived. Maybe she isn't dying after all. Maybe if I can keep her spirits up she'll come through this. Then I tell myself to stop, to step back. I can't save her.

Lydia and I help her into the club chair that we pushed over to the side window where there's no air conditioner to block her view of the child.

My mother is leaving me, going far away, and this time all the machinations, all the entertaining, all the "Look, Mommy, see what I'm doing," won't be able to bring her back.

Lourdes stands just outside the window in the bright sunlight. Inez has combed and fluffed her dark curls and slipped on an organza-covered elastic headband. A bow, like a butterfly, sits atop her head. "Where is she, Mommy?" she turns to look up to Inez. "Where is Auntie Reba?"

"In her bedroom, sweetheart. She's sick and doesn't want

to give you germs, but she wants to see her love. Say 'Hi, *tía* Reba.' She can see you."

"*Hola*, Auntie Reba," Lourdes says in her loudest, gruffest voice.

My mother laughs, but I can see tears glistening on the rims of her eyes. Lydia looks knowingly at me.

"Hello, dear Lourdes," my mother says. "I've missed our visits. How is your school?"

"Fine. Auntie Reba, I can count to twenty, the whole way. Mommy doesn't have to help me."

My mother puts her hand to her mouth. I hear a tiny whimper escape. "That's lovely. Can you count for me?" she says when she's recovered.

"*Uno, dos, tres, quatro, cinco. . .*" Lourdes counts, touching each of her chubby fingers as she progresses perfectly to twenty.

When we help my mother into bed again, she is deep within herself.

"She's a wonderful, charming child," I say.

"Yes, isn't she," she answers absently. "And so very intelligent."

THE FIRST CALL we get is from Pearl. I answer.

"How's she doing?" she asks.

"You can ask her yourself," I say. "We just got a phone installed in the room."

"Holy cow, will miracles never cease," Pearl laughs.

"It's Pearl, Mom."

"How nice," my mother says, reaching for the phone. She has weakened noticeably since her moments with Lourdes. Her hand shakes as she grasps the receiver. "Hello, Pearl. How good of you to call."

I sit listening in on her side of the conversation, marveling at how formal she remains with this woman she considers her good friend.

"Yes, it would be wonderful if you could pick us up at the hospital. I don't want to impose on Esmeralda for the drive back. It's unfortunate that Sarah never learned to drive."

But I got you a telephone, I think. And I brought over your surrogate granddaughter. Give me a little credit for that.

AFTER A LUNCH of half a cup of beef broth and a quarter of a piece of dry bread, which she keeps down, I decide to broach the question again. As I'm clearing her dishes, I say, "Did you decide? Do you want to call Hannah?"

She hugs the teddy bear to her chest, putting her cheek down on the top of his head. "I'm of two minds about it."

"What are the two sides?"

"It would be considerate of me to call her. But I don't want to burden her."

I stand holding the tray. "What do *you* want? Which side of this includes you?"

"Me? I don't understand."

"This isn't about etiquette. This is about, do you want to make contact with Hannah at this time? Or would you rather not?"

She looks at me without speaking. I see her searching for an answer.

"Look," I say. "Why don't I go do the dishes, you think about this, and we'll talk when I finish."

"Yes," she says faintly. She is far away again. "Yes, that's a good idea."

AS I WASH the dishes I'm proud of myself. I think, you're acting like an adult. For the moment you're not entangled in your childish fury. You're not constantly obsessing about your own pain, or old anger. I know this won't last, but it feels good for the moment and it's good for her. But I'm astonished that she didn't include herself in the equation. Where was *she* in this?

I RETURN TO the bedroom with a plate of peeled and sliced papaya. "I thought you'd like this. It's good for digestion, they say."

"I've decided," she says as we slip wedges of papaya into our mouths, using our fingers. She licks her thumb. "I'd like to call Hannah. It would be good to hear her voice."

I haven't told my mother, but I've contacted Hannah a number of times in the past few days, keeping her informed of the situation, telling her how bad it has become.

We decide that I will dial the number and speak first to Hannah. My mother stares at the far wall as I do. There is no way for me to know what she is thinking. Is she humiliated to have to admit to her little sister that she is dying? Does she want her sister's love? Does she want to express some old resentment? I have no sister, so I can't imagine what this means.

"Hi, Hannah, this is Sarah calling from Puerto Rico."

"Yes?" Hannah's small, strained voice says.

"I'm standing here beside my mother, and she'd like to talk with you."

"Oh," Hannah cries. Hearing this, I can see her body crumpling, in relief that this isn't the last call, in astonishment that her sister is actually reaching out. "I thought you were calling to tell me she had died. Give me a moment, please, to compose myself. Can you cover for me?"

"How's Irving?" I ask cheerfully.

"Fine," she replies quietly.

"That's good to hear." I continue in my heartiness. My mother is not looking my way. Her expression is frozen in a frown. Her finger is circling the bear's ear again.

"You can put Reba on now, Sarah. And thank you for doing this."

I sit back in the club chair to listen to the momentous conversation.

"Hello, Hannah, dear. How are you?"

My mother smiles politely as Hannah speaks.

"I'm just fine, Hannah. Couldn't be better. A little ill, but Sarah is taking such good care of me. She's quite a daughter. Coming all the way down here to look after me. How's Irving? How has he adjusted to retirement? Wasn't he about to when we last talked?"

That was twelve years ago, Mom. It's been twelve years since you've talked with your sister. You're dying. Let her know that you are sad about dying. But no. After five more minutes of formal talk, my mother says, "This is long distance, Hannah, maybe we should get off."

She hands the phone over to me. "That was very nice, dear. It was worth having Joey put the phone in. She sounded very well."

"Yes, she did." I'm too stunned to comment further.

"But I'm exhausted, dear. So if you'll just help me shift down in the bed. I think I'd like to sleep a bit."

Where was *she* in the conversation, I wonder as I hold her too-warm, sweaty body and help her to find a comfortable position. Where were *you*, Mommy?

September 1975

SARAH AND HER FATHER were taking her mother to her first day of work in the high school at Fort Buchanan naval base near San Juan. They drove off the main highway and bumped along a pitted and patched wreck of a country lane. The high grass on either side of them was packed with years of litter and their progress was marked by headless palm trees, laid bare by the latest hurricane. Through their open windows came the stench of fermenting sugar cane from the nearby Bacardi plant, mixing with the fetid odor of a polluted inlet. Sarah was in the back seat, as she used to be in childhood when the three of them went on trips, only on this trip she was thirty-three years old, unmarried, and feeling dragged down by the two of them and their inability to communicate their needs to each other. Her father drove, humming off-key, while her mother sat primly in the passenger seat, in silence. From where Sarah sat, she played at catching distorted glimpses of scenery through the large lenses of her mother's thick glasses.

Reba hadn't spoken since they left the house, when Sarah had asked her, "Are you nervous, Mom?"

"Of course not. I've taught in schools for too many years to be nervous going into one."

But Reba won't be teaching this time. Instead, the only job she could get was in the front office. She will be the school principal's secretary, a definite comedown after decades of serving as the head of the English department in the high school on Long Island.

A year earlier, Sarah's father had decided he wanted to retire, so, at fifty-eight years old, Sarah's mother again, as she had all her married life, left her beloved work to follow him to Puerto Rico. "Scott isn't happy and we both need the rest after slaving all our lives," she had said. "We'll finally have time to spend together." But after six months of lying on the beach, Sarah's father took a dollar-a-year job working for the governor of Puerto Rico, in a pivotal position designing and directing the island's first Office of Consumer Affairs, surrounded by doting young men and women who hung on his every idea. "I'm not cut out for sitting around doing nothing," he said.

They pulled up at the tall metal gate. The soldier on duty, a mainlander with a blond crew cut, held up his hand to stop them. Reba sat forward and spoke past Sarah's father through the window.

"We're going to the high school, to Principal Stalzer's office." Reba's voice was forceful.

He waved them through and Reba shrank back against the seat, letting out a sigh.

Sarah wanted to rumple her mother's wiry salt-and-pepper curls, to comfort her, to tell her it would be all right, that they would like her in this school, to say, "Remember, they are more afraid of you than you are of them." But, no, that wasn't right. That's what her mother used to say to Sarah each time she had to enter a new school in a new town in a new state as they followed her father from one place to another, whenever he was ready for the next challenge or had been pushed out the door for political reasons.

"There, over there, Scott," Sarah's mother directed him along the macadam drive lined with close-shaved pistachio grass and royal palms, their heads still on, waving majestically in the ocean breeze.

They pulled into the parking lot. Sarah's father cut the engine. Sarah heard the papery sound the palm fronds made as they slapped against each other. Her mother didn't move. Reba blew air out through pursed lips, making a "puh" sound.

"I suppose I should get going," her mother said.

Sarah wanted to tell her she didn't have to go inside to this demeaning job, but Sarah knew better. When she tried to introduce the subject before they left the house, her mother had turned on her and said acidly, "What do you expect me to do, stay home alone, painting the house over and over again? And someone has to subsidize his contribution to the people of Puerto Rico."

"I'll see you at four," her mother said. "You won't forget, Scott."

"I won't let him, Mom."

"Oh, that's right, you'll be with him, Sarah," she said vaguely, continuing to look out at the sprawling, one-story school.

Reba opened the car door and stepped down. Sarah watched her walk toward the principal's office. Her mother wore a navy blue cotton A-line skirt, a white blouse with a bow, low-heeled fake straw walking shoes. She carried her small pocketbook in one hand and her lunch in a brown paper bag in the other. She didn't look back. She was too brave for that. Sarah wanted to get out and run after her, tell her mother she would stay with her for this first day, that she could forgo driving into San Juan with Daddy.

Instead they waited until Reba slipped inside and was on her own, and then Sarah's father started the ignition. Sarah opened the door and moved into the front seat.

"I hope she does okay," Sarah said.

"Of course she will. Your mother is a consummate professional." He turned to watch behind him as he backed the car out. He broke into one of his radiant, seductive smiles. "Now let's get going. I want to introduce you to all my new cohorts and show them what a beautiful brilliant daughter I have. The governor's even set time aside to have lunch with us."

Day Eight

ESMERALDA JIJÓN arrives at nine a.m. to take us in to San Juan Hospital to see the doctor. She is the Cuban woman to whom we gave my father's clothing for the exile group.

"My love." She wraps me in her arms and heavy perfume.

Esmeralda is thirty years younger than my mother and a few years younger than I am, but as most of the women here do, she treats me like a daughter. As for me, she reminds me of all the women I used to wish my mother looked like, wearing makeup and perfume, elegantly dressed, with clanking jewelry. Today Esmeralda is sporting a double-breasted dark blue suit accented by two rows of antiqued gold buttons. Her straight skirt comes to just above her knees, showing off her shapely calves and slender ankles, made more so by the blue pumps that add two inches to her height. Her medium brown hair curls softly around her flushed face.

Driving toward San Juan, Esmeralda chatters all the way, her polished red nails tapping on the steering wheel. My mother is silent in the front seat, shrunken down, and looking even frailer outside her room. I hadn't realized how small she has become. I'm in back, sinking against the cushiony seats of Esmeralda's Saab, relieved to have someone else doing the entertaining.

"What we must do when we arrive at the hospital, Reba, is have Sarah get you a wheelchair at the main intake desk while I wait with you in the car. She can take you up to the doctor's office. You can do that, can't you, Sarah?" she calls over her shoulder as we speed along the highway.

"Of course," I say, grabbing the seat to pull myself forward and out of my lethargy. "You okay, Mom?" I touch her arm.

"I'm just fine, Sarah, you don't have to keep asking me. I'll tell you when I need anything," she snaps with her old sharpness.

I sit back, stung.

"And then I'll meet you in the doctor's office after I've parked the car," Esmeralda goes on. "You must be aggressive with him, Sarah. He can't leave her waiting like last time. What a disgrace!"

I'm certain Esmeralda blames me for his treatment of my mother. I'm a bad daughter for leaving Puerto Rico after my mother's operation. I shouldn't have gone back to New York. She probably thinks I'm starving my mother. Earlier, after she went into the bedroom, Esmeralda came back out to the living room and said, "Reba looks very badly, Sarah. Is she eating? Should she go to the hospital for a stay?" Even after I'd explained that my mother didn't want to go to the hospital, I felt Esmeralda was holding me accountable for that as well.

My mother and I have been waiting in Dr. Gold's frigid reception area for half an hour when Esmeralda reappears.

"I'm so, so sorry, all the parking places were taken. I drove around and around." She motions with her hand, nail polish flashing scarlet in the dim light. "But why are you still here? Why aren't you inside?"

I want to explain that I asked for a blanket from the secretary, who disdainfully relinquished her own sweater from the back of her chair. The office was filled with others waiting. It was all I could do. I was reluctant to push ahead even though no one looked as deathly ill as my mother, sitting hunched and shivering in the hard plastic chair.

Esmeralda rubs my mother's arms and leans down, putting her hands to my mother's gray cheeks. "You're so cold, Reba. Where is that doctor? This is not right at all."

Her heels clicking on the tile floor, she approaches the desk, and launches into an alternately wheedling and demanding monologue.

The secretary's haughtiness evaporates into fawning servitude in the face of Esmeralda's upper class carriage and Latina assertiveness. She backs her way into the doctor's office. In moments she returns to tell us we can enter. Esmeralda helps me get my mother to her feet. "You have to more forceful, Sarah," she whispers, as my mother trembles and huddles over. Esmeralda pulls the secretary's sweater more tightly around my mother's arms and shoulders, giving me two raised eyebrows, which tells me how right she feels she is and, by implication, how incompetent I am.

"Good-bye, Reba, sweetheart. I'll call you tonight." She kisses my mother and then turns to me. "You're sure Pearl is coming to pick you up?" Again her eyebrows.

"Pearl is very responsible," I say.

"Of course," she says, smiling with effort.

My mother silently takes my arm, pressing her body close to mine, and we shuffle our way through the doctor's door.

Dr. Gold is my mother's oncologist, not the man who operated on her, but the one who has done the tests and diagnoses. He was especially gracious when I said I wanted to get a second opinion from Dr. Sabran at Mount Sinai in New York. "He's a brilliant doctor," Dr. Gold said. "You couldn't do better."

Benjamin Gold is a short, slight anglo man, originally from New York City, but having married a Puerto Rican woman in the early 1960s, he has practiced here for thirty-five years. He is as soft-spoken as his face is gentle. His hair is pale blond faintly tinged with gray, and his eyes are the blue of an April sky and as penetrating as I've always thought only brown eyes could be. He always wears a *guayabera*. Today he has chosen a yellow-beige the exact color of his hair.

He examines my mother, gently prodding the huge mound that is her stomach. Her skin is mottled purple from bad circulation and the chill in the office, the flesh on her legs hangs loose, and where it still clings, the surface is puckered with dimples and stretch marks. It is only in the unfamiliarity of the office that I see how much her body has suffered, how emaciated she is, and how enormous her belly has grown in the week I've been here.

Dr. Gold says nothing as he finishes, just indicates that I can help my mother sit up. He goes back to his desk while I see to my mother's dressing. It is with great effort that she steps back into her panties, as she has no waist to bend from and no muscles left to lift her legs. I hook her brassiere in back, noting the black moles that spot her skin and the white concave spots where other moles have been excavated. How ravaged her once lithe and slender, smooth-skinned body has become. I slip her dress over her head and get her arms into the sleeves and pull the dress down over her swollen belly. She is oblivious to each action, staring straight ahead, smiling docilely each time I ask her to move this way or that. When we are about to step around the screen of the examining area, she clutches my hand.

"I'm afraid," she says.

"You mean you're afraid to know?"

"Yes." She looks down.

"That's all right, Mom. There's no shame in being afraid. Are you also afraid to ask the questions?"

She nods, her lips clenched tightly together while she fights back tears.

"Then I'll ask the questions. Do you want me to?"

Her body sags into mine. "Yes, please," she whispers. "That would help a lot."

SEATED ACROSS THE desk from Dr. Gold, my mother reaches for my hand. I take hers in both of mine. Hers are freezing cold. I try to caress warmth back into them.

"The tumor has grown considerably," Dr. Gold begins, without my having to ask the question.

He looks larger behind the desk, and in such good health. Today everyone seems to me to be obscenely robust.

"You have some decisions to make here." His hands are placed on the desk top, widely spaced, parallel to each other. I notice how relaxed they look. I wonder if he does this consciously, letting us settle into the peace he emanates.

"What are the options?" I ask.

"This is a fast-growing tumor. Whatever is done would have to be quite radical in terms of chemotherapy and radiation."

My mother exhales audibly.

"Does that mean I'd have to come into the hospital?" she asks, her fingers pressing into mine.

"I believe you'd have to stay in the hospital, Reba. These procedures can be dangerous, especially for a woman your age."

I look at her. Her features relax as her eyes sadden. The heavy crepey lids make her appear Asian. We three sit in silence. I don't want to intervene unless I have to. This is her decision. She said she was afraid, but she doesn't look frightened in this moment.

She shakes her head slowly. "No, I don't want to live that kind of life. It won't cure me, will it? Tell me honestly."

"Probably not," he says quietly. "It could buy you some time."

"But what kind of time is that? No. I've lived a good life. Suffering in the hospital is not what I call life."

I see tears welling in Doctor Gold's eyes. I move my chair closer to my mother's and put my arm around her. Her body is stiff and she doesn't relax into me.

"Then you've made your choice, Reba?"

"Yes, I have."

I feel his gaze on me and I look up. He is watching me with kindness. I can also see his mind working.

"I have one more thought," he says. "There is some

experimental therapy I heard of at the last meeting I attended in the States. It's a hormone therapy. All you have to do is take subcutaneous shots three times a day. They say it's been known to reduce the tumors. You could do it at home."

"But who would administer the shots?" I ask.

"You could do it yourself, Sarah, or Mommy could."

My mind goes numb at the thought of giving my mother an injection. I'm going to let her down in this.

"I'm not a nurse. I could never do it. Maybe we could have a nurse come in to do it."

My mother is sitting placidly, without reacting at all to our conversation. She's deep in her own world.

"I don't know if you could get a nurse to come three times a day way out in Levittown. Perhaps a nurse could teach you. It's very easy. You can practice on an orange. You'll not be injecting into the vein."

I think of the nurse who cared for my mother at home. But she'd never come three times a day. She was strict about only working a full rotation.

"Yes, Sarah." My mother turns to me. She's been listening after all. "You know what subcutaneous means, don't you? It means between the layers of the skin. An elementary physiological concept. I would hope I've raised a daughter to know that simple fact, for heaven's sake. You're not an imbecile."

"I know what it means, Mom. For a minute I forgot the difference," I say, working to get my breath back.

Dr. Gold eyes us both. He's probably seen worse inter-actions than this. But it's as if he knows everything about my mother and me, has learned our life history in that exchange. Does he know that I let her attack and don't retaliate? Does he know I get my revenge by hating her? Does he know that her cruelty will transmute into flattering kindness toward me? Does he know that I will be even angrier when she becomes excessively nice, because I'll know that only her preceding sadistic attack could release her form of perverted love?

"I'll try to do the shots, Mom. I'll do whatever I can."

"I know that, dear," she says, smiling sweetly, her tone shifting to deferential. She pats the back of my hand. "You're such a good daughter, dear. I love you and trust you completely. But I'm quite exhausted. Maybe you can get the instructions from Dr. Gold while I go outside and rest a bit in the waiting room."

After I've gotten her settled and covered her with a blanket that has appeared, I return to the office and close the door. I sit in quiet shame across from Dr. Gold.

He clears his throat.

"Will this really do any good?" I ask.

"I think it's worth a try, at the least."

"It'll give her some hope," I offer dully.

"And perhaps do some good. The results have been promising, according to the studies."

I know this is a placebo, for both my mother and me. At the same time I believe in the possibility of a miracle and know that I will purchase the hormone drugs. I will try to find a nurse to come in each day, and beyond that, I don't know what I will do because there is no way I will be able to pierce my mother's flesh with a needle.

"I understand how difficult this is, Sarah."

"Do you?" I say. A cry escapes. I pull it back.

"It takes a lot of courage to do this right."

"What is right?"

"I think you'll find the way. I trust you will. It's particularly difficult to be all alone in this."

I stare at him, thinking, No, it's not. I've always been alone with her. It's very familiar. It's easier for me to do it alone.

PEARL PULLS UP in front of the hospital. "Your chariot, ladies," she rasps, and then laughs boisterously.

I help my mother into the front seat. She sighs as she leans back as though to say, I'm home at last.

Pearl pats my mother's arm and looks at me, her large hazel eyes, with their fans of thickly coated lashes, fill with questioning sympathy.

"I'm sorry, Pearl, but I have to go back upstairs to talk to a nurse and then to Walgreen's to get medicine. This is going to take longer than I thought."

"That's okay, darlings. Don't you worry. Pearl's at your beck and call. I haven't got an iota's interest in football until the playoffs." Again she lets loose with her belting laughter.

"Oh, Pearl," my mother says. "I feel better just being here with you."

I RING THE BELL of the Intensive Care Unit and wait.

I ring again. "Please," I whisper. "Please, please, please."

"Quién es?" The intercom blares.

"Soy Sarita Ellis, la hija de Reba Ellis. Por favor, puedo hablar con usted?"

The door opens. It is the kind, middle-aged nurse with short gray hair. She is Miss Efficiency, but I always read compassion behind her stern expression.

"I don't know if you remember me, my mother was here for four days a month ago."

"Of course, *señorita,* I remember."

I feel like a child before her. We are probably the same age, but I am seven years old and I need her help desperately.

I begin to cry. I can't stop.

"I'm sorry," I say. "I don't mean to cry. But my mother is sick again, her tumor has grown. And I need help." I have to stop speaking because I am crying so hard the words are bursting out in great gusts. I am begging. Never before have I let myself be in such a position.

She steps out. The door eases shut behind her. She puts her hand on my upper arm. I breathe deeply, trying to calm myself. I love that she is touching me, but I can't look at her yet. Suddenly I know that she is not surprised that my mother's tumor grew back. I know she knows my mother is dying. She knew a month ago that my mother would soon die.

"What is it you need?" she asks.

"She has to have subcutaneous shots. Dr. Gold has prescribed them. I need someone to come each day, three times a day to give them."

"Can't the nurse on duty give them?"

Her name tag reminds me that her name is Marianela Quiñones. Back when my mother was in Intensive Care, I used to call her *señorita* Quiñones. This simple memory of familiarity brings some peace.

"No, my mother doesn't want to be in the hospital. She doesn't want chemotherapy. We're going back to Levittown where she lives." Where she is going to die, echoes in me.

"I see," she says. "Come inside, let me try to help you."

It is a relief to enter the cool, sanitary and well-equipped Intensive Care Unit again, the only area of the hospital that doesn't smack of the third world. The semicircle of the nurses' station is filled with flowers and baskets of fruit left by grateful patients and their families. I remember that when it was time to check out, I went to the local florist and bought an extravagant, showy basket of fruit for the station. The nurses now recognize me, and each comes to kiss me and inquire about my mother. When I say she is worse again, they nod knowingly. "What sadness," one says. "It is God's will," another intones.

Marianela has beckoned over the youngest nurse. She is beautiful, of medium height and slender, with long, dark silken hair that waves softly. Her face is a cocoa brown and her features are small and rounded.

"You remember Graciela?" Marianela asks.

"You were kind to my mother," I say, but in truth she was quite snippy in the beginning, and defensive. She eased up later when she saw we were not going to be excessively demanding and that we respected her position. By the end we all kissed good-bye.

Graciela smiles wanly.

"Graciela lives in Levittown on *Calle Margarita*."

"That's just around the corner from us," I say with hope rising.

Marianela explains to Graciela about the shots.

"No, no," Graciela says in Spanish. "That will be impossible. I work here and go to school. I have no extra time. I could teach you. But I can't come more than once."

"Please." I hear myself begging. "I don't think I can give my mother a shot."

Graciela pulls away from me, eyeing me warily, wondering at my intensity.

"That's all right," I say, backing off. "I'll learn, if you can come a couple of times."

Marianela takes her aside and speaks quietly but with authority. Marianela's face flushes as she talks and her hands move to her own abdomen, lifting outwardly as though my mother's tumor is growing inside of her. Her head inclines in my direction as she speaks more rapidly. Graciela nods, sneaking a look at me. She will come and teach me to inject my mother, carrying out her duty as a nurse with grace, in keeping with her name. We exchange telephone numbers.

WHEN I RETURN to the car, my mother and Pearl are deep in conversation. Pearl has settled back against her door and is idly smoking, blowing streams up toward the water-stained and ripped fabric of the roof. My mother has her hands clasped demurely in her lap, but she looks relaxed and serious, no forced smile, no underlying hostility, no attempting to act just the right way.

"Oh, hello, dear," she says as I open the back door. "Pearl

and I have been having a good conversation. Haven't we, Pearl?"

Pearl glances at me. I read that it was a very serious talk and that she will tell me more later.

My mother turns. She is in profile to me. She nods. "Yes, it's been a very good talk, indeed. Sarah is my light and you're my balm, Pearl."

I love both these women. I love that my mother is being natural and appropriate and able to have a real friend. I love Pearl for having brought this out in her. I repeat to myself, "Sarah is my light and you're my balm, Pearl." I want to practice this line so I'll never forget it.

Pearl revs the car and rasps, "Well, children," then begins to cough, a crescendo of deep, phlegm-filled hacks. When she gets it under control, she tosses what is left of her cigarette out the window. "Tomorrow I quit. What I was going to say when I so rudely interrupted myself, is that I think it's time to get your lovely mother back into bed for a little rest, what do you say? First stop the pharmacy?"

We drive west along Ashford Avenue toward Walgreen's and the pension where I stayed when my mother was in the hospital. How many times I walked this route alone, to the hospital and back. The mile-and-a-half stretch took me past the hotel that had been set on fire a few years earlier by a disgruntled employee. Each day I watched the crashing iron wrecking ball as it decimated the remaining walls of the old resort hotel. From there past condominiums, office buildings, fast food restaurants filled with tourists staying on the Condado. I walked this path in the early morning after a run on the beach and a swim. I walked it in the heat of the day after lunch. I walked it in the windy, balmy evening, in darkness pierced only by the street lights and the headlamps of the long line of stalled traffic, locals and tourists looking for fun in this good-time resort area of town.

At Walgreen's I turn the prescription in to the pharmacist, a bleached blonde woman in her early fifties.

All the while I wait, about half an hour, she eyes me suspiciously from behind the plastic bulletproof glass of her high booth. Does she think I'm a junky because I've ordered all of these disposable needles, one hundred of them, three a day for thirty days and a few extras for practice and mistakes. I felt a certain optimism when I'd deciphered Dr. Gold's handwriting, walking down the aisle. Maybe he thought this could really work. Still, it seems like a lot of needles.

LYDIA IS WAITING, watching television when we arrive. She shuts it off and helps me guide my mother, who is feeling weak and shaky, into the bathroom.

I am preparing coffee for Pearl when my mother cries out. Pearl rises from the couch, her face ashen. Lydia motions me to go to my mother.

"I'll finish the coffee," Lydia says.

I find my mother still on the toilet, her underpants around her ankles, skirt hiked up over her pale, dimpled thighs. She is staring up at me, her pupils black with terror.

"I can't go."

"You mean a bowel movement?"

She shakes her head vehemently. "No," she whispers, though to me it's more like a low whistle. "I can't urinate. I feel the pressure, and nothing comes out."

Calm down, I say to myself. You can only be helpful if you keep calm. Instinctively I feel in my pocket for Graciela's number. The paper crackles. I am not alone.

"Did you try running the water?"

"Yes, I did," she says in a tremulous voice.

"Should I hiss for you?"

She shakes her head. Her brow is knotted with worry. "It won't help. There's a blockage, I can tell."

I hiss all the same. She frowns and pushes, the veins in

her neck distending. My hand is on her back making soothing strokes. I stop hissing. She stops straining. Her shoulders slump and her head bows. If her hair weren't threaded with gray, she would be a child.

Stroking the wiry curls at the nape of her neck, I murmur, "It'll be all right. I have the number for a nurse from the hospital, Graciela, who remembers you. We can call her to put a catheter in."

She looks up, her eyes still as dark, but defeated, imploring me.

"Can she come soon? Please try to have her come soon."

"I'll do my best, Mom."

"I'm certain you will, dear."

AFTER I GET MY mother into bed, I try to reach Graciela on the phone at her mother's home, but there is no answer. Then I ask Lydia to stay with my mother while I accompany Pearl to her car. My mother seems especially troubled and I don't want her to be alone with her terror.

Pearl moves stiffly down the short path to the gate. She is subdued to a new seriousness as we make our way. She slowly gets herself into the driver's seat and lights a cigarette. I remain by her door, hand on the base of the open window. When she blows out the match, she begins to play with my fingers.

"Your mother is very brave," Pearl says. "She is resigned to dying. She doesn't seem the least bit afraid of the end. She's sad, but not afraid. We talked again about what an eventful life she's had. How rich it was with your father. How she doesn't want to suffer. I'm amazed at her, darling. You've got an amazing mother."

"I'm worried about the stoicism. Maybe it's serving her well, but I think she should at least grumble a little. Make some real demands. She talked with her sister Hannah yesterday and said essentially, Everything is just fine Hannah, couldn't be better. Why didn't she say, Hannah, I'm dying. I'm frightened. I need you."

"Because she's Reba, that's why. And because our generation and our kind learned not to complain. We were out there to do good in the world, not gripe about our own petty little needs. We had enough to eat, a place to live, good educations. We didn't live in the lap of luxury, but we had our beliefs. She's unpracticed, my dear, in the art of grousing." She reached over and opened the passenger side of the car. "Come, sit with me a minute. I can see you could use a little talk."

"Thanks, Pearl. I'm okay. I better get back. She becomes nervous if I'm away too long."

"Now you sound like your mother. Get in, kid. Relax. What's the worst that can happen? Lydia will call you."

I sink into the seat where my mother had been sitting half an hour earlier.

"Your mother's a complex person. She's smarter than just about anybody around. Am I right?" She pins me with her serious but dramatically made-up eyes.

"Yep," I say.

"But we women learned to put our needs in the background, especially in the progressive movement. Our powerful, charismatic men took center stage. Am I right again?"

"But my father loved that she was smart."

"Ha. Sure he did, as long as he got to do his work with no chains attached. You don't have to answer that, but I know from my own personal experience about being a tough professional woman and the gal behind the guy. Out in the world we could be pushy broads, but at home we kept our thoughts to ourselves. Not so good in the long run. Lots of simmering anger. Lots of it. You don't have to say yes or no, but I bet that rings true for you. Don't hold it against her, Sarah. Don't expect too much."

I don't respond. I hear what she's said. In a roundabout way, she's gently told me that the cause of my mother's anger was her inability to realize her full potential because of social and political restrictions and because my father usurped the top position in our lives. I know this argument well, and to some extent agree with it, but I also know that for my mother it was different, for my mother and me anyway. It went beyond simmering anger in our case. I can imagine Pearl being cross, fuming when she had to keep the lid on her opinions, but she wasn't cruel to her children. She wasn't cut off from her feelings. She didn't go into disassociative fugue states nor lash out physically at a toddler. The telling difference for me is that Pearl is capable of having friends. Pearl has empathy, can laugh naturally, can express irritation, can let herself go. Pearl doesn't understand that she's my mother's first real friend, the only person with whom I've ever seen my mother wholly relaxed. That's the difference. My mother didn't have a friend her entire life other than Pearl and me.

June 1952 through November 1958

THEY MOVED DOWN to Uniondale, Long Island from Burlington when Sarah's father lost his job with the Vermont Farm Bureau. In the beginning, they rented the top floor of a two-family house on a street that dead-ended at the cemetery. It was summer and Sarah spent most days with the Siciliano family, one house away. Sarah had never seen a house like theirs. The Sicilianos got all their furniture from the town dump and the place smelled of old garbage, mildew, and other rank odors; the kitchen and bathroom had no floor, just dirt and some structural beams that had been laid down years before and forgotten. There were three girls and a son named Bobby. Bobby's bedroom, which was really a glassed-in porch with filthy cracked windows where Sarah and the others played poker in the afternoons, smelled of urine. His sister Chickie told Sarah he peed his pants every night.

One evening Sarah's mother and father had gone out to a movie, leaving her at home. Sarah was brushing her teeth at the bathroom sink when she looked up to see Bobby Siciliano reflected in the medicine cabinet mirror, with a rifle pointed at her head. "Only kidding," he said, but his laugh was menacing. Sarah never told her mother. She also didn't confide to her mother that around Christmas time in her new school, when they played "I'm Dreaming of a White Christmas" over the public address system in the cafeteria, she burst into tears and couldn't stop crying, it hurt so much not to be in Vermont anymore.

The next summer her parents bought a small, postwar brick house, over the town line in Hempstead, a step up from Uniondale, but still in the Uniondale School District where

Sarah attended and her mother taught. It was a major move for her parents, who had never owned more than a second hand car. It was supposed to give them a new lease on life, as Reba said, but it was a sad place as far as Sarah was concerned. Her father had a dreary, underpaid job in New York City, going from tenement to tenement on the Lower East Side, doing interviews with families who were about to be evicted and displaced for a new, subsidized middle income housing project. When he came home, long after dinner, he would sit in the big green easy chair in the living room, watching television and drinking one scotch after another. He must have had plenty to drink before he got to the house, because he usually arrived with a slur in his speech and fire on his breath. Sarah's mother didn't say a word about his condition. She just sat on the couch, watching television and playing one hand of solitaire after another. Weekends weren't much better. He usually went back into the city for this meeting or that. Her mother would beg off, saying she was exhausted or sick after a week of teaching school. Reba would return to bed after breakfast. More times than not, she slept the entire Saturday and Sunday away, and when evening arrived, Sarah felt she had to wake her. It was too embarrassing to have her father come home and find her mother asleep, so she would gear herself up and go to the bedroom where Reba napped.

On those evenings, a wedge of light fell directly onto the bed when she opened the door, but she could hardly find her mother, she'd sunk down so deeply into the pillows and covers, so profoundly into her slumber.

"Mom," she said. "Mom, it's time to get up."

Eventually she would have to touch her, but Sarah put that off as long as possible.

"Mom, it's late, I think it's time to get up." There was a moan. She waited a second or two. Then she wanted to get it over with. She walked to her mother's bed and tapped her shoulder. It was cool and a little moist. She gave her a shake using only her fingertips. "Mom, time to get up," she said loudly.

"Oh, my," her mother moaned in her sleep-groggy voice. She turned and lay on her back with her hand across her forehead. Her mouth was slack, her eyes still closed. Her face had a slight shine to it, from the oil that had been released by sleep.

"Are you awake?" Sarah had to be sure the job was done. She didn't want to do it again.

"Mmmmm, hummm," came the usual response.

"OK," Sarah said. "I'm going out now. I'll leave the door open. OK?"

"Mmmm, hmmm."

Sarah walked to the door, but just as she was going into the hallway, her mother's gravelly voice stopped her.

"I'm so thirsty."

Sarah waited for the next line.

"Would you like to get me a glass of orange juice, dear?"

Sarah's rage at this request was the same each time.

"Yes," she answered with her hands clenched in fists. Silently she said, No, I wouldn't like to get you a glass of orange juice. I wouldn't ever like to get you anything.

But Sarah went down the stairs and into the yellow kitchen with its polished cotton curtains printed with spice jars. She got the cardboard can of concentrate from the refrigerator freezer and thawed it under lukewarm water from the tap. She squeezed the frozen concentrated juice from the can into the plastic pitcher, and then with a surge of uncontrollable fury she violently tore the cardboard to shreds.

Upstairs it was difficult to tell if her mother had dozed off again. The bedside light was on, but her eyes were closed.

"Mom," Sarah said.

"Mmmmm." Her mother opened her eyes a slit.

"Here's your orange juice."

Her mother reached for the glass. Sarah maneuvered

carefully so that her mother's hand wouldn't chance to touch her own.

"You got it?" Sarah said in her lightest tone.

"Mmmm, hmmm."

Her mother slowly brought the glass to her mouth. Sarah stood there thinking how much she disliked her mother's every movement.

"Mmmm, that's delicious," her mother said, smacking her lips when she finished. "Thank you, dear. It's wonderful to have such a good daughter. I'm so fortunate." She reached out to take Sarah's hand, but Sarah was already backing away.

Over the years there were times when Sarah went with her father, in her mother's place, to the weekend meetings. "Come on with me, chicken," he'd say. "Keep me company." Reba would agree, "Of course, go along with Daddy. I won't be much good to you today." It was a guilty pleasure to accompany her father to the meetings, which were for new members of a co-operative grocery store he was organizing on the Lower East Side or a community meeting at which the people being evicted cried and yelled and he did his best to appease them. Afterward, Sarah and her father went out to dinner at romantic, sophisticated, but understated French restaurants on Ninth Avenue in Manhattan, where the waitresses welcomed him like an old friend and called Sarah *ma petite chérie*. He drank two or three martinis before and during dinner and then they drove home. They usually found Reba waiting for them on the couch, playing solitaire. Silent, she'd look up for a moment and then down again. "Hi, honey," he'd greet her, a sheepish expression on his face. "We were a little later than I expected." "That's fine," her mother would say. "Sarah, I think you should go straight to bed. It's very late."

One Sunday night when Sarah's father had actually stayed home all weekend—reading in the back yard, trying his hand at mowing the lawn, writing reports on his yellow legal pad— the three of them were watching the Ed Sullivan show, her father with a gin and tonic in hand, her mother with her usual solitaire game laid out on the couch cushions. Frankie Laine came on and began to sing "The Cry of the Wild Goose" in his haunting, echo-chamber voice and Sarah's father joined in, starting low and building in intensity until he was plaintively bellowing out the words, "*My heart knows what the wild goose knows, I must go where the wild goose goes, wild goose, brother goose, which is best, a wandering foot or a heart at rest?*" Her mother continued to slap the cards down. "I wish you'd stop that, Scott," she said sternly, not looking up. But her father kept singing, "*It ain't no use to love the brother of the old wild goose,*" long after Frankie Laine had taken his bows and Ed Sullivan had told them to stay tuned for the rest of the "really big show." When her father hit "*Let me fly, let me fly away,*" for the third time, her mother collapsed the deck, shoved it into the box, slapped the box down on the side table, stood, and without a word went upstairs, leaving Sarah sitting alone with her father. Sarah glanced away from the Mercury car commercial and over at him. He had stopped singing but she caught him chuckling to himself.

The kids at the high school were a rough crowd, recently moved out from Brooklyn like the Sicilianos. In order to fit in, to keep from being a goody-goody, a teacher's daughter, Sarah bleached her hair platinum blonde, wore mascara and white lipstick, began to smoke and drink, and hung out with the toughest group. She was fourteen, but she dated older boys, the ones who had souped-up cars. She'd go drag racing with them on weekends, come home at curfew, sneak back out of the house to meet them and neck for hours, parked behind the high school.

When Reba caught Sarah smoking in her room, she slapped the cigarette from Sarah's mouth and called her a tramp.

"But you smoke," Sarah shouted back at her mother, for the first time in her life. "Are you a tramp, too?"

Her mother slapped her across the face again. "Don't you ever speak to me like that, young lady," she seethed, glaring at Sarah with pure hatred in her eyes.

I hate you too, Sarah thought. Hate you more than you can imagine.

The next evening her mother said cheerfully to Sarah, as if nothing had transpired between them, "Why don't we go have dinner and see a movie?"

You invite me because you have no one else to go with, Sarah thought. Because no one wants to be your friend.

Around this same time Sarah was asked to a party by Billy Kingsley, a six-foot-four senior from a high school in a neighboring town. He was a drummer in a local rock-and-roll band, a fact that her mother, curiously, seemed to like. Reba was excited, almost agitated, about the date. "Why don't we buy you a nice dress for the occasion," she said. "I want you to wear something as beautiful as you are."

Reba took Sarah to the fanciest dress store in Hempstead, a full-price establishment, though they usually shopped at the stores which sold designer clothes at discount. This was the sort of place with no racks, where the saleswomen brought out individual dresses for customers to choose from.

"I think this should suit your daughter's beautiful figure," the raven-haired woman said, on the third attempt. She held up a scarlet woolen dress, a sheath that clung tightly to Sarah's breasts, waist and hips when she slipped it on. "My, she has an hourglass shape, this one does," the woman said, standing back to admire Sarah.

If anyone had ever looked like the tramp her mother had called her, it was the bleached blonde girl with the voluptuous figure who was multiplied endlessly in the three-way mirror. Sarah was shocked to see herself. She knew her mother would never approve, but when she turned, her mother was standing there with a vague expression on her face, disappearing inside herself the way Sarah hated her to do.

"It's beautiful, Sarah," Reba said with a dreamy smile.

"Mom, it's forty dollars." They'd never spent more than twenty-eight dollars on any dress.

"Quality is worth it," her mother said, fingering the fabric, running her hand down Sarah's midriff and hip. "Quality lasts for a lifetime. You must never forget that."

Sarah wanted to push her mother's hand away. Something about the way her mother touched her made her almost shudder.

"You're right, Mrs. Ellis," the saleswoman said. "But how wonderful to have a daughter concerned about money. I should be so lucky."

"You don't think it's too tight?" Sarah asked the woman. She felt exposed in the dress, especially with her mother gazing at her longingly.

The saleswoman glanced at Reba. She was going to take the lead from the customer.

"You look beautiful, Sarah. You have a marvelous figure. You should show it off while you still have a chance." Her mother smiled sadly when she said this, and looked away. It reminded Sarah of the times when they tried things on in the open dressing rooms in the discount stores, and her mother would say, "Oh, to have a body as young as yours again."

They bought the dress. Sarah wore it to the party, but stood all night with her shoulders hunched and her arms crossed at her waist. She even begged off dancing her favorite Lindys; it was unthinkable to fling her arms out with abandon in that dress. She never wore the red dress again, and her mother never mentioned it, not once, as though the dress had never existed.

After Sarah broke up with Billy, she began to date a boy named Patrick O'Connor. Her mother was furious. "Do you know what kind of a family he comes from?"

"I don't care about that. Patrick is Patrick. I like him. You always taught me that everyone was equal," Sarah said.

"Not that kind of everyone," her mother said.

The next day Reba brought home file folders from the high school's guidance office. "Look at these," she said, slamming them down on the dining room table where Sarah was pretending to do her homework. "Look what kind of boy you're dating."

"I don't care what they say. I won't read those files," Sarah screamed, jumping up, pushing past her mother and racing to the stairs.

Reba grabbed Sarah's arm and yanked her back down into the living room. "This boy's mother is for all intents and purposes a prostitute and his father is a petty criminal. His sister pulled a knife on a girl in the hallway by the cafeteria. Is that who I've brought you up to go around with? The next thing you're going to tell me is that you want to marry one of these lower class, immoral characters."

Sarah heard her father's car pull into the drive. He was home early. He would save her from this.

Her mother rushed to the front door. Watching her mother, Sarah thought, Her behind is too big and she has an ugly haircut. No wonder all the kids hate her. Reba yanked the door open. Her husband was standing there with a startled smile on his face.

"What's going on?" he asked, coming in, grinning nervously. He dropped his overcoat and plastic briefcase on the couch.

"If you can't help in any other way, at least you could do something about your daughter," her mother said stonily. Then she whirled around to face Sarah, her voice lowering to a growl. "You're not going out for the next month. You're staying in your room and doing your homework for once so I don't have to be disgraced every time I step into the teachers' room."

"All you care about is your own pride," Sarah yelled at her. "You don't care about me. You just want to order me around. Everybody is equal in this world, negroes, everybody, except the boys I want to date. You teach me about equality and then you change the story."

"Scott, do something. Don't let her speak to me this way." Her mother was shaking, beginning to cry. "Beat some manners into her. It's the only way she's ever going to learn how to behave."

Sarah's father wasn't smiling anymore. His lips were closed tightly and his chin trembled. "Damn you," he yelled in a hoarse voice filled with desperation. He's angry at her, Sarah thought, he's taking my side. But he was coming toward Sarah with his arm raised. Suddenly his closed fist came down on Sarah's shoulder, sending her crumpling to the floor. "Daddy," she cried. He kept hitting her on her shoulders while she was down, a maelstrom of punches and grunts. She tried to rise and twist away from him, but this time his open palm came thudding down on the narrow of her back. She scrambled on all fours up the carpeted stairs while he followed her, bellowing, "You will not speak to your mother in that tone." He slapped Sarah's buttocks and thighs and finally her calves when he couldn't reach any other part of her.

She got to her room and locked the door. Sitting in stunned silence, she lifted her skirt to find the welted red imprints of his fingers on her thigh. She traced his entire hand with her own finger as the marks swelled on her flesh. Her shoulders, later bruised to purple and black, were a mean red when she examined herself in the mirror, and the precise images of his hands on her back were the same.

"Sweetheart," her father called at the door, rapping softly. "Please forgive me. I didn't mean to hurt you. You're the last person in the world that I want to hurt." He fell against the door with a thud, like the sound of his hand hitting Sarah's flesh and bone.

Sarah heard him crying out there in the hall, but she didn't open the door.

Day Eight, Evening

GRACIELA ARRIVES AFTER she's returned from work and finished dinner at her mother's. She seemed in no hurry to visit us when I called, even though I implored her, saying my mother's condition had worsened, that she could no longer *orinar,* that she needed a catheter.

She still wears her nurse's uniform with a navy blue cotton sweater on top, and she's changed into black sandals. Her toenails are painted a pale pink. Her hair is clipped back at the nape of her neck.

Graciela looks around as she enters, and I wonder how she sizes us up by what she sees. Our house is so different from the others in the development and surely not like her mother's place. Ours is not bare and poor as is *señor* Castro's, with its paltry pieces of metal and plastic lawn furniture in the living room, and card table in the dinette, covered with ripped orange oilcloth, and no rug on the terrazzo floor. Nor is our house like Estela's, where a lush garden of orchids fills her *marquesina* and reproduction Louis XV couch, chairs, coffee table and sideboard are stuffed into the living room. Our simple Danish Modern furniture and South American rug must fit no category for Graciela.

All the lights are on in my mother's room, the overhead and the bedside lamps. The square room glows pink, but is strangely lonely and stark, as if the shadows of death have stolen into the corners. My mother sits in bed with no sheet or blanket over her. Her knees are up and spread open and the crotch of her panties shows. I try to use telepathy to get her to put her legs down, but she doesn't heed me. I'm certain that Graciela is offended by such immodesty. The room is hot, but a breeze blows through as we haven't yet put the plastic cover

over the window for the night. The room smells fresh and sweet; the scent of the opened roses on the bureau fills the air. Repeated in the mirror behind them, they look like blowzy, slightly overripe women, a little the worse for wear. I go over to them as Graciela attends to my mother at her bedside. I feel the blossoms. They've gone soft, a few petals fall to the dresser top. I pick up one pink petal and one yellow petal and place them first in my palm and then rub them between my thumb and forefinger, luxuriating in their satiny softness. Tomorrow I'll throw them out. Tonight I'm just grateful to add fragrance and elegance to this too-simple room. How I long to be anywhere but here.

"There, please, Missus, can you me help?" Graciela asks.

I'm surprised by her awkwardness with the language, having always heard her speak in flowing Spanish. It explains her early resistance to us in Intensive Care. She thought she couldn't speak to us until she understood that I spoke Spanish.

"*Sí, cómo no*," I say, and we resume in Spanish.

"Can you please translate for your mother? I need to know what she is feeling, does she have pressure in her abdomen? Does she have stinging?"

I ask my mother the questions.

"No," my mother says. "I don't have any sort of pressure or pain. I just can't urinate." She smiles. "Tell Graciela I'm sorry I don't speak Spanish. Tell her how happy I am to have her here."

I leave the room when Graciela begins the procedure. I can't bear to stay. I sit on the couch with my legs up, mimicking my mother's position. I bring the petals to my nose and inhale deeply. I know what I will do with the roses. After Graciela leaves I'll remove them from my mother's room and hang them upside down to dry, from a string tied around their stems. There is great pleasure in these thoughts. The roses can last forever this way. I am euphoric at the thought, wanting to run into the bedroom to tell my mother.

We always have flowers in our apartment in New York. It's one of my luxuries, one that doesn't cause me even a moment's guilt. It brings life into the house, makes it seem a special, cared-for place.

My own apartment opens out in my imagination, the high ceilings, the white walls, the southern light flowing across the wide-planked floors on late winter afternoons. For a moment I feel I'll never get back there, never return to my life filled with close friends and Roberto.

I breathe the rose petals again. They are beginning to bruise from the pressure of my fingers. I hear nothing from the next room. I expect my mother to cry out in pain. Graciela must be being gentle with her.

I remember how I used to believe that cruelty begets cruelty, and because of that belief I decided to stop the cycle by not having a baby. I told Roberto after we'd been seeing each other for a couple of months that he should understand that I didn't want to have a child.

"Why not?" he asked.

We were sitting side by side at a bar on Broadway eating linguine with extra-hot marinara sauce and fried calamari. I didn't look directly at him as we spoke, but I could see his reflection in the mirror over the bar, partially obscured by the bottles of liquor. He was turned to me, waiting for an explanation.

"I don't want someone to hate me as much as I hate my mother."

He bent his head and began to eat, sucking up strands of linguine. I sat there thinking, now you've lost the best man who's ever come your way, this man you love totally. Why can't you pretend you want a child? Why can't you try to want a child, you foolish woman?

"I thought I'd better tell you before we got any deeper into this thing we have," I said, willing myself to stay hard-hearted.

"I could never have a child, *should* never have one. I couldn't trust myself."

"You have no doubts at all?" he asked.

"None," I said.

"I see you with children. You're very motherly, very empathic. I see how nurturing you are with your friends."

"But I'm not the children's mother. I'm not my friends' mother. I'm sorry about this. But I'm very sure of it. I didn't have a good experience as a child. I don't really blame my mother. But I don't want to hurt another human, and I'm afraid I'd have no control over it." My voice broke then.

His hand closed over my wrist and squeezed. "No need to explain. I take you at your word."

Now, not even able to look at him in the mirror, I studied the uneaten calamari on my plate.

"I have no need for children," he said slowly, his grip tighter on my wrist. "I have plenty of nieces and nephews scattered around the world. One of the few blessings of exile and the diaspora. No matter where I travel, even here in the States, I can find these young family members. As for myself, I have no desire to bring a new being into this world. Certainly not of my own blood line. I've seen enough cruelty in my life. I've borne the brunt of the state's power in Argentina. My parents and grandparents suffered because of the Nazis. I see the results of cruelty every day in my patients. How do you say it here? My hat is off to you for wanting to stop the cycle in whatever way you must. I see no honor in hubris, in believing that you may somehow be immune. As for you and me, I think this love we've found together gives more back to the world than any protoplasm we could create." He brought my knuckles to his lips. "That's my speech for tonight. Let's eat this delicious calamari."

How can I describe to him the joy I feel, I thought. How can I tell this man that I have never felt so affirmed by another being? In the end I didn't try to. I simply let my head down on his shoulder, felt the warmth of him through his shirt, and then after a moment, sat up and continued eating the crispy calamari over marinara sauce, delighting in the strong, garlicky tomatoes with their bite of hot peppers, thinking, This is the most delicious food I've ever eaten in my entire life.

GRACIELA COMES OUT of my mother's room.

"I want to wash my hands and then we can talk."

While she's in the bathroom, I go in to see my mother who is reclining on her pillows, staring up at the ceiling.

"How are you, Mom?"

She blinks. "Tired, but glad this was taken care of." She looks at me without moving her head. "She was gentle with me. It hardly hurt, but I think I'd like to sleep now."

I hook the plastic cover over the window and start the air conditioner, feeling the blast of cold air on my legs.

"Do you want your pillow fluffed?"

"That would be nice, dear." She rolls to one side, letting me take the pillows. They are damp with her sweat. I plump and turn them.

"Let me help you scoot down."

I put my arms around her waist, feeling the perspiration on the middle of her back. She wraps her arms around my neck. "Oooh," she moans, low and guttural, almost sexual. "How good it feels to have you hold me." I ease her down lower on the bed, slipping my hands out from under her body. I release her hands from my neck and kiss each palm and then place them on her tummy.

"Sleep gently," I say.

She smiles at me as though I'm the great love of her life.

GRACIELA SITS WITH me at the dinette table. She has brought extra needles and plastic vials of liquid from the Intensive Care Unit.

"Nurse Marianela gave me these so I can practice with

you. You can't use this medicine on anyone. It's for practice only."

"Can you give my mother an injection tonight?"

"No." She shakes her head as she breaks off the narrow tip of the vial. "I told you. I can only teach you how to do this. You'll have to do it on your own." She looks at me, assessing how disturbed I am. Her lips purse. "You shouldn't be so nervous. There's nothing to it. Even a child can give this sort of injection. My baby sister does it. She's ten years old. She has diabetes and our mother cannot be with her for every moment. Really, *señora*, you can do this."

I hear the reprimand in her voice.

"Of course," I say. There is no way I can explain to her why this is so difficult for me. "Just show me what to do."

She inserts the needle tip into the head of the vial and slowly pulls up the dispenser head of the syringe. She extracts the tip and holds it up.

"You see that bubble?" She points to the air bubble in the hollow of the tube.

"Yes."

"You knock it like this." She taps the cylinder repeatedly with the tip of her middle finger until gradually the bubble works up and it pops. "You don't want an air bubble going into your *mami*'s arm. It's not like into a vein, but you still don't want that."

I push away the image of Lucy's bruised and hemorrhaged veins as Graciela observes me. I am nervous and clumsy, and I can tell she is losing patience. She sighs and takes the syringe away from me to illustrate again.

"Like this," she says, exasperated, tapping the thin metal spear with more force. "Don't be so afraid."

We progress to the oranges.

"You stick it in at a slant, barely under the skin. Don't dig in too deeply."

I give it a try and am relieved at how easy it is and say so.

She frowns, her dark eyebrows meeting. "Be prepared to find skin more difficult to penetrate."

After she has supervised a few more of my practice runs at filling the needle and injecting the liquid into the orange, she deems me prepared. She clears the table, dumping the wrappings, syringes, used vials and finally the orange into a plastic bag. She ties the handles and pulls them tight. Handing the bag to me, she says, "Put this securely into the garbage because there are drug addicts in the neighborhood, especially on this block."

She means Joey. Everyone in the neighborhood knows about Joey.

"I'll take care," I say.

"May I wash my hands again?" she asks.

I wait for her at the open door. The night is balmy. I watch a young couple walk up the path to the house across the street, where a Haitian family lives between Estela's house and Mr. Castro's, and a feeling of longing for Roberto comes over me. If he were here now we could sit on the steps and talk. We could at least be outside the house for an hour or so, but within earshot.

Graciela stands beside me, hitching her medical bag onto her shoulder. I feel her studying me. I feel her pity and compassion for the first time since her arrival and I don't want it. We are not pathetic, I think. We are educated, successful people, my mother and I. We have not always been in the position where we have to beg.

"Did you know your mommy called your name each night when she was in Intensive Care?"

"She did?"

"Yes, in the middle of each night when I was on duty we would hear her calling out 'Sarah, Sarah, are you there?' And if we would come into her room, she would say, 'My daughter is outside the door trying to come in. Don't you hear her calling me?' Nurse Marianela would tell her that you were coming in the morning, that you weren't allowed in now, that she should get her sleep so she'd be rested for you. She would weep a little, but then she would turn over and go to sleep like a good child."

"I didn't know. No one told me." Sorrow sweeps through me to hear of her loneliness and how she exposed it to strangers. To hear yet again how important I must be to her. Why did I never know this before? What kept me from knowing?

"Please call me if you need more help," Graciela says. "I'm sorry I was strict. I am just too busy. I know it is very hard to have your mommy so sick."

"She's dying, and I can't keep her alive," I say. A gasp escapes. I fight the tears.

"I know that," she says. "That's why I came to help you. Nurse Marianela told me."

"I appreciate your coming, very much."

Only when she is at the gate do I realize I haven't paid.

I step out into the night. "Wait. How much do I owe you?"

"Nothing," she says over her shoulder.

"But that's silly. I must pay you. You can use it for schooling."

Outside the gate, she turns. The light from the house illuminates her round face and glistening hair.

"I don't want any money from you and your mommy. This is my little gift to you in your time of great pain. May God be with you and protect you."

AFTER SHE'S DRIVEN off, I sit on the top step with the door behind me open into the living room, half in and half out of the house. One night, a year before my father died, Roberto and I went to sit outside after my parents had retired to their room to read before sleeping. Roberto always complained that my parents sealed themselves off from the sensuous Puerto Rican nights, closing themselves into the air conditioned house. In those days my mother still smoked heavily.

"Why did they even move down here," he complained, "if all they're going to do is sit in a cloud of cold smoke?"

That night, I closed the door behind us so as not to make my mother furious that we were letting bugs in and cool air out.

The neighborhood was quiet and the black sky above was clear and packed with stars. The sweet scent of gardenias and lemon blossoms saturated the satiny air that blew around our faces and bare arms and legs. Far away I could hear the beat of a salsa rhythm and further still the faint rush of waves on sand, while all around us played the ringing song of the coquís.

We didn't speak, just leaned into each other, luxuriating in the pleasure of being alone without the pressure of my parents. Roberto caressed my leg from knee to ankle.

Fifteen minutes into our silent musings, I heard my father's shuffle in the living room. I tensed, wondering if he was looking for us. Roberto put his finger to my lips. My father came to the door, opened it a crack, peered out, closed it again, and turned the lock.

"He's locked us out," I said, jumping up.

Roberto laughed. "That's one way to get rid of me."

"Stop being so self-referential. This is no joke." I said, and began knocking on the door. "Daddy, we're out here."

I moved to the dining room window and looked in just in time to see my father, dressed in his Bermuda shorts and everyday *guayabera,* dragging along in his slippers, turning into the bedroom. "Daddy," I yelled, but he disappeared and I realized he wasn't wearing his hearing aid. We were totally locked out. The *marquesina* was bolted with a padlock. The windows had bars. All the houses on the block were connected to one another with metal bars so that there was no access to the back yards without keys. My parents had their windows sealed and their air conditioning on. There was no possibility of rousing them.

"I can't believe he doesn't know we're out here," I said. "He peeked out and then deliberately locked the fucking door."

"I told you this is his revenge on me, caused by his unconscious incestuous desire for you, his beautiful daughter. Finally he can knock the competitor out of the picture," Roberto said.

I started to laugh. "He locked me out, too. He didn't exactly keep me for himself." But there was something creepy hidden within his act tonight. It resonated with an incident that happened when I was sixteen and looking at some new snapshots taken by my best friend, photos of me kissing a boy and another one of me posing sexily in a bathing suit. My father had come up behind me and peeked over my shoulder. I'd held the photos to my chest so he couldn't look at them any longer. "What's the matter, honey? Does it make you uncomfortable to have me see you like that?" he'd teased suggestively, attempting to grab the photos away.

We sat for fifteen minutes trying to figure out what to do.

"Should we maybe go to Estela's and phone them?" Roberto asked.

"It's too humiliating. Anyway, Estela's house is dark." As were all the other houses along the cul-de-sac.

I got up again and cupping my hands to the window beside the front door, I called through the plastic, "Daddy, Daddy, we're locked out."

Nothing. No bedroom door opened. I reached over and banged on the front door.

"You're going to wake the neighborhood, dearest," Roberto mimicked my mother.

"Roberto, shut the fuck up."

"Just warning you," he singsonged.

"There he is," I said, seeing my father's naked belly and then his whole self emerge from the bedroom.

"Daddy, open the door. We're outside," I yelled, whacking the door with the flat of my hand.

My mother poked her head out into the hall and, looking irritated, spoke to my father. He turned toward us and I saw a sneaky smile twist his lips. Slowly he walked across the living room. He knew what he'd done. He damn well knew.

The latch clicked. The door opened. He was backlit, his thin hair standing in a wispy crown around his high-domed head.

"For Christ's sake, what are you doing out here?"

"You locked us out," I said, glowering at him.

A guilty little laugh escaped him. Even in the shadow, I could see the gleam of satisfaction on his face.

"Well, somebody shoulda given a shout."

I sit alone tonight thinking how much easier in certain ways it has been these past twelve years without my father.

Through the darkness I see someone crossing the street from Estela's house. It is Estela herself, dressed in a pink housedress and flip-flops, her hair set in blue and pink rollers. She carries a stacked set of aluminum bowls.

"*Niña* Sarita, I saw you sitting here in the night all alone after the girl left."

"It was a nurse. She had to put a catheter in."

"Sst, sst," she hisses in sympathy, shaking her head.

"It's not going well."

She places the bowls on the lower step and lets herself down beside me with a "humph" and another "ssst," this time like air seeping from an inner tube.

"I should ask you in," I say. "But I can't get up."

"No, no." She pats my knee. "It's beautiful out here. Your *mami* closes everything in at night."

"That's what Roberto says."

"Is Dr. Roberto coming?"

"He can't get a plane with this strike."

"They say President Clinton is sitting down with them."

"I hope so, Estela. I want him here."

"Everybody says she is waiting for him. They say she won't go until Dr. Roberto comes."

"Who says?"

"Everyone." She flutters her hand from dark house to dark house along the street.

"I'm not so sure."

All the time I chat with her, I am thinking, but my mother's not going to die. She could have weeks, months, years yet to go. I want to say to Estela, I'm going to give her injections. The shots will cause her tumor to shrink. But I say nothing, because I also know it isn't true.

"She waits for her son-in-law. It's clear," she says. "You'll see."

She rubs my knee and hums to herself.

"I've brought you food. *Arroz con pollo, habichuelas, plátanos. Mami* doesn't eat it, but I know you love Puerto Rican food. Reba turned her nose up at our food, even when she was well."

"Oh, Estela, she's sometimes a little fussy," I say, ashamed for my mother's behavior. Here were all these people being kind to her during the years after my father's death, inviting her to weddings, checking in on her, watching the house when she was off on cruises, and she had to insult them by rejecting their food.

"Don't you worry, *nena*. I understand Mommy. She doesn't feel too much for other people. She thinks only of herself. She can be a little nasty, but you have to let it roll off your back. Don't let it bother you."

She continues to rub my knee. I remember the incident with the newsboy and feel newly ashamed. This is the side of my mother I never wanted anyone else to know.

"It's okay, *nena*. I know what kind of a lady your mother is because my mother was the same."

Her pudgy face sags along the jaw line. Her dark puffy eyes meet mine. They glisten in the light coming from the living room.

"My *mami* was cold, cold, cold and mean." Estela turns away and speaks into the night. "The same as your mommy.

Don't push Mommy too hard. Don't try to get too close. Or she'll strike out like a snake. We both saw that, right? You have to stand close enough to watch and far enough away not to be hurt. But deep in her, she loves you and she waits for her son-in-law to come say his good-bye. You'll see, Estela is right in this."

With that she slips her arm around my shoulder and draws me to her. We sit together for a long time before we gather the aluminum bowls and she helps me inside with the still warm chicken and rice.

"Eat what I've cooked for you," she says. "It will make you feel better."

I SIT ON THE COUCH with a plate of Estela's food in my lap, chomping on a tender chicken leg as I dial home. Roberto answers on the second ring.

"Hi there, I was waiting for your call," he says. The television is blaring in the background.

"How can you hear with that thing going? What are you watching?"

"The news. I want to see if there is any movement on the airline negotiations."

"Should I hang up?"

"What's the matter with you?"

"I call and you just watch television. Can't you do that later?"

"What are you saying to me, Sarah? Don't you want to know if I can get the hell down there?" His voice rises.

"You don't have to yell at me. You don't want to come anyway. I bet you hope the strike'll continue."

"In that case, maybe I'll call Clinton and lobby him not to sit down with the strikers. I will tell the president of the United States that my wife doesn't want me with her, but at the same time she *does* want me there in Puerto Rico to help her help her mother to die. I'm certain he can empathize with such ambivalence."

"Is this the way you talk to your patients?"

"I remind you that you are not one of my patients, but my dear, sorrowful wife."

My chest feels as though it's going to burst, there is so much pressure building in it. I need him. I'm all alone down here. Stop acting like an idiot, Sarah.

"I'm hurting," I say aloud. "This is too hard." The tears start. I swallow the sobs.

"I know it's too hard," he says. "Your friends keep calling, asking what they can do, imploring me for your phone number. Phyllis is furious. Says you always do this, cut yourself off when you could be getting support from your friends."

I keep crying, luxuriating in the love and care I feel exists up there in my city, feeling guilty that I'm unable to accept it, angry because they don't understand that I can't have the telephone ringing day and night for me while my mother needs my attention. I don't want her to know what my life is, don't want her to compare it to her own patched-together friendships. I can't have her angry at me, envious that I'm talking with others while she's dying.

"I can't have them calling here. It would be too hard for me, too confusing."

"That's what I told Phyllis, that it's a very complicated situation, but that she's just got to accept it, the same as I reluctantly do. I said to everyone, and I can give you the whole long list of who called, that I'd let you know how much they care about you and what you're going through down there."

The tears pour over my cheeks and under my chin, dribbling onto my chest. He turns the television off and remains in silence on the other end while I cry on.

March 1947

WHEN SHE WAS FIVE Sarah went often to stay overnight with a woman who had been her nursery school teacher. Mrs. Davis and her husband didn't yet have children of their own and seemed to love having her there. Mr. Davis was short, very thin and had black hair and rosy cheeks. He wore round metal-framed glasses similar to Sarah's own. Mrs. Davis was taller than Mr. Davis, which intrigued Sarah, and much fatter, with medium-length blonde hair that Sarah's mother said would have been lovely if she hadn't given herself such a bad perm.

Each night Mrs. Davis would curl Sarah's hair in rags and in the morning would comb it out. Sarah's hair was thin and straight and didn't hold the curl well, but for about half an hour she thought she looked beautiful. Mr. Davis was a photographer and he took portraits of her in that half-hour of her beauty. Mrs. Davis would comb Sarah's hair again after each series of shots, and her husband would gently adjust Sarah's heavy eyeglasses and would from time to time remove them, spray them with the same liquid he used on his camera lenses, dry them with a scrap of yellow cloth, and carefully replace the glasses on her nose. Their fussing caused Sarah's eyelids to slip woozily closed from the pleasure of being taken care of, as did their quiet consultations with each other about the placement of lights and how she should be turned to left or right for the next few camera clicks.

Mealtimes Mrs. Davis cooked whatever Sarah wanted, or at least asked her what she liked to eat. At first Sarah could barely understand the question. How could she tell an adult what to cook? How could there be different kinds of food to choose from? In her house her mother would often cook the same meal every night for a week, adding a bit of this or that to stretch or change it, all the while in a bitter mood, complaining that she hadn't gotten an education to slave in the kitchen every night. By the time Sarah went to stay more regularly with the Davises, out on their farm in Shelburne, her mother had obtained a teaching position at the high school in Burlington. She was relieved, Reba Ellis told Mrs. Davis, finally to be out of the house where she said she was going stir crazy.

One March Sarah spent an entire week at the Davis farm. Her parents had gone to Montreal for a vacation, to get "some much needed culture," her mother told Mrs. Davis when she dropped Sarah off. Sarah and Mrs. Davis went about the farm in their galoshes, collecting eggs and putting out chicken feed. The mud was thick, oozing up over Sarah's ankles, and in order to take each next step she had to grab Mrs. Davis's hand, hang on tight and pull hard to release her foot with a great slurping sound. They laughed as they made their slow way across the barnyard, over and into the warm and smelly chicken coop. The hens clucked and squawked when they entered, wings flapping, as she and Mrs. Davis moved them off the nests, freeing up the roosts so they could scoop into the moist warm hay and take the bloody, straw-stuck eggs for their baskets.

They repeated this each morning during that week, going out before breakfast, shortly after dawn, with the sun coming up strong in the pale March sky. It was still frigid then and Mrs. Davis wrapped Sarah's neck in her own scarf, one that smelled of a mixture of soap and the murky odors of the cow barn. When they had collected their supply of eggs, they returned to the house across the muddy yard, their laughter starting up all over again.

In the bright yellow kitchen with the sun angling in

through the bank of windows over the sink, Mrs. Davis pulled a chair into the warm rays and told Sarah to climb up. Sitting on the counter, Sarah watched as Mrs. Davis plucked straw and fluff out of the dried blood, and used a rag to wash off the chicken waste. She handed Sarah the clean eggs and told her to place them very carefully into the empty pockets of the brown egg cartons. With two hands Sarah held them, feeling the lingering warmth, wondering if it was possible that baby chickens lived inside the delicate shells. When they'd packed all the cartons and stored them safely in the icebox, Sarah was given the job of cracking five eggs into a red bowl. Mrs. Davis's hand covered hers as they whisked them into a brilliant yellow froth for their breakfast of scrambled eggs, bacon and toasted bread.

The week was filled with gathering and preparing food, sewing with Mrs. Davis, and painting on an easel in Mr. Davis's studio. The three of them listened to the radio together every night while Mrs. Davis and Sarah pored over seed catalogues to plan the spring planting, after which Mrs. Davis would read to her in bed. A few nights Sarah had bad feelings in her stomach when she remembered her mother and their house on Route 7 in Shelburne. Sometimes she thought she missed her and her father, and at others she let herself think about never having to go back there to the mornings of waking up and not knowing if her mother would be angry at her or if her mother would be staring out the kitchen window and wouldn't hear Sarah even when she said, Hi, Mommy. There were the mornings when Reba would yell at her so loudly and with such fury that the colors in the room would go gray for Sarah. But she didn't let those thoughts stay in her mind during that week in March at the Davis house, because while she was there she didn't want to spoil her time. But it was also because she didn't believe her own thoughts. Sarah suspected she was only imagining that it wasn't nice at her house in the early mornings, and when she returned home she could bring back to her house the happiness she'd gathered here like eggs in a basket, and everything would finally be fine.

The Sunday arrived when her mother was coming to get her. Mrs. Davis had reminded Sarah the night before that she'd be going home after lunch the next day. She tried to act happy about it as Mrs. Davis tied the rags into her hair. Sarah told her it would be nice to see Mommy, but she had to work hard not to show her true feelings, of heartbreaking sadness at having to leave this warm, happy place. Sarah was fighting back tears, when the next thing she knew, Mrs. Davis was holding her close. And as hard as Sarah tried not to, she wept inconsolably into Mrs. Davis's soft breasts.

After lunch Sarah went up to her room to put the last few items in the suitcase that Mrs. Davis had helped her pack in the morning. On the landing she stopped to look out the window at the cow pasture. It was a favorite vista. She loved seeing the black-and-white cows on the rocky meadow, with the patches of snow and mud and early grass. She'd tried to paint it that week and was disappointed that her hands couldn't recreate the beauty she saw. Mr. Davis said that in the future she'd be able to do it, but what was most important now was to try to get the colors on the paper so she'd have the memory. Sarah didn't yet know what memory was but she was comforted that just getting the color right was acceptable to him.

Looking out the window, she saw her parents' car, the gray Plymouth, turn into the far-off gate and begin the long drive up the dirt road to the Davises' house. She stared at the sight and a dread came over her. She didn't want to see her mother. She didn't want to have to hug her and pretend she was overjoyed her mother was here. She didn't want to hear her mother's voice calling her "dear" and telling her what to do by posing questions. "Don't you want to leave now, dear?" "Don't you want to put your coat and hat on, dear?" "Don't you want to put that on the shelf, dear, and do what I'm asking you to do, for Christ's sake?"

Sarah turned around and hurried back down the stairs. Peeking into the kitchen, she saw that Mrs. Davis wasn't there. She ran across to the mud room and yanked her coat and scarf from the peg and stuffed her feet into her galoshes, snapping the top clasp on each, and opened the door. She checked the yard, and dashed out, skirting the edges of the mud, trying to stay on high ground so as not to get stuck. She made it over to the hay barn just as her mother's car was coming around the corner. Sarah stepped inside before Reba could spot her, and slid the big door closed.

Inside it was hushed and warm. The stacked hay generated its own heat by this time of year. She'd been warned not to tumble in the haymow because it could create a combustion and send the whole place up in flames. "I know how tempting it is to jump into the pile, but it's very dangerous," Mrs. Davis had cautioned on her first day there.

Sarah squatted on the floor near the sliding door. Through the slight opening, where it didn't quite connect with the door jamb, she observed the gray Plymouth draw into the drive. The car stopped by the back porch. She saw her mother through the windshield. Looking into the rearview mirror, Reba adjusted her hat. It was black, with a slight brim and earflaps that tied under her chin. Sarah's arms were around her knees, embracing them tightly. Her heart beat rapidly, making it hard to breathe. The car door opened and her mother stepped out. She wore her dark red coat with the full sleeves and flared wide skirt. Sarah knew her mother loved this coat. For a moment Sarah felt sorry for her. Her mother had dressed up to come get her. She could stand up now and run out and surprise her mother and tell her she'd missed her and that she'd been hiding just for fun. But Sarah didn't move. Reba climbed the stairs and knocked, calling out Mrs. Davis's name. "Eleanor, it's Reba Ellis." Reba waited, her hands in the pockets of her pretty coat. She looked out toward the field and then turned and stared directly at the barn door, the light flashing on her glasses, and Sarah thought her mother must be able to see through the door to where she was hunkered down. But Mrs. Davis appeared on the porch and hugged her mother and brought her inside.

As she waited, Sarah picked at a scab on her shin. It began to bleed and then she felt faint seeing the blood trickling down her leg in a long trail. She put her head on her knees to stop the dizziness and the weakness that had overtaken her. When she clenched her hands she couldn't make tight fists; it was like they were made of play putty. She began to shiver. She wished she'd worn her snow pants. It wasn't as warm in the barn as it had seemed. What was happening? Were they looking for her upstairs? Maybe her mother would give up and go back home, saying she'd return later.

Mrs. Davis opened the storm door and called, "Sarah, your mother's here." Stepping out, she looked from side to side. She called again, rubbing her arms in the cold. "Sarah, where are you?" Sarah heard her say to herself, "Wherever could she be?"

Sarah felt like she was going to throw up. The dizziness got worse. She couldn't stop herself from picking on the scabs until both her legs were smeared with blood.

Reba came out and walked down the steps. She had Mrs. Davis's shawl around her shoulders over her brown suit jacket.

"Sarah, dear, it's Mommy. Are you out there? I've come to take you home." She frowned, pushing up the nosepiece of her glasses. "Damn," she said, going up the stairs and inside again.

A few minutes later her mother re-emerged. She wore Mr. Davis's red-and-black-checked jacket and her hat was back on her head. She came down the stairs and plodded her way across the driveway, sinking into the mud, angrily pulling her feet out with each step, not laughing. She was on her way to the chicken coop, her back to Sarah.

"Sarah Ellis, this is not funny. Where are you?"

Sarah had to get away. She couldn't let her mother find her. Her mother was going to hurt her. Sarah's head was spinning as she crawled deeper into the recesses of the barn, scrambling into a pile of hay. She lay face up and pulled the matted stalks down over her, leaving just enough space to breathe. Hay covered her glasses, but she could see the door through their crosshatched pattern. Her heart raced but the dizziness was gone. She'd disappeared. She was invisible to the world. She wouldn't ever have to go home. After her mother had left, Sarah would return to the house and tell Mrs. Davis that she'd gone for a walk up by the cows to say good-bye and had forgotten what time it was. It would be too late for her mother to drive back. She'd be able to stay another night.

A long time later the barn door slid open. Sarah had been hearing their shouts. They were upset, especially her mother. Sunlight poured into the barn, reaching to where she was hidden. She barely breathed. Her nausea returned. She couldn't clench her fists again, but found she could pinch the skin on her neck, digging her fingernails in, hurting herself so she wouldn't throw up. The three adults were dark shadows in the wide, high door-frame. Her mother's arms were wrapped around her waist as she scanned the barn. Mr. and Mrs. Davis walked to the left, to the far end of the barn. Sarah knew the moment her mother discovered her. Reba said nothing, didn't call out to the other two, but strode directly toward where Sarah lay, and when she was within a foot of her, Sarah could see her mother's eyes boring in at her.

Reba whacked the hay away, catching Sarah's glasses with her hand, knocking them askew. She reached in and grabbed Sarah's wrist and yanked her to standing. She struck her on the backside and legs, jerking Sarah around, yelling at her,

"Don't you ever hide from me again." As she whipped her back and forth, Sarah caught a glimpse of Mrs. Davis putting her hand to her mouth to stop herself from crying out, and then she saw Mr. Davis start toward them as though to make her mother stop. Sarah heard Mrs. Davis say, "Tony, no." Her mother didn't seem aware of any of this as she dragged Sarah staggering to the door.

"Now you get your things, young lady. We're going home."

Outside the sun was warm, cutting through the cold. There was a heart-piercing smell of spring mud and melting snow. The sky was a deep blue with line upon line of tiny broken clouds running diagonally across, like stitching on blue cloth. Sarah wished her way up into them. She wished she could be lifted by the soft breeze and carried out to the hill where the cows were and set down. She'd walk over the top of that hill and keep walking until she reached the next hill and the next. But that wasn't possible. Instead she did what her mother demanded and went directly to the room where she'd spent the last week, picked up her suitcase, and came back down. She met Mrs. Davis at the bottom of the stairs. It was only then that Sarah realized she hadn't taken off her galoshes and had tracked mud up and down the stairs and across the hall.

"I'm sorry." Her chest began to heave.

"Oh, dear, look at your legs. No bother, kitten, about the mess," Mrs. Davis said softly, putting her hand to Sarah's cheek. "You're a good girl, remember that. I love you very much."

Sarah nodded, keeping her head down.

"We'll get you back here for another visit. How's that suit you?" Mrs. Davis wiped futilely with a handkerchief at the dried blood on Sarah's legs.

She nodded again, but she knew she'd spoiled it forever.

She felt too ashamed of what Mrs. Davis had seen to ever have it be the same here.

Her mother didn't speak as they left the Davises' driveway and turned onto the road. Sarah watched out the window while the countryside sped by, taking her further and further away.

They'd gone a couple of miles when her mother swerved off the road and pulled to a stop on the shoulder. They were parked beside a huge granite boulder. The stone glittered in the sunlight. Up ahead was a forest.

Her mother began to cry. Reba pressed her forehead to the steering wheel that she was still holding with both hands.

"Mommy?"

Her mother didn't answer. She kept crying.

"Mommy, I'm sorry." What she had done to her mother now crushed Sarah. She had hurt her. She had made her mother ashamed in front of Mr. and Mrs. Davis. Inching over to her, Sarah got close enough to smell the cigarettes and the odor that was distinctively Reba's, of old fruit like bruised apples that fell from the trees in late summer. Sarah pushed her head in under her mother's arm. She felt as if she was crying, too, but she wasn't. Her mother's arms fell around her and she pressed Sarah to her, and she sobbed harshly, as though she was having trouble breathing. Reba continued to cry for a very long time, burying her face in Sarah's hair, until she stopped and they sat breathing in and out, as though they were one while the sun shifted in the heavens and the sky turned to red, and then purple, and finally to night.

Day Nine

GRACIELA WAS RIGHT, piercing the rind of an orange is not equivalent to puncturing human flesh.

I practice for hours, filling the needles, knocking down the air bubbles and injecting the solution into an orange until a hematoma forms under the nail of my middle finger on my left hand and it is so painful to the touch that I have to change hands to do the task. I believe I'm ready, and go in to tell my mother.

Her bedroom is filled with light. The day is dry and brilliant, the sky cloudless. The beautiful weather seems to have entered her, renewed her energy and her complexion. Lydia has completed changing her bed and is helping my mother off the chair and in between the fresh sheets. While Lydia finishes I gather the drooping roses.

"I'm so glad you're finally taking those away," my mother says. "They're on their last legs, god-awful, really."

"I thought I'd dry them."

"Whatever you wish," she says dismissively. "I would throw them out."

"But I'd like to preserve them. They can be really pretty, dried. The color gets deeper." I don't know why I'm defending these damn roses. If she doesn't want them, why don't I just dump them?

"Whatever," she says. Her eyelids lower and she frowns. "You do what you like, dear."

The anger rises in me. All my sadness of the night before disappears. I feel myself glaring at her, a murderous stare.

"I think dried is pretty," Lydia says. "You'll love them, Reba. You'll see."

My mother smiles patronizingly at Lydia. "Yes, Sarah always knows the right thing to do."

I find a string in the junk drawer in the kitchen and wrap it around the stems and jerk it so violently to tie it that the string breaks and the bouquet falls into the sink. When I pick it up the heads of two roses disintegrate and pink petals fall into a heap on the stainless steel.

I hate her again. Why can't she let any feelings through? Why must she go icy on me?

Lydia comes into the kitchen carrying the bundle of used linens.

"Your mommy seems better today," she says, flashing me a devilish grin.

I burst out laughing.

"Are you going to give her the shots?" Lydia stands at the door to the *marquesina*. She wears lipstick and eye shadow today, and her hair has been washed and curled. She has on a pair of black slacks and a tailored white blouse.

"I'm going to try. I hope I do okay."

I loop the string around one of the cupboard handles, letting the roses swing over the dish drainer.

Lydia remains standing at the door, shifting from one foot to the other.

"You look nice today, Lydia. Are you going somewhere?"

"I have to be at welfare and then to Ladito's school."

"Isn't it too late to go to the welfare office?" I know these government offices in Puerto Rico. If you don't get there before the doors open in the morning, you don't have a chance of being seen.

"No," she says, fussing with a loose thread at the hem of her blouse. "I've got a special appointment with the foster care person about Ladito. My only problem is I can't get there without a car."

So this is what her waiting around is about.

"You want to borrow the car, right?"

"Joey could drive me." She shrugs.

"Lydia, why don't you just ask me directly?"

"Because you're still mad at me about the last time."

"That's not true. I'm grateful to Joey for putting in the phone. That was very nice of him."

"Joey's handy when he applies himself." She smiles. "He just takes a little pushing."

"And you're the woman to do the pushing."

"Right."

"So push him to get the car back on time and everybody will be happy."

"Right."

I sense that she's holding something back. "Is there more, Lydia?"

She looks down. "Joey and me were thinking of getting a place. For Ladito too. I've got to move Ladito out of the neighborhood, away from the drug dealers, away from his *mami*. She's getting worse. I don't want him to see her like that, all scabby and bony. It's not good for him. We were thinking a house with a little yard would be nice." Her head's still down, but I spot a nervous smile.

She wants this house, I think. That's what she's after. I try to control my suspicions, my anger. All her niceness has been a manipulation. I knew I shouldn't have trusted her.

"We're not asking for nothing free, if that's what you're thinking." She lifts her head. Her face seems more mature, sober and businesslike. No coyness there. I notice how badly sewn her deformity is and I feel sympathy.

"What is it then?" I say.

"Don't think I'm taking advantage, that I'm trying to use you, Sarah. I love you. I do. You're not like other mainland people. Not dry like them. You've got feeling in you. I see that. What I'm wanting to ask is, do you think you'd rent the house to us after Mommy dies? I'd work real hard, get extra jobs to meet the rent, and keep on Joey to get his refrigerator repair license."

"I don't know, Lydia." The rent would have to be a couple of hundred dollars a month. She could never come up with that.

"Ladito loves to play on the grass," she says.

"I know. I saw him. But I can't think that far ahead. I'm afraid I need to sell the house. I'm not rich. I can use the extra money."

"Okay, baby," she says, putting her arms around me. "Don't think about it now. I was just asking. Maybe it wasn't so good for me to ask with Mommy still alive."

"Does this have anything to do with the foster care meeting? Are they pushing you to live in a better place?"

"A little bit," she says.

"Why didn't you say so?"

"I didn't want you to do nothing out of pity."

All my suspicions of her are gone. I feel sad for all of us. "If it will hold things off for a while, tell them I'm thinking about it."

"Thank you, baby," she says. "I appreciate it."

I RETURN TO the bedroom. My mother is sitting up in bed with an open book face down on her chest. She's staring straight ahead, frowning.

"What's wrong, Mom?" I ask, but I don't really care. I'm still angry with her and preoccupied about Lydia.

"I can't read anymore."

"You mean you can't see?"

She looks up at me, her eyes magnified by her thick glasses and distorted like fish in a bowl. "I see perfectly well. I can't seem to concentrate. I read the words and they don't make sense. I always could read. What do you think it is? What am I going to do, Sarah, if I can't read? I don't understand what's happening." Her voice rises with fear as she stares at me imploringly.

I know what's happening. She is too anxious to read and too tired. Dying makes her tired. It takes too much energy to keep her body going as it deteriorates.

I sit down in the chair beside her, pulling it closer to the bed. I take her hand off her chest and hold it, caressing the inside of her forearm as she clutches me tightly.

"You're tired. Yesterday was an exhausting experience. Rest some more and maybe you'll be able to read later."

She swallows and sucks her lips in.

"I need to read. It's my greatest pleasure. I don't know what I'll do if I can't read. It's my life."

How true, I think. It's her life that she is losing.

"I know that, Mom."

I continue stroking her until her panic passes. When she is calm again, I ask, "Shall we start the injections?"

Her face is transformed with sudden pleasure. "Yes. That would be very nice, dear."

I get the paraphernalia, a new syringe sealed in plastic, a vial of the hormone, a paper towel, a pad of gauze and the bottle of alcohol. I place everything on the bedside table, break open the plastic around the needle, insert the needle into the vial and drop it all on the floor.

"Shit," I cry.

"Sarah, why do you have to be so clumsy?"

"I'm sorry. I'm nervous."

"Of course," she says, sighing. "I suppose you should get another dose and start again. But please be careful. It's expensive."

This time I don't drop anything, but, as I'm trying to tap out the bubble, liquid squirts into the air, losing half the dose.

"At this rate I'll never get my medicine," my mother says through tight lips.

"Hey, Mom, I need practice, is all. I'll get it down."

"I'm sure you will, dear." She is at her most disingenuous now.

I swab the inside of her arm with alcohol, working to keep my anger under control, and then the moment arrives when I must pierce her flesh. I angle the needle. Touch the tip to her skin, and hesitate.

"For Christ's sake, just push it in," she commands. "Don't be so afraid every step of the way. That's what's wrong with you. You're always so afraid of everything. How did I raise a daughter to be so frightened?"

I push against the resistant flesh. It is more like a stiff coating of rubber or plastic than the porous peel of an orange. Then in one awful moment it pierces the surface and is in. I can barely breathe; I am repulsed and terrified. How could Lucy have shot into her own veins?

"Push the damn plunger," my mother growls.

I do as she says and watch it move down the cylinder emptying the liquid into her arm. I pull up to remove the needle, leaving a spot of blood on the gray-beige surface of her skin. All my pent-up energy leaves me in one whoosh like the liquid leaving the syringe. I am becalmed, peaceful. I actually did it.

I dab the puncture wound with more alcohol. "Now I can really be a nurse," I say, laughing. "I can change bedpans, regulate the intravenous machine, and puncture you with shots. We're in business. You can stay sick as long as you want."

"That's not funny," she says. "I don't wish to be sick."

"I know that, Mom. Just trying to add a little levity to the situation."

"Well, I don't feel like laughing." She rubs her arm and pouts.

"Damn it, Mom. Give me a break, will you?" I'm shocked to hear myself talking back to her. I haven't done that since I was a teenager. "All this is difficult for me, too."

"Certainly not as difficult as for me."

"No, you're right. But I don't make it harder for you. And you could do the same for me by not berating me, at the very least." I stand up abruptly. My anger is like a solid brick. I feel in complete control of it. There's no threat of it boiling over into rage. It is too firm for that.

I observe my mother's mind working, doing its calculations.

She smiles shyly.

"You're doing such a fine job of taking care of me. I couldn't ask for more, dearest."

I don't want to feel pleased by this admission of hers, but it is entering me, softening the edges of my cube of anger. I know she's afraid I'll abandon her, that it's the only reason she's being nice. But I think, Maybe this is all it ever would have taken to make her consistently treat me nicely. All I would have had to do was stand up to her. It's what Roberto contends. "No one ever put her in her place, not your father or you. You both allowed her to treat you however she wanted."

"Thank you," I say to her. "I appreciate that." I gather up the medical supplies and leave the room.

Day Twelve

MY MOTHER IS EATING less and less. A few bites of toast in the morning, a sip of tea or coffee. Three spoons of soup for lunch, a nibble of macaroni and cheese for dinner. I'm careful to bring her small portions on salad plates, hoping she won't notice how little she's eating. I don't want her to grow more frightened or perhaps I myself don't want to face this indication of decline. Her systems are shutting down one by one. She vomits more frequently. I've learned to stay in her room for an hour after she's eaten her food. It doesn't usually take that long for her to regurgitate most of what she's taken in.

"I think I'm going to be sick again," she cries.

"It's okay, Mom. I'm here."

I put the plastic bowl under her chin and watch as barely digested bits of what I've fed her come up along with black bile from the depths of her stomach. I wash her face with a damp cloth and brush her teeth with a dab of toothpaste.

"Now lie down and rest," I say as I ease her onto her pillows.

Her face is gray and small, frightened as a newborn kitten.

"I'm eating nothing," she says. "I've hardly eaten anything for days. And even that won't stay down. I can't live like this."

"You're getting some nutrients each time," I say. "And you're not exerting much energy."

"I'll say," she laughs bitterly.

"We could go to the hospital, Mom. We could get you fed intravenously."

"No!" she rasps angrily, beginning to cry. "I told you, I

don't want to go back there. It's too awful. I want to stay here."

She closes her eyes and in moments she is breathing deeply, sound asleep.

I call Dr. Gold's office. I sit on the couch with my knees up, my arm over my head to hide myself from the incriminating eyes of the world. My hand grips the receiver tightly and presses the mouthpiece into my jaw as I wait for the doctor to come on the line.

"Hello, Sarah, this is Dr. Gold," his kindly voice sounds in my ear, entering my body, expanding my heart. I begin to weep so violently I'm unable to speak.

"Calm yourself, Sarah. Try to tell me what it is."

"I'm killing her."

"How are you killing Mommy, Sarah?"

"I'm starving her to death. I don't want to kill her. She doesn't want to go to the hospital. Can't I feed her intravenously here in the house?" I continue crying as I speak, at the same time trying to stifle my sobs and keep my voice down so my mother won't wake and hear me.

"Sarah." He pauses and waits for me to stop weeping. "Sarah, you could do that. We could set up a system in the house."

"Could you? Thank you." Relief is like a heavy, warm wool poncho on my shoulders, tamping down my terror and sorrow.

"We could, but I think it wouldn't be the best for everyone, including Mommy."

"Why not?" My panic rises again.

"Because what we're looking for is a merciful death."

I begin to moan.

He goes on. "We're not looking for a way to prolong life. Do you understand?"

I can't answer him. I can only rock forward and back.

"This is the best, Sarah, in your mother's case," he says, speaking over my rhythmic moans. "It's the kindest thing you can do for her. But it takes enormous courage and I can understand if it's too difficult for you. But it's what I would do if she were my mommy."

Tears wash my face as I continue to rock. I hear myself whimpering, but I don't care; I've abandoned all dignity in front of this man.

"If you can do this, my hope is that she will die a painless death. If this works out the way I anticipate, she will sleep more and more, for longer and longer periods until finally she doesn't wake. These tumors can be painful, but so far so good, and if the progression of the cancer continues as it has been, she'll just slip away. Sarah, can you speak to me? It would help if you could."

After a few moments, I hear myself say, "I'll try to be brave. But it's so hard."

"I know that. But I believe you're strong enough to do this for Reba."

Before hanging up, I ask, "Should I keep giving the shots?"

"Why not?" he says. "As long as she notices, you might want to keep giving them. Do you understand?"

"Yes," I say.

Day Thirteen

WHEN LYDIA ARRIVES the next morning, she brings along Ladito. She asks permission for him to play in the backyard and then sends him out.

"He loves it here," she says, as we watch him run from end to end and then throw himself in the grass and lie there looking up at the sky.

I want to say, Stop manipulating me, but I hold my tongue. I even suspect that she's told him what to do to win my heart. Because that's what's happening. I can't help but identify with his joy, romping in the backyard, remembering how many times I longed for such a place to play. How magical and luxurious it would have felt to me at seven years old.

But I have come to count on having this house, selling it, adding the extra money to my savings. I make a modest living from my writing. Roberto has some patients who pay full price, but he has a tendency to give discounts when an interesting case comes along, and lately he's been doing quite a few torture survivors from Argentina for free. "How can I turn my back on my fellow *porteños*, when I got out in time and they didn't?" he says.

"How did it go yesterday?" I ask Lydia.

We are at the dinette table having coffee. She has brought me an Egg McMuffin from the local McDonald's.

"It went okay," she says, taking a big slurping drink of her milk coffee. "I told them what you said to say. That keeps them happy for a while. I just don't want them to put him in the foster care system. I'd die if I lose my Ladito." She dips the last of her biscuit in the coffee. "One thing maybe I can do, if it's not good for you to rent to us here, is move in with my daughter. She lives out in the Carolina urbanization. It'd be tight for her, but she said she'd do it so I can keep Ladito. But not Joey. She won't have no Joey in her house."

Which could be for the best, I think.

"It would be too hard for you to live without Joey?"

"Sarah. . ." She pauses, turning to look out the open louvered windows in the direction of Estela's house. "He may not be that much, but he loves me. He don't hit me. He's good-looking, you can see that. And he's nice to Ladito. Ladito loves him, loves to have a man. The only thing is, Joey's a mama's boy, and he does drugs. My thinking is, if Estela is just across the street, like here, for example, it's not so far for him to run home when he has to see her, and I can get him back easy enough. As for drugs, we're working on that." She pauses again, her face losing it's bony contours. It's as though the flesh has suddenly slipped and bloated at the same moment. She looks at me. I see a depth in her dark eyes, in the silence she meets me with, a profundity I'd sensed, I suppose, but not completely believed before. "Life's hard, you know. We can't get everything we want. For me, Joey's pretty much of a prize. I'm no beauty contest winner, but I'm a good person, and Joey's a good enough person himself to see that. I'm willing to go a lot out for him, to try to give him what he needs to make a life for himself before it's too late. He's got a right to happiness, too, like everybody."

As we sit there I don't care whether she manipulated me by bringing Ladito here. I don't care if she's had her eyes on the house the whole time she's come to work. I trust this woman, trust that she wants the best for the little boy and for Joey. As I think about it, I begin to admire that she's been playing me so well, so professionally. It's a job to get what you want and need, especially if you don't have all that much to begin with.

"How would a year be, Lydia? A year in the house with you watching over things. I don't want to take my mother's stuff back with me, only the good dishes and a few other items, and I don't want to have to try to sell all her belongings now. It would be too painful."

Lydia sits forward, hope firming up her face again. "I know how to take care of Mommy's things. You see that. You see how nice I keep it here."

"I do. Why don't we say that you pay me $100 a month, which will cover the mortgage, you pay electricity and all that, and you keep the place nice. We'll do it for a year, and see how it goes."

"Oh, my God," she says. "Oh, my God, is this true?"

I nod. I think of Mrs. Davis and Sonya and Roberto and all the other people who've been good to me along the way. Lydia is all those people for Ladito. It's the least I can do for her and him.

"Oh, my God. I'm going to wait to tell Ladito in a couple of weeks. It'll be my birthday present for him. Oh, you'll see, I'll keep the house real, real nice."

A peace comes over me as we finish our coffee. Lydia goes on about how she's going to make a garden in the backyard if that's okay with me and how she'll fix this and that up. And I think how maybe this will work out fine. I won't have to do anything about the house right away. I won't have to bag all my mother's possessions the way she had me do my father's. The house can rest for a while, find its own serenity and maybe a little happiness. The money can wait. A little boy will have a backyard, if only for a year.

Day Fifteen

I SPEND MORE TIME in my mother's room, sitting, often in the dark, as my mother slumbers. I wait for her to wake and begin talking. She's started to talk a lot, telling long rambling stories of her life. These are not the set pieces that I know so well, those repeated vignettes that used to reveal her true meanings when she least intended. Like the one about the time she taught me to bake a pie when I was seven years old. "It was a lemon meringue, my best pie, but I concentrated so on helping you that your pie came out better than mine. It took me days to get over being angry at you." Or the blustery winter day when we had to cross Route 7 to catch the bus into Burlington. I must have been five. "I had you take my arm so you wouldn't fall on the ice and then *I* slipped and it was you who braced my fall and held me up instead." Or the Manzanar Camp tale. "The Issei woman who baby-sat for you while I taught at the school was so funny. When we were leaving camp for good, she told me she was afraid I wouldn't be able to care for you properly on my own." Or on the beach when I was six. "I sat on the shoreline with the other mothers. They were astounded that all I had to do was call your name in a certain tone of voice and you'd stop doing any mischief." Or the summer we'd lived in Chicago and my mother had gone to work in a welfare camp, bringing me along because my father was down in Arkansas. I would have been two and a half. "I had to leave you in the dormitory with the welfare mothers and their children at night because I was assigned to a teenage girls' cabin. You began to wake earlier every day, crying at the top of your lungs. The director of the camp was furious at me, ready to fire me. So I had to get up at four or five in the morning and take you out of there. I would put you in the bow of a rowboat and row you around the lake until you stopped screaming. So you see, I didn't have an easy time of it either."

But today's stories seem consciously meant to leave me with information she's never wanted to reveal before.

"You know your father wasn't the paragon of virtue you like to think he was," she begins late in the afternoon, just before darkness falls in its abrupt tropical manner. "I know you love him more than you do me."

"Mom, that's not true."

"Of course it is. I've always known that. But he wasn't perfect." She turns her head to look out the window at his tree. The light on it is ardently golden. She lies in silence for some time, long enough for the sun to dim and the backyard to go from dusk to sudden nighttime. I let her prolong the silence even though I want to ask, Whatever do you mean? This is the first time she's ever come close to directly criticizing my father. Except for her deprecating taunting of him or her irritation with the way he smacked his mouth while eating or her stony silences, she never criticized his very being or called into question his goodness. The few times I talked back to him in her presence, she turned on me, the way she had gotten him to attack me that one awful time, seething, "Don't you ever speak to your father in that manner, ever again. You are to respect your father, young lady."

She sighs. "I never told you this, but after you were born, Scott wouldn't sleep with me or rather, couldn't, for the longest time. Maybe it was my fault. I insisted that he come into the birthing room. He was horrified by it, all the blood and screaming, and he couldn't have intercourse after that."

The evening sounds have not yet picked up. I sit in the stillness, stunned by what I'm hearing. More than the subject of my father's impotence, I am upset by the inference that my birth was the death knell of their sexual intimacy.

"What I really hated," her disembodied voice begins again, "was the way he was dishonest about it. How he led me on. We'd be at parties and he would put his hand on my neck or around my waist, sliding it up close to my breast and I would think, Tonight it's finally going to happen, and I'd become all excited in anticipation. We'd go home, I'd get ready for bed. I would slip in beside him and nothing would happen. Nothing. He couldn't do it. He didn't really even attempt to. He'd tricked me, you see."

I want to defend my father, saying, Well, at the party he probably thought he could. I want to say with all the cruelty I can muster, Maybe he found you too unattractive. I remember, as I control that dreadful impulse to hurt her, how as a child I wished she smelled as good as other mothers and that she would fix herself up as other women did.

"I often wondered if he had extramarital affairs," she says. "But there was never any evidence of more than silly flirtations. I don't think he was man enough to go off on his own."

The coquís begin their song directly outside the window. The savory aroma of frying onion enters our room, wrapping us in another family's warmth.

"Mmm, that smells good," she says. "Inez is such a good cook."

"She is," I say, relieved to be on safe land again even though my blood pumps too rapidly through my veins.

"Sarah?"

"Yes, Mom."

"I forgive you for not loving me as much. Your father was a real charmer. And he thought the world of you. There was no defense against his charm."

February 1978

SARAH'S FATHER ARRIVED unannounced at her door one cold, slushy February day. Sarah had moved in with Roberto a few weeks earlier. She'd barely settled her belongings into his rent-controlled apartment on a side street off Central Park West. It was a beautiful place in a small five-story building with high ceilings and satiny wooden floors, backing onto a quiet yard filled with tall old trees and small snow-covered gardens.

At ten on that Saturday morning the intercom buzzer blared through the apartment, going on and on as though it had become stuck.

"What the hell is that?" Roberto came out of the bathroom holding a towel in front of his naked body.

Sarah couldn't answer the call until the buzzer quieted.

"What is it?" she said angrily into the receiver.

"It's your dad!" her father's voice yelled. "Let me in."

"What are you doing here?"

"Let me in. I can't make sense of what you're saying."

"God damn him. God damn him anyway," she shouted as she pushed the button to release the lock. She knew he'd been in Washington negotiating a funding package with OSHA, for the governor. He'd called during the week, but never made mention of plans to visit. "What is he doing coming here, not even asking if it would be convenient for us, poking his nose into my life?"

"That's exactly what he's doing," Roberto said, flicking the towel away to expose his genitals. "Snooping around his daughter's new bedroom."

Sarah had to laugh. Then she sobered. "And do you know what day this is?"

"I'm afraid to find out."

"It's February 11, my mother's birthday. New York City is not where he should be today."

He had done this all her life, shown up at her schools at times when parents weren't invited, or more recently at the freelance jobs that she took to supplement her writing, saying, "Just thought I'd drop in and see how you're doing," and he'd plop himself down in the chair beside her desk and begin talking about his own latest accomplishments. "Got the mayor to bend," he'd say, or "I just showed up at the Commissioner of HRA's office, my old friend from way back, and was he ever surprised. Ended up giving me everything I wanted." She'd sit there cringing with embarrassment as people whom she barely knew in the new office walked by, checking him out, and also from imagining what the commissioner must have thought of him just showing up.

The doorbell rang, as insistently as the intercom had. She opened it to find him in a light blue summer blazer and darker blue slacks, with no overcoat.

"Daddy, where's your coat?"

"Forgot it," he said, smiling his old standby sheepish grin. "Got on the damn plane in San Juan in the blazing heat and would you believe it, I didn't notice I'd left the coat at home until I got into D.C. It was nippy in Washington this week, but nothing like up here. Didn't remember what real winter can be. Honey, aren't you going to let me in?"

No, she thought. I'm going to block your damn way and watch you steamroll over me.

"Why didn't you at least let us know you were coming?" she said, reluctantly standing aside so he could enter.

"What's the matter, you got something to hide? Did I catch you by surprise?" He chuckled suggestively, as he walked by her and went through the foyer directly into the living room, where he set down his black plastic briefcase and brown suitcase next to the couch.

"Is this guy Roberto here?" he yelled into the air and then turned to Sarah who stood in the archway of the living room.

"Yes, Daddy. Roberto is here," she said, trying to keep her voice calm. "You caught him in the shower. He'll be out in a minute."

"This morning I decided on the spur of the moment to come up and see you two as long as I was on the mainland, and maybe spend the night." He went over to the window and looked out. His jacket was wrinkled and pulled tight across his backside. His shoes were badly run down at the heels.

He can't even care for himself properly, she thought. Still, it didn't excuse this behavior.

"But it's Mommy's birthday. You shouldn't be here, you should be down there with her, taking her out to dinner."

"Honey, you know birthdays don't mean that much in our family. Especially not to your mother. I've been away on plenty of birthdays. She doesn't care." He turned to Sarah. "Really, honey, don't you go worrying about that."

"Well, you could have called."

"You said that already," he said sharply, as the lids of his eyes drooped and his mouth went pouty. He nervously brushed his right hand over the top of his sparse hair. "I'll go in a few minutes if that's what you want. I don't want to impose myself on your life."

"Oh, Daddy," she said. She went to him and put her arm around his middle, feeling dense rolls of fat under the two layers of fabric. "Of course you can stay, but maybe next time you could give us some notice."

As she brewed coffee for her father and he buried himself in her copy of the *New York Times*, her anger returned. She remembered the story her mother told repeatedly, almost obsessively, of a birthday in New Philadelphia, Ohio. They'd recently moved down there from Chicago, she and her mother.

Her father was in Washington, finishing up business for the War Relocation Authority. "Your father was away," her mother always started the story, and then proceeded to tell it in exactly the same words each time. "I didn't know a soul in that godforsaken town. It was my birthday and I was feeling desperately sorry for myself. I needed someone to acknowledge the day, so I taught you to wish me happy birthday. You were barely four at the time. You were such a dear. All through the day you took special delight in my pleasure—You'd run into whatever room I was in and fling your arms around my legs and shout, 'Happy Birthday, Mommy.' And I'd kneel down laughing and half crying and hug you and say, 'Thank you, darling, thank you, my best little companion.'" Here in the recounting Sarah's mother would begin to laugh. "I woke up the morning after my birthday to your bounding into my bed, screeching, 'Happy Birthday, Mommy' with pure delight across your sweet little face. It took the better part of the day to get you to understand that birthdays lasted only one day, and that was what made them so special. How disappointed you were, but finally you stopped."

Roberto came into the kitchen as they were drinking coffee, dressed in his herringbone coat and red scarf. He looked handsome and vigorous to Sarah. She longed to put her arms around his neck and give him a passionate kiss.

Her father rose from his chair. "There's Roberto," he yelled. "Thought you were hiding from me."

Roberto embraced him. "Never, my dear friend. But I have bad news. I must be out all day. I hope you'll be here when I get back."

Her father gave Sarah an inquiring look.

"Daddy's spending the night," Sarah said.

"*Maravilloso*. We can have dinner together. Sorry I can't stay even for coffee but in half an hour I'm on a panel dealing with the latest controversy between the object relations people who believe the genesis of our psyches lies with the mother

and the Freudians who swear by the Oedipal complex."
Roberto's eyes twinkled mischievously.

"Roberto," Sarah warned, suppressing her laughter. "As
you said, you're going to be late."

When they heard the front door close behind Roberto,
her father said, "I'm sorry, sweetheart, but I don't understand
a word he says. He's got a pretty thick accent there."

She could hear Roberto saying, "What your father doesn't
understand is how there can be another man in your life. He's
adamantly deaf to that possibility."

Sarah took her father to buy a winter coat even though he
resisted, saying he could borrow one of Roberto's for the
weekend. "No, you can't," she'd said. "They're too big for
you and anyway you need something to get you to the airport."
She wasn't about to let him get away with wearing Roberto's
clothes for any longer than the taxi ride to Macy's.

He looked shrunken in the mirrors as he tried on the coats.
His face, tanned a dark brown, was narrower than it had ever
been, and there seemed to be no flesh covering his cheekbones. His dark hair had gone completely white around the
temples. He looked elderly to her for the first time, not vital
and not well. Familiar guilt began to creep in. It said to her
that she shouldn't have been so hard on him. She warned
herself to not let him wheedle his way into her heart.

"Should I do this?" her father fussed, looking at the price
tag attached to the sleeve. "Spend money on something I
hardly have an opportunity to wear? You know how your
mother is. She doesn't like to spend money unnecessarily."

"Daddy, it's on sale. Rock bottom. It's only thirty-five
dollars. It won't break the bank."

"Oh, boy. You know I don't like to spend money on
myself. Even more than your mother. It's the old Depression
mentality. After fifty-odd years, I still can't shake it."

"Daddy, buy it. Just take the leap and buy it. I don't want

you shivering through the streets and you can't take Roberto's coat with you."

"Okay, okay. But you don't have to get so huffy about it." He looked at himself again in the mirror. His shoulders sagged. He sighed. "Sometimes I hate it that I look like such hell."

Back at the apartment, Sarah insisted that he had to call Puerto Rico.

"Honestly, sweetheart, it's not a problem. Your mother isn't expecting a call. I remember once when your mother had to be up in Albany to meet Board of Education officials about Regents' exams on her birthday. I called her to wish her happy birthday. I was feeling pretty much like a sad sack with her gone, and all she had to say was, 'That's not necessary, Scott. I know you love me.' Your mother's a very loving person, you know."

"I'm sure she is," Sarah said. "All the more reason that she needs a call from you."

He flopped down on the couch instead of going to the phone.

"I know you and your mother have had some trouble over the years," he said, his face set in his most earnest expression. It was the face that appeared when he ran a meeting of farmers, or organized people into a cooperative. It was an open face, square-jawed, serious, with a high, smooth forehead. This was her father at his handsomest. He was momentarily the young father she had adored. "Especially when you were a teenager. I know Reba and you had real friction then."

"A little bit," Sarah said, feeling wary. They'd never come near this subject before.

"It was some kind of misunderstanding, I suppose," he said. He was watching her carefully, probably gauging how far he could go.

She looked at her hands, thinking, This is how he works the people at those meetings.

"Maybe I should have been around a little more," he said softly. "Maybe I could have done a little arbitration."

"Maybe so," Sarah said. There was a time when she had longed for this, but now all she wanted was for him to get out of that private place in her, to stop prodding, to stop trying to enter her thoughts and feelings as though he were pushing past the barrier of her flesh.

"One thing I used to wonder about," he continued. "I often thought that in some of those pretty anti-Semitic places we lived, the business of us not having a stated religion and your being half Jewish might have been a burden on you. I know it was for your mother."

His words came as a shock to her system, tilting her world on its axis.

"It was a little difficult at times," she said cautiously, while trying to get her emotions to settle down. "But not all that bad." Don't give in to his charming ways, she kept saying silently. Don't tell him anything you don't want him to know.

She looked up and met his dark brown soulful stare.

"Maybe Roberto heals that part of you, chicken. Maybe it's good that he's Jewish."

"Even if you can't understand a word he says?" she chided.

Her father threw his head back and laughed full out in his old infectious way.

"Got you, Daddy," she said.

"Guess you did, sweetheart." His laughter simmered down. "But no matter what, no matter how idiotic I may act at times, just know I want whatever brings you happiness and peace of mind."

He went to take a shower to get cleaned up before Roberto got back and before he called Reba. Sarah washed the dishes they'd left. He'd won her over in the end but she didn't care.

For all her father's enraging qualities she still loved him, adored him really, and on occasion he had earned that adoration. He'd told her before he'd gone to shower that he recently remembered how worried he'd been about her when her friend Lucy had died. "You were so depressed, I was frightened for you. You locked yourself in your apartment for over a week. It was a bad time for you."

Back in the living room, hearing the rushing water of his shower, she recalled how he'd come to her Lower East Side apartment. He'd sat for hours in comforting silence on the big green easy chair with the nubby upholstery. It was the chair they'd carted from place to place throughout her childhood. Mute with sorrow, Sarah had occupied herself imagining him sitting in that chair in each of the apartments they had rented, in Ohio, in Burlington, on Long Island. The arms still held his odor and the stains of his sweat. Then she'd seen Lucy curled up, the way Lucy used to do, in its deep pocket of a seat, with her skinny legs tucked under her, and Sarah had started to cry for the first time since finding her best friend overdosed and rotting at the kitchen table.

"That's good. It's good to cry," he'd murmured. "You don't have to talk. But allow me to say a few things. If I've learned one thing in my long years of working with people, it's that there's only so much you can do for another human being. You can listen to them. You can try to help them find the way, but some people are too fragile for this world. Often it's the fragile ones you attach to the most. The curious thing is that often those who seem the strongest on the outside, who take the most chances in life, are the people who constantly battle their own insecurities, fighting demons you had no idea existed for them. Your friend Lucy struck me as a very adventurous girl. But she had a troubling fragility, and a deep cynicism that comes from dashed hopes. I don't think your friendship, strong and loyal as it was, could repair the kind of psychological damage that she seemed to carry."

"I'm out of the shower," her father's voice called, "but where the hell are the towels?"

She brought a towel from the linen closet and put it into his hand which he reached out from behind the door. He's minding his manners, she thought, not overstepping the boundaries for once.

She had been comforted by his words that night and by his mere presence, but memories of Lucy's death still plagued her, still woke her in the middle of the night. Even *he* couldn't erase that.

Washed, groomed and smelling of Roberto's aftershave lotion, her father placed the phone call to Levittown Lakes.

"Hi there, honey," he shouted into the hall phone, his rounded back to Sarah, who listened from the living room. "I just called to wish you a happy birthday. I'll be home tomorrow afternoon. I'm with Sarah in her new apartment."

He was silent and then he laughed. "I told Sarah birthdays didn't matter to you, but she was adamant. She bawled me out and said I shouldn't let you down."

He listened. "I miss you too, honey," he said. "Okay, I'll get her, honey," and he beckoned to Sarah.

Sarah went over to him and put her hand on his back, which drew a broad, winning smile from him.

"Here she is!" he announced as though he were the emcee on a late night television show.

"Hello, dear," her mother said, the waves on the cable line distorting the timbre of her voice.

"Hi, Mom, Happy Birthday." Sarah's words echoed back to her, sounding forced and phony.

"That was so sweet of you to send such an extravagant gift. It really wasn't necessary and your father also said you were worried that I'd feel lonely by myself on my birthday. You know birthdays aren't that important to me," she said. "But I don't know if you remember the time we were in New Philadelphia, Ohio. We'd just moved there and I didn't know a soul in that godforsaken town. Your father was away in Washington, D.C. finishing up some work for the WRA and you were. . ."

Sarah didn't interrupt. She just listened all the way through to the bittersweet end of the story.

Day Sixteen

TODAY IS HOTTER and more humid. When you live in the tropics for any time you can feel the minutest of climate shifts from day to day and season to season. Differences that would go unnoticed by visitors and tourists are dramatic to people who live here. Just as September heat can kill with its intensity, slamming you against the pavement every time you go out, November can feel like springtime with its lighter humidity and daytime breezes. But today could be September. There's no way I can take my morning jog. I wear my bikini around the house. It's too hot to put anything more on. At ten a.m. we decide to turn the air conditioning on in my mother's room.

"It's ungodly hot," my mother says, mopping her face with a washcloth I keep refreshing.

She has forgone breakfast today. "Too hot to eat," she said when I brought in dry toast and coffee. "I'll wait until lunch."

I give her her shot, and then Lydia and I change her bed at eleven and give her a sponge bath as she sits in the chair. "I don't feel up to going to the bathroom," she says.

This is the first time she's not made the ten steps to the bathroom. She's always insisted on going back and forth to the toilet and the shower as if not making the effort would be giving in to death. As I wash her, lifting her arms, swabbing down her thighs, and over and under her distended belly, I wonder what goes through her mind. Does she feel she's giving up? Or is this a brief hiatus, a time to husband her strength for the next battle tomorrow when it's cooler?

I help her back into bed, cover her fresh body—dressed in a newly laundered yellow nightie—with a threadbare sheet. We change and wash one of her three sets of sheets every day. They're wearing out. Yesterday my mother and I went through a Company Store catalogue. "I want to buy you something for being so nice to me," she said. I replied that I was being nice because I loved her, that I didn't need to be paid back for my services. "No, no," she said. "You misunderstand. This is for me. I want to do it." We picked out a set of pale blue-and-white-striped French cotton sheets, with duvet cover and pillow shams. After I'd finished calling in the order, I told her how beautiful I found them. "More lovely," I said, "than anything I'd ever buy for myself." "That pleases me," she said, her eyes closing. She immediately dropped off to sleep. As I watched her rest I thought, She never contemplated buying new sheets for herself, even though it was her earlier comment about how worn her own sheets were that had triggered her decision to order these for me. She knows she's dying. She tells me that she knows by these coded acts of generosity and by offering me never-before-told stories; I must remain alert to them. How much easier these messages are than the twisted ones I worked to decipher my whole life.

After lunch I untie the roses from where they still hang over the kitchen sink. I hold them upright and see that the heads don't topple or sag. The drying has been a success. They have become deeper in color, now ocher and a dusty pink. Their petals are smaller and more closely clasped. They are rather pretty, I think, proud of my effort. I decide to put them in the tall, narrow, cobalt blue depression glass vase. Clipping off two inches of stem, I release them from the string and arrange them in the vase. I'm about to run water in when I remember there's no need. They're already dead.

Vase in hand, I open my mother's door quietly. She's awake.

"What is that?" she demands.

"I've dried the roses. Aren't they pretty?"

"No. They're desiccated and ugly. Don't bring them in here. I don't want to look at dead roses. You can have them in your room if you like, but get them out of here. They're horrid. Take them out!" She shouts. Her hand is trembling as she points to the door.

I step back, quickly shut the door, and stand in the hallway as the heat of the day closes down around my bare, exposed skin. I meant no harm, I say to myself. Honestly, Mommy, I didn't mean to hurt you.

I dump the roses into the garbage can by the outside door in the kitchen and let the lid down with a metallic thud. Sinking to my haunches, I put my forearms on the top of the can, lay my head down, smell the garbage odors, and think of Roberto and how much I wish he were here. He would make a joke of this. He would laugh at me, voluptuous in my bikini, bringing dead flowers into the room of a dying woman. He would transform it into a gentle mistake filled with unconscious stupidity and good intentions, not one that revealed my old anger at her, my competitiveness, my hatred.

How many times in my life have I been intentionally cruel to her, I wonder? How many times did she feel the stab as I went blithely on, turning the knife? I'm her daughter. Why did I think I could escape the family heritage, believe myself to be without cruel impulses?

When I return to her room she is leafing through her checkbook.

"Hello, dear," she says, glancing up as though nothing has happened. She looks energized and cheerful, more vital than she has in days. "Why don't you sit down and make yourself comfortable. I'd like to go over some bills that need to be paid."

There is no hint of anger, no reference to what has just transpired. I tell myself not to dwell on anything.

I notice how bony her chest is above the scoop neck of

her nightie and feel a twinge of pity. The flesh hangs loosely on her upper arms, while the nubs of her collarbone jut out under skin that is almost transparent, it is so thin.

She finishes writing a check for the phone bill and puts down her pen.

"Oh, my," she says breathlessly. "Look at this check."

I take it from her.

"Look at the signature. It's not mine anymore."

She's right. I would never have recognized this shaky, cramped script as hers. Only the R of Rebekah resembles what I know. After that it falls away into indecipherable scratches.

"In Scott's last months his signature became feeble. I only registered the fact after he died. I didn't want to see the inevitable, I suppose." She places the flat of her palm to her bony chest. "We had such a long life together. We were ripped apart when he died, like Siamese twins when they try to separate them." She laughs. "What a grotesque image. But we had become so close down here in Puerto Rico, closer than we ever were."

I am amazed to hear her say this because what I remember was a silent house, with the windows shuttered against the light, when they were here together. Outside the confines of their house it was better, in the cabañas at Boquerón, sitting on the beach with the other expatriate couples, but even there it was only marginally more upbeat. After a day or two my mother would grow resentful of my father's popularity, turning sour and insulting at dinner parties.

But maybe I can never know what went on inside their marriage. Marital closeness can be based on incalculable elements—silence for instance. What I love most about Roberto is that I can be silent with him. I don't have to perform. We can be in a car for hours, driving somewhere, never speaking, and by the end of the trip I am filled with an overwhelming sense of closeness to him. It is a strange place, marriage. I'm sitting ruminating when I realize my mother has turned out the lights and is talking through the darkness. Only a sliver of brightness enters through the slit where I haven't closed the door properly.

"We had a very long marriage, but it wasn't my first."

"Yes," I laugh. "You had three before."

"No, only one before."

"Mom, c'mon. Who was he, this lucky guy?" How odd. This is not the sort of joke she's ever made. But I'm enjoying it.

"His name was Bill Anderson. He was a senior at the University of Washington when I was a freshman. He was a drummer in a jazz band. I was very infatuated with him and when he was graduating he asked me to run off and marry him. And I did."

I can't speak. This is too much concrete detail, told in too matter-of-fact a voice to be anything but the truth.

"My professors and the dean of women got wind of it somehow and tried to dissuade me. I told them no one had ever loved me before. Not my mother or my father, not my sister, and certainly no boy or man. I didn't think very highly of myself, you see, didn't think I was pretty. This man adored me. He made me feel capable of being loved."

She pauses. I sense from the thick aura of emotion permeating the room and the expression on her face, which I can now make out in the darkness, that she is very far away, back there in the 1930's. I wait for her to speak. As unsettling and strange as this revelation is, I want her to go on. I wonder if those fugue states she fell into all my life were when she recaptured this Bill Anderson and his love for her.

"I went away with him one weekend toward the end of the semester, up to his family's farm outside of Bellingham. His father was a minister, and he married us."

"What?" I can keep silent no longer. "A minister can perform a marriage for his own son?"

"Well, he did and it was legal, so legal that when Mother

tried to force an annulment, she had difficulty. Mother did not like Bill, but she never dreamed I would marry him." My mother smiles. "Poor Mother, for all her control, she couldn't stop me." Her voice is wistful and triumphant. Then she sucks in her lips and a tiny cry escapes.

"What happened to the marriage, Mom? Did you go live with him?"

"No," she whispers.

I'm bursting to know more, but don't want to push her. I can see she is in pain.

"No, Mother forbade me to see him once I came home. She told me she had gotten an annulment, but she was lying. Apparently she forced Bill to move away. He was going to be leaving after graduation anyway. I never heard where he went."

"You never heard? That's impossible."

"No, back then it wasn't impossible. We didn't have such easy methods of communication. And I came to my senses, you might say, and settled down to school. I excelled, and then I met Scott, and we fell in love, and he broke through the glass wall I'd built around myself."

"Did Daddy know?"

"What?" Her voice comes from far away.

"Did Daddy know about this Bill Anderson?"

"Oh. . ." She fades off.

I wait.

"Oh, I suppose he did."

She supposes he did? I am incredulous. My father must either have known or it was kept a secret from him.

"Yes," she says, returning to the present. "Yes, Scott knew. Anyway, he had to know because when we went to get the marriage license there was a little problem. It seems the annulment didn't go through in Washington State. We had to postpone the wedding in Seattle."

But my parents didn't marry in Seattle, they married in Palo Alto because my father was at Stanford.

"So you see, your father did know and he was very understanding. Your father was always understanding of complications."

An impulse to laugh rises from my belly to my chest. My mother is a bigamist. My mother, who was so upset with me for dating the wrong boys in high school, who wouldn't let me out of the house with some of them, who denigrated my choices by bringing home the school records of the ones she considered the worst, who warned me what could happen if I ended up with them. It was she who called me a tramp and slapped me silly when she caught me smoking cigarettes even though she smoked two packs a day. My mother who bought me a sexy red dress I didn't want, for a date with Billy Kingsley. Finally, her vehemence about my behavior makes sense. Billy Kingsley. Bill Anderson. Both drummers. She confused my life with her secret desire, with her conflicting shame. She pushed me to buy that inappropriate red dress because she, my complex, contradictory mother, wanted to wear it herself.

"I'm exhausted," she says. "I have to rest." She slips down lower in the bed and pulls the sheet up under her chin. I have completely adjusted to the lack of light and I can see she is at peace with herself. Her face is radiant, her eyes are dark and glistening. She looks like a pretty young woman who has fallen in love.

"I am so relieved. I've never told anyone about it for over fifty years. It's like a heavy weight has been lifted from my conscience."

"I can imagine," I say softly.

"You can? You don't hold it against me?" she asks plaintively.

"Mom, of course not. I wish you'd told me earlier."

She nods. "But I don't think that would have been possible, do you?" Her hand grabs air, reaching for mine.

I sit forward. Her hand is cold and wiry, all bones and tendons, no protection any more. She grips me tightly.

"I don't suppose so." I caress her thin skin that is as soft as talcum powder. "We only tell these stories when we're able."

"How wise. What a wise child I have."

She drifts off to sleep. Her hand gradually relaxes, but I keep holding on.

WHEN I REACH Roberto on the phone, the first thing I say is, "My mother is a bigamist."

"What are you talking about?"

"Just what I said. She was married to another man before my father and I don't think she got a proper divorce."

"This is astounding. It never occurred to me that she carried such a burdensome secret. Poor dear woman."

"It feels weird. It's like a shift of the continental plates. My father wasn't her first husband and he may not have known about it."

"Scott didn't know? Did she lie to him or was it a sin of omission?"

"I'm not sure. With her you can never tell." I think of the way she spoke with Hannah, never letting on that she was terminally ill. And how she twisted matters in buying me the red dress. "Maybe by now she doesn't know herself whether or not she told him."

"That's possible. Your mother has great powers of denial."

I laugh. "You don't have to tell me that."

"Was she relieved after she told you?"

"Very. She seemed cleansed in body and soul and as if she could breathe again."

"She probably never told him."

"She did say that she'd never told anyone for fifty years."

"Then I'm positive she never told your father, Sarah. I think she kept this dark secret all to herself."

"That's so sad."

"I agree. It accounts somewhat for the narrow band of her emotion."

"What do you mean?"

"That she expresses her emotions within a very limited range."

"Do you think so?"

"Sarah, are you kidding me? Your mother has the emotional range of a muskrat."

"This keeps making me sadder."

"Then be sad for a while. It's better than being angry at her all the time. For once, don't let your anger get in the way of your sadness. Let it just happen. Try it out to see how it feels. She has earned a lot of sympathy with this confession. That's what I think anyway. She doesn't want to carry this to her grave, but it couldn't have been easy to tell you."

I sigh deeply and then sit in silence, listening to the coquís right outside the window. I wonder if my mother used to daydream about this Bill Anderson. Did she recall him playing drums? Did they go to little jazz hangout places where the air was thick with smoke and the rhythms of the music? I imagine her in a sophisticated, clinging, red rayon dress, sitting at a table close to the dance floor, sipping a whiskey and smoking a cigarette, her head thrown back as she lets out a long stream of smoke. It is his solo. His eyes meet hers as he begins to build the riff, driving the intensity. She feels the drums through her entire body, pulsing, beating like blood through her genitals.

Roberto's voice startles me through the receiver. "The negotiators are making headway in the talks, so I may get down there in time."

I pull myself out of the dream, remembering the business at hand. "Please let that be true. Estela says my mother's waiting to die until you come. Estela says that the whole neighborhood knows she's waiting for her son-in-law."

"If they only knew."

"Maybe they're right. Maybe her love for you is another mystery to be uncovered."

"If that's true, my lovely, I think I should start hiking to Puerto Rico. I have a very good chance of walking on water."

When I hang up the phone, my mother, young and beautiful, is weeping inconsolably on her bed in her parents' apartment. Her mother has told her that the mess with Bill Anderson has been taken care of, that she is free to go on with her life. Her mother has said to her that she will get over this foolishness in a few weeks and in the future will thank her for intervening. My mother is prostrate with grief on her bed, with her arms spread wide, her hands gripping the bed posts. Her pillow is soaked with tears. She wants to suffocate on her own tears. How can she live if she can never again lie down with him in a grassy meadow, as they had at his father's farm, hidden from view behind a stand of trees? How can it be that he will never caress her breasts as he did? She wants him to enter her again, looking down at her as he moves enticingly, making her plead that it last forever. But there will be no forever. She cries out. How can she live without him? He made her feel human and loved. He made her anger go away, untied her knots of rage. Mother, she weeps, your daughter is sad, desperately sad. You have abandoned her to her sadness.

Day Seventeen

"SARAH, I WANT YOU to go to the linen closet and get the metal box from behind the towels and bring it to me."

My mother cannot sit up today. It is morning, when she usually has more energy but today she has asked again that the air conditioner be left on and that I bathe her in bed and bring the potty to her and give her her shot. Lydia and I changed the sheets with my mother in bed, rolling her carefully to one side and the other while either Lydia or I held her emaciated body so she wouldn't fall. The linens, when I crumpled them, were stained yellow with sweat and held the smell of sweet rotting matter.

I come into the kitchen and rest against the refrigerator.

Lydia is washing up, though there are almost no dishes. My mother ate nothing for breakfast. "I can't," she said, when I asked for her order. "Maybe I'll eat lunch."

"*Mami's* not so good today," Lydia says.

The water rushes into the sink as she finishes swabbing down the stainless steel sides.

"No, she's not."

"It looks close to the end. I can tell. I've done this enough."

"How close?" I can barely stand; I feel faint and breathless.

"Three or four days."

I calculate and realize it could happen on Thanksgiving.

"What if it happens on Thanksgiving?"

"What do you mean?" She has turned off the water and is drying her hands on a cloth towel, standing with one leg lifted, her bare foot resting on her knee.

"Will the funeral home take her on Thanksgiving?"

"Of course, they have to."

"Lydia, I don't know a funeral home. What should I do? Does Estela know a funeral home I can use?"

"I'm sure Estela knows a funeral home."

"Sarah, where are you?" my mother cries weakly from the bedroom.

"Oh, no, what's happening now?"

I run in. My mother is lying where I left her. She hasn't vomited.

"Where did you go? I thought you were getting the strong box." She struggles to breathe.

"I was talking a moment with Lydia about something, Mommy. I'll be right back."

Lydia is waiting in the hall.

"I'll ask Estela about the funeral home," she says. Her brow is furrowed. "You have to rest, baby. You can't do this all yourself. You've got to sleep, too. I think it's time to hire the nurse again. She can come at night." She puts her arms around me, and I give in to her ministrations, let her pat my back, allow my head to fall to her shoulder. I know she's right. I've been sitting up with my mother until one or two o'clock, afraid to leave her alone. Even when I go to my own room, I wake every hour to listen, and often I rise and look in on her. I'm terrified she'll die and I won't know it, and then I'll go in and find her dead. I remember Phyllis warning me not to be alone when death arrives.

"Can't you come nights?" I ask Lydia.

"No, baby. I have to take care of Ladito. But I'll be here every day and you don't have to pay me extra. I'll help you through this."

"I'll pay you."

"No, no. You're already giving me enough."

I find the rusted green box behind the stack of mismatched, frayed bath towels. I get it out and close the louvered metal doors to the closet, noticing that the rust is working its way through the white paint job. Our world here feels shabby and poor.

I pull the chair to the bed, placing the strongbox beside my mother. I help her to sit up higher and at a comfortable angle. Her hands are trembling so much it takes numerous attempts for her to open the box. Sensing that she doesn't want me to intervene, I control my intense desire to reach over and unlatch the lock. When it's open she slowly lifts out two sets of folded papers that quiver with a life of their own in her hands.

"These are the wills, dear. Everything is left to you."

"Mom, I know that, you don't have to. . ."

"Be quiet. I want to go over this once and for all. These are the wills. The financial papers are in the top right-hand drawer of the cabinet in the dining room. You'll find all the stock certificates and the name and phone number of the broker on the top of the stack. The car is yours, and the house, of course. Today you must go to the bank and get the signature papers so you can sign the checks. There's also a savings account of some thousands of dollars. As soon after I die as possible, go directly to the bank and take out all the money, preferably the same day."

"Mom, must we do this?"

"Yes. I'm exhausted, but we must get this taken care of. Now, please, take the box so I can lie back."

I hold the box dutifully on my lap. How can she be doing this? I could never be so resolute and strong.

She lies there breathing with effort.

"This is tiring you out. We can do it later."

"No. I want to do it now. Give me a moment."

The room is silent but for the whir and rattle of the air conditioner and her labored breathing. I browse the wills written nineteen years earlier when they first moved down to Puerto Rico. The paper is yellowed newsprint with an outer wrapping of faded purple construction paper, the cheapest quality. They are written in Spanish and English. In my mother's case only her family names appear, holding to the Spanish tradition. As far as these records show, she never married my father after all. Rebekah Kahn Goldberg. Goldberg being my grandmother's name and Kahn my great-grandmother's. It took moving down here to officially document that past. A Jewish matriarchy. How accurate. My mother handled all the money in our family, earned more than my father, kept the house, was solely responsible for me, and moved our household from place to place. Her mother was the same and her mother before her. I'm suddenly filled with remorse at how hard I've been on her. Where did my hatred come from? Why couldn't I have been more compassionate? Why couldn't I honor her accomplishments?

"You'll find about four hundred thousand dollars in one of the brokerage accounts and one hundred thousand in the other."

"That's half a million dollars. How is that possible?" I start to laugh. "You mean you accrued half a million dollars?"

"Yes, I have. I don't think it's particularly funny."

"I'm amazed. You're stunning me. How did you do it?"

"I saved and I invested well, no thanks to your father. He would have given it all away." She stares straight ahead, her eyelids blinking. "Now it's yours."

"I can't take all that money."

"Then give it away as your father would have. Do whatever you want with it. I saved it for myself so I wouldn't be a burden on anyone. So your father and I could take care of ourselves. But we won't be needing it."

Her chest rises and falls like a heaving sea as though speaking is too much for her. Her eyes close.

I know what she has just said is true. Much as I'd like to think she saved it to leave it to me, I know differently. This mother of mine did not want to be dependent on anyone and she expected the same of me. How many times had she said to me, "I want a daughter who is independent, who can take care of herself." All those years of stretching the food, making my dresses, upholstering, turning my father's frayed collars, and rarely indulging what she considered my frivolous desires. I remember another story she loved to tell. "When you were four and we were living in Shelburne, we went into Abernathy's in Burlington. You spotted a stuffed animal in the toy department. It was a little lamb, made of actual lamb's wool. You clutched it and held it to your cheek. I told you that we couldn't afford toys. I could see you loved that lamb and wanted it so. You put it down on the counter, minding what I said, being such a brave, grown-up girl, but you couldn't control your feelings and the next I looked, tears were streaming down your face."

I can't help wondering if she chose the savings account over the stuffed toy. The teddy bear lies in its usual place beside her on the bed. How perfect that I picked a child's stuffed animal to give her comfort in my absence.

"Maybe you'd like to give money to Israel, Mommy. Plant some trees."

"It doesn't interest me, Sarah. If you wish to, do it." She has retreated into her cold dismissive voice.

"Can we leave some of the money to neighbors and to some of your friends in the bridge club?" I ask this, thinking with pleasure that if the amount of money is as big as my mother says it is, I can easily rent the house to Lydia.

"I'm not interested in writing a codicil. If you want to, you do it after I'm gone." She turns away from me to lie on her side. "Now I would like to rest."

Even as she is dying she can summon up coldness. It must take enormous energy to maintain this defense against, at the very least, sadness and fear of dying. But maybe she is indeed through with life. Her practicality, her no-nonsense approach is coming to her aid when she needs it most. She would often say to me, "Why do you have to get so hysterical, Sarah?" or; "Why don't you have more confidence in yourself?" or; "Don't be so afraid of every turn in the road." She would tell me that her mother was a fretter. "Mother worried over every little move she made. She was a tyrant as a physics teacher and later as dean of girls at the high school, but she fretted endlessly over how much meat to buy at the market, or if she had spoken rudely to a neighbor, which of course she always had. She invariably insulted people with her arrogance. I never understood how she could be both people, totally haughty and completely fearful. You must have inherited her fearful side, dear."

I'm still sitting in the dark beside my mother's bed when she wakes. It's after seven. She has slept all day. She has eaten nothing.

"Sarah, are you here?" she says groggily.

"Yes, Mom, I am." I cover the bed table lamp with a bandanna and turn it on.

"Have I been asleep for long?" She squints against the light.

"Quite a while."

"Did I miss my shot?"

"We can do it now."

"If you would, dearest. That would be nice of you."

I get the bag of paraphernalia from the kitchen. My eyes are smarting from tears that don't fall. My throat is tight. It is easy to fill a fresh syringe and smack up the air bubble. I've become expert in the procedure. If only I weren't deceiving her.

I insert the needle into her frail arm. The skin slips against fragile bone; there is barely any flesh beneath this skin.

"How good you're getting at that," she says. "I'm proud of you."

Wiping the puncture wound with alcohol, I say, "I need

to get some help for the nights. I need to call Ana Llosa to come back."

"Why, Sarah?"

"I'm getting exhausted, Mom. I need to sleep through the night." Remorse overtakes me, threatening to close me down. "I really need the help."

She takes my hand. "I'm sorry to be doing this to you."

"It's nothing, Mom. I'm just getting tired."

"Of course, but couldn't we ask Lydia? I like Lydia so much more. I feel comfortable with her."

"I asked Lydia. She has Ladito to take care of. She can't be here all night."

She sighs as she rhythmically pats my hand. "Then call Ana. She's so stern is all."

Day Nineteen

ANA LLOSA IS COMING tonight and it's none too soon. I was up almost the entire night. My mother slept intermittently, waking and wanting to talk or to be sponged down because she was feeling feverish. At two in the morning I gave up trying to sleep and remained in her room, sitting in the chair wrapped in my quilt, dozing as best I could.

I'm still here. It is just past dawn, but the sky is gray. The air conditioning is on and the room is frigid. My mother wants it that way. My legs are curled under the blanket; only my head is uncovered. My mother sleeps peacefully with a mere sheet over her. Her bony arms lie on top of the blue fabric, bracketing her slip of a body.

I sit here thinking of nothing much. I am too bored to think. Waiting for someone to die can become tedious. Or is it my tamped-down terror that causes the boredom? What will I do if she dies now while I'm alone in the house? What will I do with her body? I haven't yet summoned the courage to call the funeral homes. Estela said she had no funeral parlor in particular to recommend, but she helped me mark the Yellow Pages, pointing out the establishments she knew to be reputable and not expensive.

"This is where people from here go," she said. "Stay in Levittown or Cataño. The places in San Juan or Río Piedras will rob you." She fanned her hand to indicate robbers.

As I listened, I thought, We don't have to go with someplace inexpensive, we are rich as we've never been before. But it's too strange a concept, too new, to change our way of doing things.

I decide to begin calling after breakfast. I still fear my mother will die on Thanksgiving, two days away.

The phone rings. I go quickly into the living room.

"*Sí*," I answer.

"It's me, love. The strike is over. Clinton got them to agree."

"So you're coming?"

"I'm going to try."

"Do anything to get a ticket, Roberto. Pay three thousand dollars. We can afford any amount now." I've already told him about my mother's money. "But please, get down here. I think she's going to die very soon." I'm whispering so she won't hear me, half choking, my throat is clogged with phlegm. "Can you come today?"

"No, they just settled and they won't be flying until tomorrow and I have to notify my patients. But tomorrow first thing, if I can get a ticket. I'll start calling right now. I'll try for the earliest flight."

"Please do everything. You've got to make it."

Half an hour later, Roberto calls back.

"I got a first class ticket on the earliest flight out of Newark tomorrow. I'll arrive at eleven a.m. in San Juan."

"I'll ask Joey to pick you up."

All the time we talk, an interior litany is playing; She's going to die tomorrow. After she sees Roberto, she's going to die.

I go back to my mother. I sit for hours as she sleeps. She doesn't wake at all for breakfast, nor when Pearl calls to see how she's doing, nor when Lydia comes to help change the bed and do the dishes.

"She's sleeping," I say out in the kitchen.

"She didn't wake up?"

"Not since three or four in the morning."

"This is the end, *niña*. She's just going to keep sleeping."

"Roberto's coming."

"Sweetheart, how good. Then she can die in peace. Does she know it yet?"

"No, he only called a few hours ago."

"Tell her first thing she wakes up. Let her get prepared."

"He doesn't come until tomorrow."

"Mommy can last that long if she knows."

I tell Lydia that Ana Llosa is coming for tonight and what my mother said about wishing it could be Lydia because she feels more comfortable.

"Did she say that?" Lydia smiles. Her stitched-together lip rises high over her false teeth. "*Mami* said that about me? I told you, old people like me. They know I care about them."

When we return to the bedroom my mother is awake.

"Hi, beautiful. How's my baby?" Lydia honks nasally, clearly delighted at being wanted.

"I'm all right, Lydia," my mother smiles up at her. "It's so nice to see your friendly face."

"We have news for you. Good news," Lydia says. She sits on the bed and brushes my mother's hair off her damp forehead. "Roberto is coming. Your son-in-law."

My mother turns to me with a questioning, hopeful look. "Is that true, Sarah?"

"Yes, the strike is settled. He'll be here tomorrow."

She smiles broadly, her face lighting up with total joy. I can't believe what I'm seeing.

"He's really coming down to see me? He's taking time off from work and flying all the way down here to see me?"

"Of course, Mom." What does this mean to her? Does it tell her she is about to die? But why would she be surprised that her son-in-law would take the time to see her while she's so sick? She thought he wasn't going to come, that she wasn't important enough to him. This is what she feels about herself, that she is so inconsequential that her son-in-law wouldn't take a four-hour flight to see her on her deathbed.

"How good of him to do that. How wonderful." Her eyes

are open but she's no longer looking at us. She is solidly inside her pleasure, at least that's what her serene expression tells me.

As of this afternoon, my mother has eaten nothing for forty-eight hours. She has barely kept a few sips of water down. I am losing my courage. I call Dr. Gold's office and get Alicia, to my relief. She is his amiable nurse, young, pretty, gracious, so unlike his imperious secretary.

"The doctor's not in, Sarah. Can I help you?"

"My mother hasn't eaten anything for two whole days. Dr. Gold said this is merciful, but I don't think I can do this."

"Sarah, I know your mommy's case. I've spoken to Dr. Gold. We love your mommy, but she is too sick. And she decided herself not to have intervention. She's right. You're mommy's right. You must stay brave."

I am weeping so hard I can't speak. I am trying to control the sobs so my mother won't wake. I hear Lydia coming in the side door.

"I can't do this. It isn't right." I'm killing her, I think. I've hated her all these years and now I'm seizing the opportunity to kill her. These people don't know this about me, don't know what an evil daughter I've been.

"Sarita," Alicia soothes. "Sarita, I did the same with *mi mami*. I had to let her die when her time came. It is cruel to prolong such a life. This should be painless for your mother. She should just sleep more and more, God willing."

"But she doesn't look as though she's dying when she's awake. She speaks clearly. She says what she wants." They don't know how many times over my life I've wished her dead. Now I don't want her to die, but I must not be able to control my unconscious because I am killing her. Sweet Alicia can't possibly imagine such a person as I am.

"But she doesn't eat, Sarita. If she was supposed to live, she would be hungry and eating on her own. Let her be. If you can't, you bring her in and we'll take care of her, but I think she wishes to remain at home. Isn't that right?"

"Yes."

"Then leave it that way if you can. We love you and your mommy. Remember that."

When I hang up I am convulsed with sobs. My head is pressed into the gold throw-pillow on my lap. Lydia sits beside me and wraps me in her arms.

"You're doing right by her. You're doing right," she croons.

Estela arrives a little later with more bowls of food. She has made *pasteles* for Thanksgiving as well as an *asopao*. She sits with me and makes me eat. I unwrap the plantain leaf from around the *yautía* and plantain meal, which is filled with meat, raisins, olives and capers. The spicy sweetness goes down easily and warms my soul.

"It's good to eat. You need your strength for what is coming, *nena*," Estela says. She is dressed in her business clothes, a two-piece black-and-white dress with a white piqué collar. Her dark red, dyed hair is nicely coifed in a short bouffant.

"Lydia says you feel bad letting your mother die."

I nod, afraid if I speak the damn tears will start again. I'm tired of crying.

"It's the correct way to do it. You're a good daughter. Even though she wasn't always the best mommy, you have been good to her."

I shake my head. "I haven't."

"Yes, you have. I know. And I know how hard it had to be. Remember, I know Reba very well."

After Estela leaves I feel fortified enough to call the funeral home. I begin by calling Ortiz Funeral Home in Cataño.

A woman's voice comes on announcing that this is indeed

the Ortiz Funeral Home "at your service for your grieving needs."

"*Buenos días,*" I say.

"*Buenos, cómo puedo ayudarle?*"

"*Mi mama va a . . .*" I begin, but as I try to speak the word *morir,* I choke on my sobs again.

"*Su mama es muerta?*" the woman asks.

"No," I say, and then can't go on.

"What did you call for then?" she asks.

"She is going to die. She may die tomorrow or the next day. *Día de gracias.*"

"I don't understand. Your mother is not dead?"

"No," I continue to cry.

"Then I don't think we can help you. Good-bye, *señora.*"

"No, no, please. My mother is dying. If she dies on Thanksgiving, are you open? Can you take her?"

"You know she's going to die then?" Her voice has grown cold. She must think she has a murderer on the phone. But then she may be right. I am killing my mother.

"No, I don't know it. I fear she will."

"I see," she says, though clearly she doesn't. "If she dies, then you call us, *señora*, but not before."

ANA LLOSA ARRIVES at seven o'clock. She is to stay through until seven in the morning and return again the next evening, "If I'm needed," she says solemnly after she's been in to see my mother.

"She doesn't look good," Ana says, standing erect in the doorway to the kitchen where Lydia and I are making coffee and a snack.

Ana is taller than I am, at least five-foot-eight and heavy-set. She must weigh close to two hundred pounds, with a large shelf of a bosom, a big belly, ham-hock arms, and dense calves showing below the hem of a pristine, starched nurse's uniform.

"She isn't good," Lydia says. "She hasn't eaten nothing for over two days."

"Tsk," Ana sounds, shaking her head.

"She can't eat, Ana. We've tried," I answer defensively.

"It means the end," Ana says. "Three days without eating and they die."

Ana gets down to business. She boils water to wash the few dishes, wipes down the counters, the top of the stove, the cupboard doors, and gets the mop out. Lydia and I stand idly by giving each other looks that say, Get a load of her. Lydia starts to giggle and leaves the room, going into the bathroom.

"You don't have to clean, Ana. I can do that."

"It's important to have everything in order," she says, giving the counter a final swipe. "Do you have painkillers, morphine?"

"No, she has no pain." I remember Phyllis telling me that it is a big step to give pills to help someone end her life. I am grateful that it hasn't come to that. After the past few days, I see I wouldn't have been able to do it. This is bad enough.

"She could in the end," Ana says. She stands with her arms folded over her middle, between her huge breasts and her bulging abdomen.

"You're right." Lydia returns, sobered. "I told Sarah that it can be very bad in the last hours."

"I'll call Dr. Gold tomorrow," I say. "But he never mentioned anything to me about morphine. Never told me to get it."

"Tsk." Ana does her reflexive head shake. "Doctors aren't here in the home in the end. They don't see what happens."

"You're right, Ana," Lydia says. "I know, I've gone through this many times. Those doctors come and sign the death certificate after all the ugly mess is gone by, and it's been me who held the person and cleaned up."

Oh, God, I think, get me out of here. I don't want to hear their stories. I don't want to feel so inadequate. But I reassure myself that it isn't going to happen like that with my mother. As Dr. Gold said—and Alicia too—if everything goes the way it has, she'll sleep more and more until she doesn't wake up. I leave Lydia and Ana to their escalating tales of disastrous death scenes and go into my mother's room. The lights are on. She is propped up on her pillows with her eyes closed, but they open as I enter.

"Hello, dear."

"Hi, Mom, Ana's here."

She nods.

And from this ordinary exchange, one we've had five times a day—Hello, dear; Hi, Mom—I am swept with love for this woman lying in her bed. I am transfixed by her tiny, heart-shaped, sad Jewish face and the dark, almost black eyes meeting mine, this face I've known all my life. The face I looked up into as a baby. I imagine her soft young visage bent over me, staring at me with kindness. Did she marvel for a while at what she had created as she lifted me into her arms, letting my downy baby skin slip against her flesh, reveling in my fragility and solidness?

"I love you, Mommy," I say.

She smiles and I see how cracked her lips are, how yellow her teeth have become.

"I love you too, dearest," she says, the familiar touch of formality still in her voice. But this time I embrace it as her last remnant of dignity.

I perch on the edge of the chair, but have no words for this moment other than what has been said. It is my mother who finally speaks.

"Tomorrow I'd like it if you would cut my fingernails and toenails and maybe shave my legs. I've become quite unsightly. I'd like to be cleaned up a bit."

IN THE MIDDLE OF the night I come awake with a shock. My heart is racing so fast I fear I'm dying. I try to listen beyond my heart and hear my mother in the next room. No air conditioning. No breathing. My mother is dead. I'm alone in the house with her and she is dead. I begin to tremble and I try to sit up and can't and I wrap my arms around my waist telling myself that I must get up and go in there and see to her. But maybe I should wait until morning when I can go to Estela for help. There's a rustle of a body shifting in the next room. I leap up and go to her door and look into the darkness.

"*Niña*," a voice says. It's Ana. I'd forgotten about Ana.

"Is she all right? Did she die?" I whisper.

"No, no, *niña*." Ana rises slowly.

I make out the shadow of her large frame against the window. She comes to me. I smell the starch in her uniform, the emerging odor of her body seeping through soap and perfume.

"Go back to sleep, *niña*," she says as she touches my bare shoulder. "I will call you if anything happens. It's important that you sleep tonight. Your husband will be here tomorrow. You want to look pretty for him."

She walks me slowly into my room. I am the failing patient.

"Tomorrow will be a difficult day," she says. "You need your rest."

Day Twenty

ANA LEAVES AT SEVEN, to return in twelve hours, "or earlier, if I'm needed," she says. I take up her position in the chair beside my sleeping mother. I sit there for three hours as the light changes and the sounds of the day begin: the cocks' crazy crowing that goes on and on well past dawn; the dogs' barking that passes from one house to the next like dominoes falling; Inez clanging the breakfast dishes in the sink as she gets Lourdes ready for nursery school; her car starting up and sending a gust of exhaust into our room as she honks for Jorge to come and yells that they're going to be "*tarde como siempre;*" the man calling, from his truck parked on our street, that he has oranges for all of us to enjoy; the whisper of the first wind through palm fronds; the first pass through the neighborhood of the *Independentista* truck with its loudspeaker reminding us to vote for liberty. I check my watch. It's ten. My mother is still asleep. Roberto should be here in a few hours. Thinking of seeing him fills me with a thrilling pleasure. My mother said she had become unsightly. The same holds true for me. When she left, Ana reminded me to wash my hair. "Your husband is coming. You should be clean, at the least."

As the tepid water sprays over me in the shower, I allow myself a little guilty pleasure. I'm able to stand in the shower and soap my own body and rinse the soap off myself. I'm able to know the joy of complete cleanliness. It is a luxury that my mother no longer has.

I dress in a fresh bra and panties, khaki shorts and a new white tank top. Standing before the bathroom mirror, I observe myself for the first time in a week, really seeing the woman before me: I am shocked at how vigorous she seems. My skin is firm, smooth and brown from my daily runs. I've lost weight but my shoulders and arms are rounded and the muscles lightly defined. My face is open and though there are laugh lines around my eyes and frown lines between my brows, I am strangely unscarred by what is happening in this house. In my mind I have become my mother, my body rotting away, emaciated, loose-skinned and lined. I touch my shoulders, my arms, expecting thin surface flesh to slip against bone. But I am as solid as the oranges I practiced on.

Returning to sit by my mother, I say to myself, This is the deathwatch. We are alone together in this as we've always been alone together on our journeys. I recall a trip so long ago that I know I can't be remembering it myself. My mother had to have told it to me. It is 1945. The war is almost over. We've left Manzanar Camp and my mother and I are on our way to Chicago, but my father has gone on to another camp in Arkansas to help close it down. We haven't seen him for many months. I've taken to attaching myself to any man in sight and following him around and crawling up into strangers' laps to rest against a male chest. But we are just the two of us, my mother and me in the car traveling from California eastward, with all our belongings, intent on crossing the continent. After Chicago we will meet my father in Ohio, where we are to live with him. The light glares as we cross deserts and plains. It is broiling hot. This light and heat, these are my own earliest memories. It must be summer. My mother has fashioned ice holders that she ties around our wrists and necks to keep us cool. She sings, "She'll be coming round the mountain when she comes," and "The old gray mare, she ain't what she used to be." At roadside stands we buy milkshakes with eggs in them for nutrition, because that's all we can afford. But at the end of the trip, when we know we'll make it, my mother says, "Let's splurge. Let's split a chicken-in-the-basket." We sit at a picnic table beside the road, eating the most delicious fried chicken I'll ever have and drinking frosted steins of root beer with a scoop of vanilla ice cream floating in each. That evening as we're searching for a motel, my mother pulls the car onto the shoulder of the road and shuts off the ignition. The sun is setting behind us, turning the hills to the east a rich magenta, and the puffy clouds in the deep blue sky a pale pink. "Come here," she says. I scoot over beside her and she puts her arms around me. She holds me close against her slender chest. "You've been my best little companion on this trip. You helped me so much. I don't think I could have done it without you."

My mother wakes and smiles as though she's been having the same dreams and memories.

"I feel wonderful," she says. "Better than I have in days."

My hopes rise. Perhaps she isn't going to die after all. Maybe my warm thoughts have infused her with new life. Maybe I can save her after all, have the power to keep her with me now that I have felt her love.

"Do you want your injection?" I ask. Maybe they too are helping; they're not a placebo after all.

"Let's let them go today, Sarah. I'd rather have you clip my nails and shave my legs. I don't want to overtire you, dear. Roberto's coming."

She is being more sensible than I am. She has always been more logical, more mature, less prone to flights of hope and sorrow. She knows she is going to die. There is no fooling her. It is she who wants to conserve her energy for his visit.

I get the nail clippers from the medicine cabinet. Sitting on the bed with my back to her, I clip the thick twisted nails of her toes and massage her narrow feet, gently soothing her bunions.

"How good that feels," she murmurs lazily.

I think of the sinning woman washing the feet of Jesus. *And he said unto her, Thy sins are forgiven.*

Shifting around to face her, I take her right hand. I used to shudder when this hand touched me, used to jerk away. Did she realize that I pulled away from her? She must have. It had to have hurt terribly to have her only daughter hate her touch. I keep my head down so she won't see my tears as I clip the age-striated nails at the tips of her delicate fingers. My tears drop on the back of her hand but she doesn't acknowledge them. I douse her dry, flaking calves with soapy water from a bowl and run a razor over the sparse hairs. After I've finished, I give her a long leisurely sponge bath from the belly up in front, turning her to wash her back, behind and upper thighs.

She is all bones and loose flesh except over the huge bloated belly that is now as large as a full-term pregnancy. She gave birth to me. I am giving death to her. I am bringing her out of life.

I find a new nightie, noticing when I fish in the drawer that there are only five left. The one I choose is a pale pink gingham with a pink satin bow on the shirred yoke.

"Good choice," she says. "This is my favorite. Do you remember how I used to shirr the yokes of the dresses I made for you?"

"Of course I do."

"I was very proud of them. Prouder than they merited. But it felt very domestic to me, quite accomplished in that realm."

"It's amazing you could find the time to do it with a full-time job."

"Do you think so?" Her eyes widen. "How nice of you to say that. I was never certain if you appreciated it. I know you preferred store-bought clothes, especially when you were older, but we really couldn't afford them."

The question flits silently by: Were you saving money even back then?

"I think I'll rest a bit," she says, closing her eyes. "I want to look beautiful for your husband too."

By two in the afternoon, Roberto still hasn't arrived. Just as I'm about to burst with anxiety and loneliness and fear, Lydia comes into the bedroom and beckons me out.

"Joey called. He said the plane was late leaving Newark and wouldn't be in until four this afternoon. I told him to stay at the airport. Was that all right?"

"Of course." I rest my elbows on the counter top, my face in my hands, faint with hunger and the tension of waiting.

"It's okay, honey. He'll get here in time. Mommy will wait." She has her hand in my hair, massaging my scalp. "You want me to stay? I can. I told my daughter to pick up Ladito. He can be with her till I get home."

I can only nod. The comfort of her froggy, nasal voice, the familiarity of her knowing exactly what I'm feeling without being told, seems like the greatest gift. The unquestioning, undemanding gift of empathy. She can't be faking this. I would know.

At four my mother cries out in agony. There are no words, no names called, only a wrenching horrific, guttural wail. Lydia and I are drinking tea in the dinette. We look at each other. I see the knowledge in her eyes as she nods. We race into the darkened room.

When she realizes we are there, my mother tries to stifle her cries.

"It hurts so much," she whimpers. "I am in so much pain."

But she isn't supposed to have pain, I think frantically. Dr. Gold said she shouldn't have pain. I scrabble around in the drawer of her night table, looking for the codeine pills I remember she was prescribed after the operation. I find the bottle and give her one tablet, holding her head as she drinks the water.

"I'm going to call the doctor," I say.

I dial his office from the living room. I don't want her to hear my alarm. He isn't in. Alicia says she will try to find him.

"Don't you have morphine?" she asks.

"No, I didn't get any. She hasn't had pain until now. Alicia, she's in terrible pain."

"Didn't hospice call you?"

"No," I say, my voice rising in fear. "Can Dr. Gold call the pharmacy?"

"Let me see," she says. But I hear doubt in her fading voice.

"What's the matter? Tell me what it is, Alicia." I hear the insistence in my voice and caution myself to calm down.

"Nothing is the matter," she says, but I know she's not telling me everything. "Let me hang up, Sarah. I'll call you back."

Back in the bedroom my mother says the pain is subsiding. But that she is burning up. I put my forehead to hers as she did to test my fevers as a child. It is clammy and cold. I feel her hands and cheeks. They are cold as snow.

"You're hot?" I ask again, disbelieving.

She is throwing her head from side to side and pushing down the blankets.

"Yes, dammit, I'm on fire. Do something, please."

In the kitchen Lydia says this is what happens. "They get cold outside as they burn up inside."

We dump ice cubes into a blue plastic bowl.

"Rub her down with these," Lydia says. "I'll bring you more. I'm calling Ana. She should come early."

"Do you think Roberto will make it in time?"

"She's trying her hardest to wait for him. I can see that." Lydia says. "If she can she will."

For the next hour we apply cubes to my mother's face, chest, arms, belly and legs. As soon as the ice cubes touch her cold flesh they melt as though they are licked by fire, as though she is a furnace with a roaring flame within. Lydia works on my mother's face while I do her legs and feet. Then we trade. At first I am afraid to put the ice directly on her skin, that it would be too shockingly cold, but each time I do, she moans, "Thank you, thank you. I'm burning up. This gives some relief."

Ana arrives and so does Estela. Inez comes in a little later when Jorge gets home to look after the girls. It takes all five of us applying the ice to keep my mother calm. We put the orange bandanna over the lamp, turning the light in the room to terra cotta. As we bend and reach to rub my mother down, our shadows loom large and slow-moving on the ceiling and the walls. My mother writhes, thrusting up her distended belly, as Lydia swabs her face and neck and I work on her right arm and chest. I catch a glimpse of my mother's shadow in the center of ours, lifting and falling, like a woman in the agony of labor. Estela hasn't taken the time to change, and in her white linen work dress she looks as much like a nurse as Ana. Estela draws the ice expertly along my mother's left arm, turning the arm, moving the ice to the inside, pressing it into the sensitive spot in the bend of the elbow where the veins are closest. The wet skin of Inez's bare, rounded arms looks as though it's been painted a deep burnt sienna. She's taken up her station at the foot of the bed; her torso, clad in a red knit camisole, stretches long as she reaches up to my mother's hips and with both hands rhythmically rolls the ice cubes down the scrawny thighs and calves to my mother's ankles and the soles of her feet. Ana spells us when one of us needs a rest.

We decide that Ana should go to the bodega down the alley at the end of the cul-de-sac to get some five-pound bags of ice. As she leaves I ask her if she will ask the pharmacist about morphine, because Dr. Gold has not called back.

"They'll not have morphine, *niña*. It's not possible."

"Why not?" I look up from my mother. I can't believe what I'm hearing. What could she mean, they don't have morphine? This is ridiculous.

Following Ana to the living room, I ask her again. "Why wouldn't they have morphine in a pharmacy?"

"Because of the drug addicts. It's too dangerous. They could get killed from holdups."

I had been calmed by tending to my mother with the other women, but on hearing this my anxiety almost chokes me. Even with a prescription, I can't get the morphine in the neighborhood. I call Alicia. She hasn't been able to locate Dr. Gold.

"But I'm trying everything, Sarah. How is Mommy?"

"She's in worse pain. She's burning up. And the nurse says they don't sell morphine here because of the drug addicts."

"They don't sell it even in San Juan," she says quietly.

"What? Not in San Juan either? How am I supposed to get it? What am I supposed to do? How can I help my mother?"

"We have it at the hospital pharmacy. Let me get off and try to reach Dr. Gold before the pharmacy closes. It shuts down at seven."

I check my watch. It's five. This cannot be happening. How could I have been so irresponsible, such a fool?

"Please, Alicia. Please try harder."

My mother has resumed her moaning. "Sarah, help me."

Estela and Lydia are trying to soothe her with endearments. Inez is icing her chest. I begin again on her face.

"Mommy, I'm doing what I can," I say, trying to speak evenly, but my voice catches.

She touches her freezing cold hand to my shoulder. "I know you're trying, dearest."

A car pulls into the driveway, followed by the clunk of the padlock on the *marquesina* gate. This has to be Roberto. But I can't leave my mother. I am working on her legs when I feel his presence. I look over my shoulder to see him at the door, standing there in blue jeans and rumpled white shirt, his round face stricken, mirroring the emotional scene in this room filled with four women tending to my mother who is thrashing in pain.

"Mommy, it's Roberto. He's here for you."

Her body stills. We cease our ministrations. Each woman stands back holding the ice high, letting it drip down her arms. My mother's face lights with unmitigated joy.

"Roberto," she sighs. "Roberto, how good of you to come." She holds out her scrawny wet arms.

He goes to her, brushing past me, sits on the bed and folds her into his arms.

"Rebekah," he croons. "Rebekah, I thank God I could get here."

"I want to talk with Roberto alone," she says tremulously to all of us.

Roberto indicates with a thrust of his chin that we should leave.

Lydia is sitting in the corner of the couch by the window, her head thrown back, her eyes closed. Inez sits on the other end, with her hands clasped between her knees and her head down, praying. Estela is in the easy chair by the phone, looking through the phone book again for funeral homes. I'm too agitated to sit down. I keep walking to the front door and back, looking out for Ana.

When I see her large form appear under the streetlight at the end of the cul-de-sac, I step out into the night and meet her at the gate.

"What did the pharmacist say?" I ask, knowing the answer.

"No morphine, but he gave me Duragesic patches. Tomorrow he needs a prescription from your doctor to cover them. I told him the *señora* Mainlander was dying. He said he knew. He'd heard. He gave me the drugs even though he could get in trouble. I told him I'm a registered nurse, so he agreed.

"Thank you, Ana." I hug her solid body. "At least we have something to give her."

"But we must get the doctor's permission before we apply them. I can't prescribe."

When we enter, Inez stands, wiping her hands down her wet arms. The front of her knitted shirt is darkened to blood red and her khaki skirt is soaked. "I must go home, Sarah. I have to make dinner for Jorge and the girls. I'll bring you back some food."

"Inez, thank you, but you don't have to bring food." There is no possibility that I can eat.

"You see what I said," Estela is saying. "She waited for him."

What is my mother saying to Roberto?

"She's right," Ana agrees from the kitchen where she opens the freezer and puts the ice inside. "*Señora* Reba has kept herself going for him," she says, nodding. She turns and begins to fill a pot with water for tea.

Roberto emerges from the room but sinks back against the wall by my mother's door. He is pale and stricken. The skin around his lips is gray. Rubbing his eyes and then his face, he doesn't budge from there.

I go over to him. "What is it? What did she say?"

Lydia, who has risen stiffly from the couch, walks past us into my mother's room.

"It was awful," he says, moving us away from her door, into the kitchen and out into the *marquesina*. The humidity closes in. I am surprised at how hot it is. The house has kept cool from my mother's air conditioner.

Roberto again slumps against the wall as if he needs its support to remain upright.

"She turned the lights out so I wouldn't see her and she begged me to help her die. I said I couldn't, that as a doctor I couldn't do that. She pleaded again, grabbing onto me, pulling me close. She said she couldn't ask you, that you'd be too upset, but she wants to die. It hurts so much, she said. She can't stand the pain." He begins to cry, his head down, his body shaking. I put my hand on his shoulder.

"She must love and trust you," I say.

"How would I ever have known that?" he asks, raising his hands as though imploring a higher power.

"You wouldn't," I say, " because she didn't let you know." Another lost opportunity, I think.

"And then she said that if I couldn't help her to die, she wanted to go to the hospital, but only if she could return to the Intensive Care Unit. Could she do that?"

"No, they'd never take her. They know she's dying. It was hard enough to get her a bed when there was some hope."

"Maybe she thinks they'll help her die."

"No. What she wants is their loving care. They were especially kind to her there," I say, sorrow overwhelming me.

The phone rings inside.

"Sarah," Lydia calls. "It's Dr. Gold."

"What is happening?" Dr. Gold asks when I get on the phone.

"She's in hideous pain and she wants to die and I have no morphine. All I have is leftover codeine from her operation and Duragesic patches that the nurse wrangled from the pharmacist," I say, my anger seeping through even though I'm trying not to sound accusatory.

"Oh, dear God. At least you have the codeine and the patches. I didn't think it would happen this quickly," he says.

"But I told you, Dr. Gold, that she wasn't eating."

"Sarah, forgive me. Sometimes doctors don't want to see the inevitable either. But that's no excuse. Oh, God, I'm so terribly sorry. I was blinded by my hope that it would be a painless death. I've been remiss. I should have had hospice working with you. You would have had morphine."

"I blame myself," I say. Why did I let myself believe her death would be painless? For all my bravado about helping her to die, I didn't even prepare for the end with a stash of morphine. "But, Dr. Gold, she's suffering and I don't know what to do. I'm not prepared. I can't protect her."

"Sarah, give her two more codeine tablets. Let's see if she can hold them down. And then apply one of the patches. Place it on her neck, on her artery," he says. "Can you have someone come in to the hospital?"

"Yes, my husband just got here."

"Good, have him drive in right away. He should come to my office. I'll wait for him. And I'll have the morphine. In half an hour, if the pain continues to be intolerable, put more patches on her neck and back. Keep putting them on. We have nothing to lose. Do you understand what I'm saying?"

"Yes," I say, and begin shaking.

I ASK LYDIA to give my mother the codeine and to apply the patch while I deal with Roberto's trip to San Juan.

Ana volunteers to go into San Juan with Roberto. She will drive because she knows the way to the hospital and the labyrinthine route through the hospital corridors to Dr. Gold's office.

"It will be faster if we take my car," Ana says, picking up her purse. She waits while Roberto and I leave the room for a minute.

"Maybe she can go alone," Roberto says to me in the bedroom. We have closed the door against my mother's moans. "I can stay here and help you."

He has his arms around me, holding me close for the first time since he has arrived. It is as though I am melting into his body. I am tempted to say, Stay here, take care of me. Let me sleep in your arms until this passes.

But instead I say, "No, you have to go with her. It's better if Dr. Gold releases the morphine into your hands. And Ana said she doesn't want to be alone carrying morphine through San Juan."

"So we can both be shot by addicts."

He and I begin to laugh, stifling the sound against each other.

"This is terrible," I say.

"You're allowed," he says, sobering. He holds my hair back from my face in a ponytail. "You take care. I'll get back as soon as I can."

As Ana and Roberto pull away in the car, Estela comes out on the steps with the Yellow Pages under her arm. She has taken her pumps off and carries them by the heels, in her other hand.

"I'm going to start calling the funeral homes. But I don't want to do it here. Reba shouldn't know what I'm doing."

I'm about to say, But she wouldn't understand, and that she couldn't hear through her agony, and that she wants to die, but I stop myself. Estela doesn't want to be here for the end.

"See you later, Estela." I kiss her on her soft cheek.

"May God be with you, child."

I hurry back into the bedroom. Lydia continues to ice my mother who by now is groaning in one continuous sound like an organ with the stops out. Lydia lets up when she sees me in the door.

"I'll be back in a minute, sweetheart," she says to my mother who doesn't notice that Lydia has left the ice cubes to melt on her chest, the skin of which is flushed from the cold, a raw red like a giant strawberry birthmark.

"Do you want me to stay?" Lydia asks. "I was going to leave at eight."

Leave? It never occurred to me that Lydia would leave. I can't be alone. What if my mother dies before Roberto and Ana return?

"Please don't go, Lydia. I can't do this on my own. What if. . ." I can't say it.

"I'll stay. Lydia will stay with you. Lydia understands. I've done this many times before."

MY MOTHER HAS dropped off again. Her mouth is wide open, a dark gaping hole. She draws in raspy, guttural breaths. I start to relax, thinking that maybe this is all it takes, a few codeine tablets and one patch, when she wakes up screaming. She insists that all the lights be turned back on, that the cloth be taken from the lamp. "I need light. It's too dark in here." Roberto's name is not uttered, nor is mine. It is Lydia that she implores.

"Lydia, give me something for the pain, I never felt such pain." She holds her mammoth belly in both hands and rocks from side to side like an infant in a crib.

"I can't tolerate any more of this. Please, Lydia, another pill for the pain."

"We have to put on more patches," I whisper to Lydia.

Before I can open the plastic wrap on a new patch, my mother begins violently vomiting up undigested pills.

"Oh, my nightgown is all dirty," she whimpers, brushing her hand through the black bile. "My pretty nightgown."

Lydia helps me cut it off, this time down the front.

"Noooo," my mother laments. "You're ruining my favorite nightgown."

"It's okay, Mommy," I say, wadding it. "Don't you worry." I can't lie to her. I can't tell her I'm going to repair it as good as new.

We place a towel over her emaciated chest, instead of disturbing her further by dressing her again. The room smells of vomit and that peculiar odor of bile that I associate with Coca Cola, the sweet caramel they use to color it. The floor is wet in puddles where fallen ice has melted. The sheets are soaked and streaked with black.

My mother starts screaming. Lydia quickly applies the

patch to her neck, just under the first one, on her main artery, which pulses rapidly.

Strands of Lydia's hair have escaped her ponytail and hang stiffly before her ears. Her tee shirt is as filthy as the sheets. Her eyes are puffy and there are pouches along her jaw line. Muscles strain in her arms as she lets my mother back down onto her pillow, telling her, "Reba, relax, my little child. Take it easy. We're going to help you through this."

My mother grasps her arm, gazing at her pleadingly. "Please make it fast."

I rip another patch from its package and slap it on her chest. I try to open another one but I'm trembling so badly I can't tear the plastic. Lydia puts her hand over mine and says, "Maybe you should call the doctor. Ask him how many we can put on at once."

I know the answer, but I call him all the same. I need him to give permission again. I dial Dr. Gold's number and pace in front of the couch, before the spot where my mother would sit when she took my calls or placed hers to me. In one ear I count the rings, silently begging him to pick up; in the other ear I take in the singing of my beloved coquís.

"Yes," he answers.

I fight back tears. I know what I am asking and what he will say.

When I present the question, he answers patiently. "Keep applying them. Put all of them on if necessary. We don't have to worry about an overdose anymore." His voice is resigned. "And by the way, I've just said good-bye to your husband. He and Ana should be back with the morphine within the hour."

Too late, I think.

He gives me his home number. I can barely write legibly, terror has so overtaken me. In a calming voice he says he should be at his apartment in fifteen minutes. Then he says, "Sarah, my heart is with you. This is the most merciful way of doing it. Remember that."

I let Lydia know what Dr. Gold told me. She nods. She is sitting high on the bed, her back against the headboard with my mother's head on her chest, soothing her face with yet more ice. My mother's teeth are clenched and her eyes are closed in pain. Her breath hisses through her teeth.

"Mom, Dr. Gold says we can give you more pain killer."

She opens her eyes and looks at me. She reaches up with her trembling hand and pats my cheek.

"That's good news," she says.

I can't believe that she is dying. She is so alert. What if Dr. Gold is wrong about this, too? What if she isn't dying? How could he have believed in a painless death in the first place? He must be an idiot. But this is my fault, not his. I'm the daughter. If I'd had the morphine she could just slip away. Did I unconsciously want her to suffer? Or was I too afraid that I would kill her before it was time? I shouldn't have let Phyllis talk me out of it. But I stop berating myself and everyone else because my mother begins to thrash so fiercely that Lydia can barely hold her to the bed.

I shake the entire box of patches onto the bed table and as fast as I can I release them from their packaging, Lydia sticks them to my mother's skin, on her neck and chest and back and breasts. We apply ten before her frenzy subsides.

"Oh, that's better," she slurs. "Oh, the awful pain is gone."

The peace is short-lived because when she tries to speak again, she can't. "I caaannnt taaaaak," she tries to say, signing frantically, pointing to her mouth, opening it, touching her tongue and shaking her head.

"Can you move your tongue, Mommy?" I ask. What have I done to her?

She shakes her head. Her eyes grow wide and she lurches forward out of Lydia's grasp and begins to crawl to where I am standing near the foot of the bed. She is coming toward me like a desperate child in need of a parent, shaking her head back and forth, her mouth open, her tongue out, but no words come, only a guttural growling emerges.

She grabs my hands. I raise hers to my lips. Her hold is like steel, cold and rigid. As I search her eyes and she stares into mine, as though trying to take me into her being, I witness death entering her and her heart-shaped little face with its pointed chin transforms into a skull. Her eyes sink in, her teeth are bared like a wild animal's, her cheekbones stand out more and more sharply under her thin darkening skin.

I must look frightened because Lydia comes to us and touches my mother. "Reba, do you want Sarah to have to go through this last part?"

My mother stares more intently at me; there is a violence of longing in her look, as if she wants me more than anyone has ever wanted another, and then she shakes her head, pulling my hands to her face and kissing each one. Then she drops them and shakes her head again, still boring into me with her eyes that are liquid with tears.

"All right, Reba darling. Come to Lydia. And, Sarah, you go in the other room. Mommy and I will do this."

I wait in the living room, kneeling on the couch with my arms wrapped around my head to keep what is going on in the other room away from me. As sounds emerge, my mother's groans, Lydia calming her, I squeeze my arms tighter and hum to myself. I am in another place far away and yet here. She dies and I can't be with her. My mother's kindness has set me free. Her generosity has saved me from witnessing the moment when she leaves herself and me.

"Sarah," she cries out.

"Oh, no," I whisper. "No, Mommy, I can't. Please just die now. Die in peace." I dig more deeply into my arms, into the musty fabric of the couch.

Silence from the next room. It's over. I begin to weep. After a while Lydia comes out and sits with me. My head is in her lap.

"Thank you, Lydia. I just couldn't do it."

"It was better that you weren't there. It was very bad. Everything came up. But then after she called for you, she said, Give me my baby, and she reached for the little bear you brought her and put it on top of her head and closed her eyes, turned over, curled up like a little baby herself, and that was it. It was all over. So sweet. You'll see how sweet she looks when I get her cleaned up."

I shake my head adamantly. "I can't. I can't see her dead." The tears pour out unrestrained.

Ana and Roberto pull up and come rushing in the front door. Roberto's shirt is plastered to his chest with sweat. His eyes search the room. Even Ana has lost her composure. She has rivulets of perspiration running down the sides of her flushed face. They stop once inside, hearing the silence of the house, realizing.

"It's all over," I say.

"Shit," Roberto says, tossing the white pharmacy bag of morphine on the table.

"Did you write down the time of death?" Ana asks Lydia. "You must document the time."

"Nine-seventeen," Lydia says.

"Very good," Ana says, wiping at the moisture on her brow with a pale blue handkerchief.

"You can help me wash her, Ana," Lydia says, lifting my head from her lap.

"Is it bad?" Ana asks. She dabs at her upper lip.

"Yeah," Lydia says. "Everything came up."

Ana calls Estela and she returns, announcing that she has phoned the police and the funeral home. Her hair is half in curlers and half out. She wears her flowered housedress and flip-flops.

"The police?" I ask. I've remained on the couch. Roberto has come to sit with me, taking Lydia's place. He holds me against his damp body.

"Yes, they must take the body to the morgue." Estela becomes officious. "When there's a death in the house, the police always come."

"I don't want the police," I cry angrily.

"Don't be difficult, Sarah, they have to come. It's the same in New York," Roberto says.

"I don't want them here," I yell, surprising myself. I try to get up, but Roberto won't let me.

"Stop acting stupid," Roberto admonishes, tightly clenching my upper arms, turning me around to face him. "Look at me. What do you want, the body to stay here forever?"

Avoiding his eyes, I begin to wail. I know I'm acting crazy, but I feel insane. I don't even know why I'm crying. But great sobs are rising up, barking out, screaming. I want to yell that I want my mommy, but I can't. I feel a force taking over my body, my senses, my hopes, my sorrows.

Ana and Lydia leave the living room. Inez has appeared at the open front door. Roberto is still holding me, as I struggle to escape his grasp. I have to get out of this house. Why doesn't he let me go? Despite my resistance he murmurs endearments, but I can't stop crying, can't stop making a display of myself, as my mother would have said. Calm down, Sarah, for heaven's sake, you're making a display.

Then Ana offers me a cup of tea. Through my howling I have heard them conferring in the kitchen, "She needs tea, something to calm her, she is becoming hysterical with grief. She will hurt herself." Exhausted, I give in to Roberto. I let him pull me gently to him. Still weeping, I slide down until my head is on his chest.

The tea has whole leaves floating in it, hard, ovate, dark green.

"It's *manzanilla*," Ana says. "It will calm you. You must get control of yourself."

The tea is hot and savory. I sit up to drink it. When the

cup is finished, my crying subsides and a powerful calm comes over me. I can hardly hold the cup. Lydia grabs it as my grasp loosens. My body slackens and rests again in Roberto's arms.

"There, she is settling down. The grief is too much for her. The death too hard," I hear someone say.

I want to answer, No, no, no, you are wrong. It's a relief. I never loved her. But I know it is I who am wrong and the speaker correct. I needed her too ferociously to find my way to love.

Later, I don't know how long since I'm in such a blissful haze, blue light flashes from outside through the louvered windows and the open door. It is accompanied by a siren.

Opening my eyes, I see that Mr. Castro is here in my father's best white embroidered *guayabera*, along with the Haitian couple and their daughter from across the street, Inez and Jorge, Lydia, Ana, Joey and Estela.

A tall thin man in knee-high leather boots saunters in. He has coal-black hair slicked off the forehead of his arrogantly cocked head, a thick black mustache, a gun on his hip, and blue reflective sunglasses covering his eyes even though it's nighttime. He's a caricature of a Latin policeman. I feel an urgent need to laugh. No, I say to myself, you can't laugh, you're in mourning. What will everyone think of you? But again the hysterical urge to giggle at this asshole. I press it down.

"Who is the family of the deceased? Where is the deceased?" the policeman demands in a booming voice, lifting his sunglasses to reveal dark eyes that widen as he waits for a response.

Roberto gets up from the couch. He shakes his legs to adjust his jeans and tucks his wrinkled shirt down into his pants in back.

"Are you the husband?" The policeman's eyes open so wide they look like they'll pop out.

"Yes, I am," Roberto says.

"No, no," Estela jumps in. She too has to stifle laughter. "He is the son-in-law."

The policeman frowns and postures more, his chest expanding, one leg extended to the side.

"*Jesus mío,*" Lydia whistles beside me.

I step on her toe and shake my head.

"I'm the daughter," I say. "It's my mother who died."

"My condolences, *señora,*" he intones in his basso voice. "And where is the body of the deceased?"

More questions are asked. Forms filled out. We will have to get a death certificate from the doctor and go to the morgue the next day to retrieve her body, the policeman instructs.

"But tomorrow is Thanksgiving," I say. "Is the morgue open on Thanksgiving?"

He frowns at me, his chin pulled against his neck. "Of course, *señora*. Death doesn't wait on holidays."

I suppress my renewed desire to laugh. But then he says, "It is time to take the body," and all silliness leaves me. "You may go in, *señora,* to have your last moments with the deceased."

"No. I can't."

"Someone must say good-bye, Sarah," Lydia says. "You can't let her go without a good-bye."

The room is silent. Everyone is staring at me.

I shake my head, looking down. "I can't. I can't look at her. Please, I'm sorry."

"I'll go." It is Roberto. He puts his arms around me and whispers, "I'll say good-bye for both of us."

I go out to the *marquesina* and sit on the old painted kitchen chairs and look out into the dark back yard. Lights are on in the house on the other side of the chain-link fence. I press against our gate, holding onto the wrought-iron bars, and look toward my father's tree. It is illuminated by the light coming from my mother's room. A shadow passes over the leaves of the tree. I remember her telling me that she couldn't view my father's dead body in the hospital. Like mother, like daughter. I hear the bed scuff and scrape on the terrazzo floor.

"I'm sorry, Mommy. I'm just not brave enough to say good-bye."

After the blue lights and siren have pulled away and good nights have been exchanged and I've heard gates clanking and doors shutting along the cul-de-sac, Roberto comes out, pulls over another paint-spattered chair and sits beside me.

"Have a beer?" he asks, holding up two bottles by their necks.

"Sure."

We drink the beer down. It is cool, fizzy and delicious.

"That was pretty medieval," he says, "the bedroom full of women icing her."

"It got more intense after you left."

"I'm sure," he says.

I tell him how Lydia took over in the last minutes of my mother's life.

"She's a good, decent woman," Roberto says.

"I want to give her the house. So she can live here with her little Ladito, and maybe Joey if he can pull his shit together, which I doubt. I'll tell her that my mother left it to her in the will. It's worth about twenty-five thousand dollars. With the money we're getting, we won't need the house and all the bother of selling it."

"It's your money and your house."

"It's both of ours. You can have your say."

"The other money we can share," he says. "And I agree, it's quite enough for us. You decide about Lydia and the child."

We sit in silence finishing our beers.

"I've decided," I say. "I want her to have the house for herself and Ladito."

"That's what I thought you'd do. It fulfills a need in you, but it's also generous."

"And I want to leave the car to Estela and give five thousand to Inez for Lourdes. I'll say my mother left it to Lourdes for her schooling. Is that all right with you?"

"I agree with that as well."

"I want them to remember my mother fondly."

Roberto laughs softly. "I do believe they will."

WHEN WE GO INSIDE, I walk immediately to my mother's room. It is utterly transformed. The sheets have been stripped and the towels, ice trays and buckets, water glasses, codeine and aspirin bottles, the plastic packaging from the patches, Kleenex, bedpan, and syringes have been cleared away. The floor is scrubbed and the throw rugs have been taken up. My mother's spirit isn't even in the room. That is the greatest shock. I expected to find an aura of her remaining, expected to feel her presence, smell her, hear her voice, sense a familiar gesture, but absolutely nothing is present. Just four peach walls, a dresser, a mirror, a bed, a chair, a bed table and a lamp.

Roberto comes up behind me and puts his arms around my waist, pulling me close, his cheek to mine.

"How can she go so quickly? I feel nothing of her here," I say.

"She said she wanted to leave. She was done with life."

"But why didn't her spirit stay?"

"Your mother wasn't much into spirit, I don't think. She didn't like anyone dependent on her and she hated needing anyone else."

"Even though she did need us, desperately," I say, thinking of these last day and hours.

"Yep, in her own way, I guess. But don't romanticize it too much, Sarah."

"Oh, let me, please, just for a little while." I sink further back into him.

In bed, as Roberto snores beside me, I think of how my

father inhabited the house for years after his death even when my mother had me clear out all his clothes and belongings. He hung around in the corners, in the air, in the limbs of the tree in the back yard. He is still there, even now; he hasn't gone off with her. But she, my mother, his wife, has definitely left for good.

As I fall off into sleep, I think, I wish I missed her more.

A Week After Thanksgiving

PEARL AND I REACHED a compromise. Even though my mother's memorial service was to be on Saturday, and it is forbidden by Jewish law to say kaddish on the Sabbath outside of synagogue, Pearl agreed to intone the opening lines. That seemed right in the end, given my mother's conflicted relationship with Judaism.

The ashes were not ready for the service. Roberto and I had her body delivered to the Levittown Lakes Funeral Home and we returned each day to retrieve her ashes. But we were always greeted with "*Mañana*. Your mother's ashes will arrive tomorrow." It had something to do with sending her to San Juan to be cremated as there was only one crematorium in Puerto Rico. "But it is getting very popular on the island and we are straining the facility," they said by way of excuse.

We finally reclaim her ashes a few days after the simple service at the bridge club where, to my relief, twenty-five people showed up, and I cried, which I always feared I wouldn't be able to, telling the story of our journey across the country in 1945 and how my mother sang to me.

Roberto and I take the black plastic box down to my mother's favorite beach. We've heard it's illegal to spread the ashes in a public place so we find a side road and park the car in a secluded area. We take our towels and a cotton blanket to sit on. I carry the black box. Somehow I hadn't expected the ashes to be in such a utilitarian container. A plastic urn, a somber jar, but this cube of rough plastic is so impersonal. And heavy. It must weigh five pounds.

We scramble under the bushes, finding our way to the

shore. After a number of false starts, we locate a path that takes us to the beach. We enter a grove of tamarisks. "They are so elegant and romantic," my mother used to say about these tall, feathery-branched trees she loved so much. "They look particularly beautiful against the sky, don't you think?"

No one is close by, very few people are in the water. It's winter. Most are sitting in their cars in the far parking lot, with the doors open like wings and the music blaring. It was where my mother used to park and walk down to the water. She felt safer with people around, she told me, "and not so lonely."

The sun is high and blazing hot but the air is dry, so it's comfortable as we spread our faded blue blanket in the open. The sky is bright blue, many shades darker than our blanket. It is midday and high cumulus clouds sit on the horizon, far out to sea. There may be an afternoon thunder shower, but at the moment it is a perfect day at the beach.

"She'd love it here today," I say, sitting down on the blanket, my legs curled under me, the box on my lap.

Roberto sinks down beside me and puts his arm over my shoulder. "She'd say, 'It's the most beautiful day I think I've ever seen.'"

"And then she'd say, 'I'm so glad Scott and I came down here. It was a good decision. I've never known more beautiful skies anywhere.'"

We sit watching the undulation of the turquoise ocean, watch the gentle lapping of waves in this protected cove.

"Well?" Roberto says. "Should we do it?"

"Yes, but how?" I'm trying to find a point of entry, turning the box around and over, hearing the hiss and feeling the heave of the shifting ashes inside.

For the next few minutes we try to pry open the box, to no avail. It is sealed shut.

"I'll have to use my knife," Roberto says. He digs in his pants pocket and brings out his Swiss Army knife and for the next fifteen minutes he attacks the box, stabbing it, carving at it, pulling away the thick resistant plastic, bending back the stiff sides, until little by little we have smashed and ripped and stomped into submission the box containing my mother. We are cursing, laughing and saying, "This must be her final plan for torturing us." When it is open, we are met with further packaging, this time a thick, transparent, sealed, plastic bag. We peer into it.

"The pieces are so big," I say. "And they're all different colors, even black. I thought it would be dust particles, as in 'dust to dust.'"

"It looks like chunks of bones," Roberto says, grimacing. "This is horrible."

"I don't even think it's her," I say. "I sort of hope it isn't."

I imagine them burning many bodies and scooping out the chunks and pouring them into waiting bags. "This is for the Ellis family, and this is for the Gonzalez family, and this is for the Sanchez family. They'll never know the difference." But the more I examine the thin slices of bone in all their varied shades of beige, white, gray and black, I think I recognize my mother in them, the very essence of her living being, and I am filled with a familiar mixture of love, remorse and revulsion. This is my mother, for better or worse. This is the woman who will always be in me. The smells and images of these last three weeks descend on me and my breath catches noisily in my throat. Will I ever forget our last journey together?

"I did everything I could for her. I only wish I'd done more earlier," I say.

"That wasn't possible," Roberto says. "You had a big failure of communication. I don't think you ever could have overcome that. I mean, how much did you two really talk while she was dying?"

I shake my head. "It wasn't really about talking. You're probably right."

We slice open the bag, carry it to the edge of the water, and wade in. When we are up to our chests, I empty the contents of the plastic bag into the blue ocean and we watch as my mother, caught in the currents, swirls around and around our bodies, gradually dissipating as the waves ebb and flow, sending the particles out to sea and back.

MARNIE MUELLER
is a former Peace Corps volunteer who served in Ecuador.
That experience became the basis for her debut novel
*Green Fires: Assault on Eden, A Novel of the Ecuadorian
Rainforest,* which won a Before Columbus Foundation
American Book Award and a Maria Thomas Award for
Outstanding Fiction. *Green Fires* was also selected for the
New York Public Library's "Best Books for the Teen Age,"
and Barnes & Noble's "Discover Great New Writers." A
German translation, *Grüne Feuer,* was published in 1996 by
Goldmann/Bertelsmann. As a result of the publication of
Green Fires, her experience in the Peace Corps, and her
long history of political activism, Peter Jennings
interviewed her for his ABC NEWS documentary *The
Century* and also included her as a first-person "voice of
the twentieth century" in his book of the same title.

Her second novel, *The Climate of the Country,*
published in February 1999, dealt with the forced
internment of Japanese American citizens and immigrants
in the U.S. during World War II. Mueller was in fact the
first Caucasian born in Tule Lake Japanese American
Segregation Camp in northern California, where her father,
a pacifist, and her mother, a teacher, worked. *The Climate
of the Country* met with rave reviews, and the Gustavus
Myers Outstanding Book Awards 2000 awarded it an
honorable mention. An Italian translation, *L'Aria Che
Respiravamo,* was published in the fall of 1999 by
Corbaccio, Milan.

Her third novel, *My Mother's Island,* is perhaps her
most intensely personal novel to date, relating the intimate
story of a daughter's reluctant but dutiful journey of
reconciliation with her dying mother, for whom she has felt
resentment and rage. Although the novel is set against the

backdrop of McCarthyism and post-war anti-Semitism, its center is the daughter's death watch and the painful probing of the psychological contradictions within the family unit.

Both Marnie Mueller's parents maintained a life-long commitment to fighting for social justice. Because of her father's work as a political organizer, she lived in many parts of the country. In 1963 she joined the Peace Corps and spent two years in Guayaquil, Ecuador. She subsequently worked as a community organizer in New York City's East Harlem and South Bronx neighborhoods, Director of Summer Programming for New York City, Program Director at Pacifica Radio's WBAI-FM in New York, and as an events planner. She currently lives in New York City, devoting herself to her writing and volunteer work in community action projects. Her short stories and poems have appeared in numerous magazines and anthologies including *Quarterly West, The Minnesota Review, The Laurel Review* and the *Village Voice Literary Supplement.*

CURBSTONE PRESS, INC.

is a nonprofit publishing house dedicated to literature that reflects a commitment to social change, with an emphasis on contemporary writing from Latino, Latin American and Vietnamese cultures. Curbstone presents writers who give voice to the unheard in a language that goes beyond denunciation to celebrate, honor and teach. Curbstone builds bridges between its writers and the public – from inner-city to rural areas, colleges to community centers, children to adults. Curbstone seeks out the highest aesthetic expression of the dedication to human rights and intercultural understanding: poetry, testimonies, novels, stories, children's books.

This mission requires more than just producing books. It requires ensuring that as many people as possible learn about these books and read them. To achieve this, a large portion of Curbstone's schedule is dedicated to arranging tours and programs for its authors, working with public school and university teachers to enrich curricula, reaching out to underserved audiences by donating books and conducting readings and community programs, and promoting discussion in the media. It is only through these combined efforts that literature can truly make a difference.

Curbstone Press, like all nonprofit presses, depends on the support of individuals, foundations, and government agencies to bring you, the reader, works of literary merit and social significance which might not find a place in profit-driven publishing channels, and to bring the authors and their books into communities across the country. Our sincere thanks to the following foundations, and government agencies who support this endeavor: Connecticut Commission on the Arts, Connecticut Humanities Council, Daphne Seybolt Culpeper Foundation, Fisher Foundation, Greater Hartford Arts Council, Hartford Courant Foundation, J. M. Kaplan Fund, Eric Mathieu King Fund, Lannan Foundation, John D. and Catherine T. MacArthur Foundation, National Endowment for the Arts, Open Society Institute, Puffin Foundation, and the Woodrow Wilson National Fellowship Foundation.

Please help to support Curbstone's efforts to present the diverse voices and views that make our culture richer. Tax-deductible donations can be made by check or credit card to:
Curbstone Press, 321 Jackson Street, Willimantic, CT 06226
phone: (860) 423-5110   fax: (860) 423-9242
www.curbstone.org

IF YOU WOULD LIKE TO BE A MAJOR SPONSOR OF A
CURBSTONE BOOK, PLEASE CONTACT US.